Escape was impossible...

From the bathroom Rafe heard the shower start and his mind was filled with images of Jenna's graceful body and shapely legs.

He had to see her. Too soon, he would be an angel again and the moment would have passed. Jenna would no longer be available to him. He was well aware he was playing with fire. How could he see her naked and not make love to her?

"Jenna, may I come in?" he asked while pushing open the door.

She peered out at him, her body a tantalizing outline. "Rafe...?"

His throat constricted. He couldn't speak. Instead, he untied his silk pajama bottoms. They slid from him, puddling at his feet.

"Can we do this?" Jenna asked through trembling lips. "What will happen?"

"I don't care," Rafe replied huskily. Never in his existence had he wanted anything more. It was love that burned within him. Love for Jenna.

"Are you sure we should make love?" she whispered.

In his heart he was sure it was what he wanted; in his mind he was sure it was a mistake. He closed his eyes, unable to think when they feasted on Jenna's beauty. But right now he didn't want to think. Instead, he took a step closer....

Dear Reader,

Last year we brought you a quartet of
AVENGING ANGELS—the sexiest angels this side of
heaven, to be exact. And you loved them so much that
we're bringing you two more of these very special
heroes.

Whenever there is injustice, the Avenging Angels are
on the case, ready to right the wrong, but often not
ready to deal with the pleasures of the flesh.

Here, Cassie Miles, who was one of the originating
authors of the quartet, is back with Rafe's story.
This *Real Angel* is about to learn a thing or two
about life and love.

We're delighted we could bring you more
AVENGING ANGELS!

Regards,

Debra Matteucci
Senior Editor & Editorial Coordinator
Harlequin Books
300 East 42nd Street
New York, NY 10017

A Real Angel
Cassie Miles

Harlequin Books

TORONTO • NEW YORK • LONDON
AMSTERDAM • PARIS • SYDNEY • HAMBURG
STOCKHOLM • ATHENS • TOKYO • MILAN
MADRID • WARSAW • BUDAPEST • AUCKLAND

ISBN 0-373-22443-5

A REAL ANGEL

Copyright © 1997 by Kay Bergstrom

This edition published by arrangement with Harlequin Books S.A.

® and TM are trademarks of the publisher. Trademarks indicated with ® are registered in the United States Patent and Trademark Office, the Canadian Trade Marks Office and in other countries.

Printed in U.S.A.

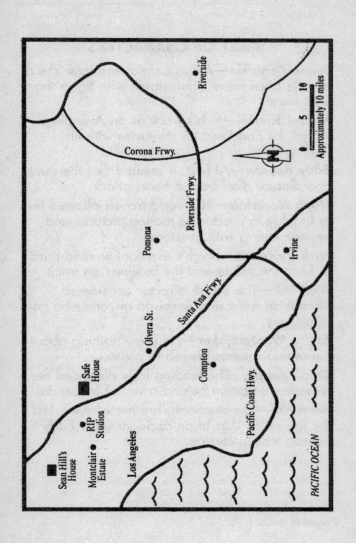

Approximately 10 miles

0 5 10

N

Riverside

Corona Frwy.

Riverside Frwy.

Pomona

Irvine

Santa Ana Frwy.

Olvera St.

Safe House

Compton

RIP Studios

Pacific Coast Hwy.

Montclair Estate

Los Angeles

Sean Hill's House

PACIFIC OCEAN

CAST OF CHARACTERS

Jenna Denardo—As an animal wrangler she'd always been more comfortable with tigers than with men.

Rafael Santini—In his work as an Avenging Angel, he had lived for centuries without finding love.

Eddy Benson—At first, it seemed that the stunt coordinator died from a heart attack.

Hugh Montclair—His world travels allowed him to indulge in producing motion pictures and experimenting with livestock.

Nick Vincenzo—Hugh's assistant worked hard to keep the estate and the business on track.

Alex Hill—The British director considered himself an artist and despised anyone who got in his way.

Taylor Wannamaker—He knew nothing about the animals it was his job to protect.

Dinah Aaron—The leading lady disguised her ferocious ambition behind a veil of innuendo.

Sean Hill—The stuntman, brother of Alex, lost the use of his legs in an accident while Eddy Benson was in charge.

Chapter One

Jenna Denardo peered into the tiny freezer of the half-sized refrigerator and contemplated ice cream. Devil's food chocolate chunk or low-fat heavenly hash? The hash was less caloric, more saintly. But it wasn't strictly necessary for Jenna to maintain the sleek body of a high-fashion model. Though she worked in the motion-picture business, her career as an animal handler kept her on the sidelines. She didn't need to worry about being front and center, where a camera would add ten pounds to her short, muscular frame and cause her long curly, dark blond hair to look like a mass of sandy frizz.

With sinful abandon, she grabbed the pint of devil's food. Humming along with the classical music on the late-night radio, she sat yoga-style in the middle of the lumpy sofa bed in the tiny dressing room at the rear of Soundstage 7. For the past three days and nights, this room had been her living quarters at Roybal International Productions—referred to as RIP, Rest in Peace, because the movie studio hadn't had a hit in such a long time.

The large room adjoining her dressing room had been modified to house the animals being used on this production: two llamas, five little pigs, six monkeys, lots of

birds, one ancient tiger and an eight-foot reticulated python.

She spooned into her ice cream and took a huge, de-
lectable bite. There was nothing better than chocolate!
Not even sex, if she remembered correctly. It had been
a long time.

Unfortunately, not even a mountain of chocolate could
rescue this movie project. Soundstage 7 was *not* a happy
set. Tempers were flaring. The director wanted to kill
the stars. The stars wanted to kill the stuntmen. And
everybody wanted to kill the artistic director, who was
taking forever to set up the scenario for a Garden-of-
Eden sequence that used all of the animals Jenna had
brought from the ranch she owned with her mother.

Three whole days, and only four scenes had been
filmed. Everything seemed to be going wrong.

She swallowed, savoring the cold, sweet ice cream.
Mid-slurp, she paused. A noise? A thud? Like the ware-
house doors on the soundstage slamming shut.

Strange. It was after eleven o'clock, and production
had shut down at six. Nobody should be here.

An intruder? Even though the movie lot was situated
in a run-down part of Hollywood, access was limited
and watchmen patrolled on a regular basis.

She turned off the radio and listened hard. Quiet
cloaked the atmosphere. She shrugged. Nothing to worry
about.

As she dipped into her ice cream again, Darius the
tiger let loose with a booming roar. In the menagerie
room, the monkeys made a sudden chatter. The pigs
squealed. Several varieties of birds joined in with loud
whistles and screeches.

Jenna knew her animals well enough to know that
these were not wails of hunger or discomfort. These

sounds signaled a warning. Their world had been invaded.

Her protective instincts activated, she leapt off the bed and whipped open the door to the adjoining menagerie room. Though she saw no one in the semidarkness, her animals continued their cries. In the center of the room, the birdcages rattled beneath their covers like angry ghosts. The monkeys scolded. Three of them, the capuchins, swung toward her. They bared their teeth. Their tiny fingers clenched the bars. The hair on the backs of their necks stood up.

She picked up her cell phone and called the front office. A tired voice answered, "Pete here."

"This is Jenna Denardo on Soundstage 7."

"The animal woman," Pete said. "What's up?"

"I think somebody's in here."

Her animals continued their racket. The noise echoed, magnified like a jungle movie being played at high volume.

"Can't hear you," Pete said.

"I might need your help. Can you come over here?"

"I'm not going in there with your snakes and tigers, young lady. Get your critters under control and—"

"Fine." There wasn't time to argue with him. The reaction from her animals told her that something was wrong. "I'll call back."

Jenna tucked the flip phone into the pocket of her pink sweatpants. With her matching sweatshirt and fuzzy slippers and a trace of chocolate on her lips, she wasn't exactly dressed for intimidation. But the right accessory made all the difference. She took a few careful steps backward, reached under her pillow, grabbed her snubnosed automatic and expertly checked the ammunition clip. After a moment's hesitation, she removed the safety.

In the menagerie room, she turned on the overhead fluorescents, causing an even more hysterical response from her animals. First, she went to the box where Selena was coiled within a bag. The python appeared to be safe and quiet. Then she circled the birdcages to the large enclosure where five piglets huddled together on a bed of straw. Beside them were the llamas.

There was no intruder in this room.

She stared at the door that led onto the soundstage. From outside, the tiger roared. The danger was out there.

Her fingers closed around the doorknob. She yanked it open and slipped outside. The cavernous interior of Soundstage 7, huge as an airplane hangar, was dimly illuminated by work lights. There was a clutter of technical equipment and a complete set for the Garden of Eden. The outer walls were lined with other dressing rooms, offices and a kitchen. There could be a dozen bogeymen hiding in here, and she'd never see them until they were right next to her.

Moving swiftly across the concrete floor, Jenna went to the heavy iron cage that held the tiger. Darius was an old beast, declawed by the carnival that had once owned him, but his coat was lustrous and handsome. In the care of Jenna and her mother, he had regained his vitality.

As she approached his cage, he slapped the bars with his huge paw. Nothing should frighten a Siberian tiger, the largest of felines, yet Darius stalked back and forth, distinctly tense. His long tail snapped like a whip.

In her peripheral vision, Jenna caught sight of movement, and she whirled to face the threat. Among the shadows, she saw no clearly defined form, but she sensed a presence. A shiver went through her. Someone was there, hiding amid a forest of props, lighting equipment and cameras.

A loud groan distracted her. She pivoted in time to see a man staggering toward the door to the room where her animals were kept.

"Hold it!" she yelled.

Stumbling, he turned to face her, and she recognized him. Eddy Benson, the stunt coordinator. "Eddy? Are you okay?"

As she watched, he crumpled to the floor. His watery blue eyes looked up at her, pleading for help.

"My God, Eddy. What's wrong?"

Though she saw no wound or injury, he was obviously in pain. She redialed the office on the cell phone and shouted into it, "Pete, call an ambulance."

"What?"

"It's Eddy Benson. It looks like he's having some kind of fit. He needs medical attention."

"That's bad news. Eddy's got heart problems."

From somewhere in the vast building, she heard a scraping noise. She dropped the phone with a clatter.

"Who's there?" She braced her gun in both hands.

Standing lights, props and shadows surrounded her. So many shapes in the dim light. They ranged across the concrete floor like a dark army.

Eddy groaned again, and she was torn. Should she let down her guard to help him?

Still holding her gun, she got behind Eddy, hooked her arms beneath his shoulders and pulled him inside the menagerie room where the light was better. She slammed the door and knelt beside him.

His entire body spasmed. A harsh, guttural cry issued from his lips. He grabbed her arm, pulled her close.

His teeth chattered violently, as if he were trying to

speak. His wiry body shuddered against her. He was burning up with fever, sweating. His gray hair was plastered in damp strands across his forehead. Was he having a heart attack?

When she attempted to move away, trying frantically to remember basic CPR procedures, he tightened his grip. His jaw clenched. A thin dribble of blood trickled from the corner of his mouth.

"It's okay, Eddy. I'm here."

He stared into her eyes, somehow disbelieving. His breathing steadied to a painful rasp. Not knowing what else to do, she held him, rocked him as if he were a child. For several minutes, they stayed in that position, with the animals screaming and Eddy trembling.

Where was the damn ambulance? She could feel him losing strength, dying in her arms. The animals knew. They seemed to sense the approach of death—a chill shadowy presence.

"Hang on, Eddy," she urged him. "It'll only be a few minutes more."

Please don't die. She prayed intensely. It wasn't the first time Jenna had cradled death in her arms. Three years ago, her father had died in a car accident. He'd lost control on a winding, hillside road. Crashed into a tree trunk. Jenna had been following in the truck. She'd witnessed the whole hellish spectacle, had heard her mother's screams from the passenger seat...and then the terrible silence as her mother, Kate Denardo, passed from consciousness. Though she'd survived the crash and her physical injuries had healed, Kate had never regained her vivacity and wit. Nowadays, she hardly ever left the ranch.

Sometimes, death was harder on those who were left behind.

"Please, Eddy. Don't die."

Finally, Jenna heard the soundstage door crash open. Help was on the way. Someone would save Eddy Benson.

He stiffened, then a stillness came over him. His arms and legs went limp as a rag doll. He exhaled a thin gasp.

"Stay with me, Eddy. Don't give up."

But it was too late. She could feel him slipping away. The cries of Jenna's animals modulated. The sounds were less frenzied and more mournful.

As the paramedics appeared at the door, she heard a rattle in Eddy's chest. A single word escaped his lips, "Francis."

AT ELEVEN O'CLOCK in the morning, Rafael strolled into the Brentwood Smoking Club. Although women were allowed as members, there was a strong flavor of masculinity at this private club in Beverly Hills. The resonance of primarily male voices created a low murmur. Lustrous oak wainscoting lined the walls. The carpeting was billiard table green. Furniture was solid, heavy and man-sized, precisely comfortable for Rafe's broad-shouldered, six-foot-three-inch frame.

In the temperature-controlled cedar room with floor-to-ceiling humidified lockers, he trailed his fingertips across the brass plate etched with the name, "Rafael Santini." It was one of his many aliases. Rafael Santini. Rafe Sabat. Ralph Sanders. Ron Sukahara.

He unlocked the humidor and removed a wooden box filled with handmade Havana cigars. The redolence of pure tobacco, rolled firm on the thigh of a young señorita, assailed his senses. His tongue whetted in anticipation of the first draw as he removed two cigars from the box. There were some sensual delights that surpassed celestial ecstasy.

Rafe found a leather armchair in a private corner near the picture window, offering a panoramic view of milky smog, rooftops and royal palms. In a subtle gesture, he signaled to one of the white-coated waiters. Rafe was ready for his double espresso.

After he had clipped the end of his cigar, he crossed his long legs and adjusted the trouser crease of his charcoal gray Armani suit, subtly striped with midnight black as dark as Rafe's long, thick hair tied in a ponytail at the nape of his neck. He reached into his inner suit coat pocket and removed a small book that he usually carried with him. The Bible.

As the waiter delivered the espresso and turned away, Rafe was left completely alone. He snapped his fingers to spark a small, blue flame, which he used to light his cigar. Such small miracles were among the privileges of being an angel.

The first taste of his cigar was ambrosia, deeply satisfying. The thick coffee added to his contentment. Rafe settled back to read the Book of Psalms, poetry for the soul.

After only a few moments, a muscular gentleman in tennis whites settled into the leather chair beside him. Without looking up, Rafe acknowledged the presence of the other. "Good morning, Mike."

"That's Saint Mike to you, my boy."

"Then this is an official visit."

"Yes, it is."

Mike was usually more casual, not like some of the saints who were tiresome with their insistence on titles and entitlements. Ironic, Rafe thought. The righteousness of souls derived from the few short years of actual human life, rather than from the ages of angelic existence.

As a mortal man, Rafe had been less than exemplary. In an ancient land that no longer existed, he'd been a thief and blackguard, living by his wits and his physical strength, which was, without exaggeration, formidable. Ultimately, he was apprehended for his crimes and incarcerated in a stinking hole of a jail, where he witnessed the suffering of innocents and underwent an epiphany. He'd repented and received divine forgiveness.

At the moment of his execution, Rafe had been recruited by Saint Michael himself into the ranks of the Avenging Angels. Saint Michael of the flaming sword. Saint Michael, the patron of policemen.

Rafe owed this virile saint a debt of gratitude that could not be repaid in one hundred lifetimes. Turning his head, Rafe gazed upon his mentor. "Cigar?"

"Don't mind if I do. Cuban?"

"Of course."

Mike accepted the cigar, rolled it between his fingers and savored the fragrance before he neatly clipped the end. "I like this place. Some of our friends in high places—literally in high places—don't approve of such creature comforts."

"I have no choice," Rafe said. "In my work with the International Department of Avenging Angels, I frequently deal with men of wealth and power. I need to look like one of them."

"By the way, I'm mightily impressed with your work in Latin America and the Pacific Rim," Mike said. "Your vengeance has been exact and proper."

A compliment? Though Rafe didn't wish to be suspicious, he sensed that Saint Michael was leading toward something unpleasant. "What's my next assignment?"

"It isn't exactly your kind of job. Nothing political. However, this assignment comes from the highest authority. It's about the death of a man named Eddy Benson."

"I don't recognize the name." Rafe routinely worked with presidents, excellencies and heads of state.

"Eddy Benson was a stunt coordinator for the movies."

Rafe felt his lip curl in a sneer. He had little use for the superficiality of the motion picture industry and the people who ran it. For the most part, they were ill-mannered—dull and frantic at the same time.

As Saint Michael explained the circumstances of Eddy Benson's death, Rafe's disdain grew. Why should his talents be wasted on such a trivial death?

"I assume by your presence," Rafe said, "that Eddy did not die of a simple heart attack."

"Know this, Rafael. It wasn't his natural time to die. Eddy was a good man, conscientious in his work. In his twenty-one years as a stunt coordinator, there was only one serious accident. Two years ago. Though it wasn't Eddy's fault, he mourned the tragedy. At that time, he rediscovered his faith."

Rafe didn't really care about Eddy Benson's tawdry little life. If he was to be stuck with this tedious assignment, he wanted it solved as quickly as possible. "Was he poisoned?"

"I don't know. The autopsy will be performed within a few days. You will investigate this death and report directly to me. I've cleared your schedule."

"Very well." Rafe tasted the smoke of his Havana cigar.

"Do you think this job is beneath you?"

Assuredly, it was. In his international work as an

avenger, Rafe had manipulated the rise and fall of empires. He had been matched against some of the most heinous criminals of history. In the grand tapestry of human events, this little murder of Eddy Benson was an infinitesimal snag. Yet, Rafe knew better than to voice his opinion. "I will complete the assignment to the best of my ability."

"It might be good for you to be involved in something that was less than earthshaking."

"Why?"

"Arrogance, my boy. Pride is a sin."

"And too much humility is a bore."

Saint Michael puffed on his cigar and chuckled. "Well, Rafe, we'll never have to worry that you might become boring."

WITH EDDY GONE, Soundstage 7 was even more chaotic than usual. Jenna stood in the semidarkness, watching as the grips rearranged the Garden of Eden to suit the vision of Alex Hill, the director of *Alien Age*. Before working on this film, Jenna had great respect for Alex, an Englishman who had directed an award-winning BBC children's series. He was, however, out of his depth in working with adults. He vacillated. He was moody and indecisive. Sometimes, he even second-guessed himself.

"Excuse me," came a deep voice from behind Jenna's right shoulder. "I'm looking for Hugh Montclair, the producer."

"Good luck. I haven't even met the man, and—"

When she turned, Jenna was struck speechless, her gaze riveted to the handsomest man she'd ever seen in her life. He was tall and had a great body. His Levi's outlined muscular thighs, and his fitted, custom-made work shirt spanned well-developed shoulders. His thick black hair fell loose to his shoulders. His eyes were a mysterious blue. He was so gorgeous that he seemed to glow.

"What is it?" he asked.

"Sorry." She shook her head but didn't look away. "It must be a trick of constantly standing in bright light, then shadow. It looks as if you're...shimmering."

"I'm not," Rafe assured her. "I'm not a star."

He studied her curiously. Very few mortals were so perceptive in detecting his angelic aura. "What's your name?"

"I'm Jenna Denardo, the animal handler for the film."

"Pleased to meet you." He knew from Saint Mike that Jenna Denardo was the woman who'd discovered the body of Eddy Benson. "I'm Rafe Santini. Could we talk for a moment? Privately?"

She glanced toward the set where technicians were adjusting lights and rearranging the greenery. "We can talk privately all you want," she said. "It's going to be a while before they're ready for my animals. Come with me."

He followed her past a caged tiger and into a separate room where she closed the door behind him. This area, filled with caged animals, was well lit, so Rafe assumed that his aura would be less noticeable. Yet the woman, Jenna, eyed him suspiciously.

"What?" he asked.

"It's strange. The animals generally react to the presence of someone they don't know, but look at them."

"They're well behaved," he said.

"Trust me, Rafe, this is a very rude bunch."

He reached toward the tall cage where four spider monkeys had ceased their play to watch him. With attentive calm, they scampered toward his hand and sat in a neat row. Their behavior was typical in Rafe's experience. Humans, with all their supposed sophistication, were generally unaware they were in the presence of angels. But animals, even the lower species, responded with instinctive reverence.

"Amazing," Jenna said. "You've been around animals before."

"I lived in Africa for a time."

Though he enjoyed her puzzlement, Rafe knew he shouldn't be so conspicuous. In a quiet thought, not unlike a prayer, he sent a message to the primates. *Dance for me.*

Immediately, the spider monkeys began darting around their cage.

"That's more like it," Jenna said. "I'm always worried when they're quiet. It means they're plotting something."

"Do you really believe that?"

"That monkeys are mischievous? You bet I believe it."

"Can they think?" he queried. "Can they plan? Do they feel emotions?"

"I believe they do. Surely, they experience love and rage. I've seen it."

"Some people would say your opinion was anthropomorphic and foolish."

"But you wouldn't, would you?"

Not unlike the creatures she worked with, this small woman with the mane of curling blond hair seemed attuned to him on an unusual level. In some strange way, he felt he'd known her before. Her taut body, clad in snug black leggings and an oversized red cotton sweater, appeared familiar to him, as if he knew the details beneath her clothing, the scent of her flesh, the softness of her skin. Her dark eyes shone with an odd intimacy.

But this was impossible! He couldn't have known her before. Rafe couldn't remember a single detail of his earthly existence. It had been centuries ago, and there had been no grand passion during his mortal life. He hadn't been the sort of man who gave himself to love. His only alliances with women were sexual, marvelously sexual. Distracted, he exhaled a brief sigh. Sex was a pleasure he hadn't indulged in for a long time—centuries. Lust, of course, was forbidden to angels.

He strode across the room. "It was in this room that Eddy Benson died."

"That's right," Jenna said. "Are you a cop?"

"No."

"Then why are you interested? You're not a reporter, are you? Because if you are, I have no comment."

"Why not? I thought all movie people loved the media."

"Not me. I don't want to see Eddy's death sensationalized on the front page of some cheesy tabloid." She bristled. "He was a good guy, and it wouldn't be right to—"

"Calm yourself. I'm not a reporter."

"Then tell me why you're here."

"I'm a stuntman," Rafe said. He hadn't precisely formulated his plan of action, but this direction felt right. As a stuntman, he could be on the set. He'd have ample time for investigation because he would only be called upon occasionally to perform simple physical feats. "I'm looking for a job."

"Did you know Eddy?"

"Only by reputation," Rafe said. He repeated the

words of Saint Michael. "I've heard he was conscientious in his work."

"That's right." She strolled to the enclosure, where two llamas gazed haughtily through their thick lashes. Jenna reached inside to stroke one and then the other. "Eddy was a pro. I'd worked with him on another project and liked him a lot. I'm sorry he passed away."

Rafe sensed a thought that was deeper than her words. "Was he murdered, Jenna?"

"That's an odd question."

"I've heard rumors."

"Well, you can forget about murder," she said. "He wasn't wounded. Not as far as I could tell."

"Heart attack?"

"I don't know. This seemed different. More like a seizure or something. He had a hard time breathing, and he was weak as a newborn kitten." She frowned. "Actually, his symptoms reminded me of a really bad case of bronchitis or flu."

"A virus?"

"Maybe."

Rafe nodded, considering. There had to be a reason Saint Michael had assigned him to this seemingly unimportant case. If Eddy Benson had been killed by a deadly virus, the implications were as far-reaching as the spread of Ebola. "What else can you tell me, Jenna?"

"Eddy was incredibly hot. Sweating like a pig." She smiled fondly at the piglets in their pen. "Pigs really aren't that gross, you know. Their reputation as slobs is undeserved. In fact, they're very like humans in their metabolism and bodily functions."

"Perhaps, then, their reputation is deserved, after all. Much of human behavior is despicable."

"Well, we can't all be sublime." She grinned. "Okay,

Rafe, you're looking for Montclair, the producer, and you want a job. Do you belong to the union?''

"Of course." Paperwork was never a problem for Rafe. Given a few moments, he could create any necessary credentials through various angelic resources or his human contacts. But he didn't want to discuss his cover story. His intellect had been sparked by her mention of viral infection. He was thinking of poison gases, virulent disease, a plague that would sweep like wildfire across densely populated southern California.

From outside the room, they heard a sudden commotion. Loud shouts echoed. Then, a scream. There were crashes, and the noise of people running across the concrete floor.

When the roar of a tiger exploded, Jenna cringed. She flung open the door and stared. "Damn!"

Darius stood outside his cage. His huge head swung from side to side. He sniffed the air and growled, appearing to enjoy his power to terrify these puny human beings who ran from him.

Though declawed and trained, Darius was still a wild animal, not a house pet. He weighed over four hundred pounds. From his nose to the end of his long tail, he was ten feet in length. His shoulder height was three feet. With one lazy swipe of his paw, he was capable of flinging Jenna across a room. She had to respect his physical strength and predatory instincts.

The director of the film, Alex Hill, dashed to Jenna's side. "Thank God, you've returned. Get your animal back in his cage."

Easier said than done. "What happened here?"

"We were arranging the set and needed the tiger to check the lighting. You didn't seem to be about, so I told one of the crew to fetch the beast."

Darius threw back his head and roared.

Within her breast, Jenna felt a similar primal fury. No one should have gone near her animals. If Eddy had been here, this never would have happened. "Why?"

"Well, the tiger seemed rather tame. Yesterday, when you walked him through his paces, he was utterly gentle."

She didn't bother to explain that she used severe restraints for handling Darius. All that was important now was to get her tiger back into his cage before he injured himself...or someone else.

Before she could act, Darius sprang. In a majestic lope, he charged toward the lights of the set. Gracefully, he avoided the tangle of wires on the floor and the forest of klieg lights and reflectors.

"No!" Jenna shouted. She strode after the tiger, exuding a courage that she didn't truly feel. "Darius, no!"

He paused and turned his head toward her. Though tigers were fearsome stalkers, their eyesight wasn't keen. Nor was their sense of smell. They responded best to auditory commands.

"Sit!" she commanded.

He snarled, and raised his paw in a threatening gesture as she approached.

"Sit!" she repeated. "Darius, sit!"

Jenna was well aware of the peril in getting too close. She was completely unarmed. If she'd been thinking, she'd have grabbed the tranquilizer gun in her supplies. Or her whip. But there wasn't time.

She needed to gain immediate control. But how? Even if she managed to hook her hand through the tiger's collar so she could lead him to his cage, Darius might break and run. With his powerful strength, he was capable of yanking her shoulder from the socket.

She was only five feet from the big cat. "Darius, sit! Stay!"

He took one stride toward her. Almost apologetically, he reached out with his huge paw and batted her arm. The blow staggered her, but Jenna remained on her feet. If she'd fallen to the floor in front of him, Darius might assume she was prey. He might be old, but there was nothing wrong with his teeth.

From the corner of her eye, she saw Rafe step up beside her.

"What are you doing? Get back, Rafe."

"Let me help."

"He doesn't know you," she said. "He might—"

"Darius," Rafe said softly. He went down on one knee, putting himself at eye level with the animal.

The enormous cat cocked his head. His fierce eyes gleamed like amber jewels. He made a low rumble in the back of his throat. His tail lashed. The muscles in his haunches tightened, preparing to leap.

"Darius," Rafe whispered.

A crashing door at the rear of the soundstage distracted the beast. He looked away from Rafe.

Jenna saw two of the studio guards. They entered the room with their pistols drawn.

"Hold it!" she yelled as she stepped around Darius and positioned herself in front of the tiger. "Put down those guns!"

"No way, lady. That's a dangerous animal."

"Please, give us a chance. Please."

The guards exchanged a glance. "What do you need?"

"Silence," she said. "Everyone, please be quiet."

"You got it," the guard said. "Now, step aside."

"No." She stayed in front of the tiger, her arms outstretched, shielding him with her body. "Please, all of you. Silence."

An eerie stillness descended upon the soundstage, as if everyone had caught their breath at the same time.

Jenna looked over her shoulder at Rafe and the tiger. They hadn't moved. Caught in a private rapport, man and beast stared at each other. As the hush wrapped around them, they seemed to be communicating in nods and frowns. The tiger relaxed his powerful musculature. He blinked lazily. Slowly, Darius lowered himself to the concrete floor and turned his head to one side, conceding natural dominance to Rafe.

When Rafe stood, the tiger stepped up beside him. Together, they walked through the clutter of movie-making equipment toward the iron cage.

Jenna kept pace beside them, still protecting Darius from the overzealous guards. In Eden, she imagined, Adam must have been like Rafe. Unafraid, he was master of all he surveyed. The rivers bent to his will. The beasts obeyed without question.

He held open the door to the cage, and Darius calmly walked inside.

When Rafe locked the door behind the tiger, the soundstage erupted with applause. No one clapped more fervently than Jenna. This incident could, so easily, have ended in tragedy. Overwhelmed with gratitude, she flung herself into Rafe's arms.

As soon as her body made contact with his, a shock went through her. It was a jolt, as if caused by high-voltage electricity. She'd never felt anything like it before. Immediately, she recoiled.

Who was this man? What was he? No ordinary human being had the willpower to dominate a Siberian tiger.

As she stared at him, Jenna shuddered inside. She'd never met anyone like Rafe Santini before.

Chapter Two

Regular activity resumed on the soundstage. The guards holstered their guns and left. The art director returned to his set, signaling to the grips which props should be repositioned. The gaffers fussed with their lighting equipment. Other members of the crew and cast meandered past the catering tables to chug coffee, nibble on dried-out sandwiches and brag about their role in this real-life drama.

Jenna stood apart. Didn't these people realize what they had just witnessed? Were they too jaded by movie magic to recognize the real thing? In her heart, she knew she had just seen a miracle. There was no natural explanation for the way Rafe had stared Darius in the eye and directed him back to his cage.

"That was fabulous," Alex Hill exclaimed. He raised his voice. "I don't suppose anyone happened to catch that fabulous moment on film?"

There was a mumbled chorus of negative replies.

"Pity."

Alex Hill, outfitted from head to toe in black, stroked his goatee thoughtfully as he scanned the faces of his crew through his round, silver-rimmed glasses. His gaze finally came to rest upon Jenna.

In his eyes, she saw a sly comprehension. He knew. Alex knew—as she did—that there was something unearthly about Rafe Santini, something beyond pale, everyday experience.

Rather than feeling relieved that somebody else saw the strange magic in Rafe, Jenna was worried. Alex was smart without being wise. Though he acted like an artsy British fop, he hadn't achieved a position of power in the movie industry without being a master manipulator. He wouldn't hesitate to use anyone, even Rafe.

"Well, Jenna," he said. "Won't you please introduce me to your friend?"

"This is Rafe Santini." She inhaled a deep breath, struggling to suppress her apprehensions. "He's a stuntman."

"Really?" Alex grabbed Rafe's hand. "Consider yourself hired, Rafe. While I watched you subdue the savage beast, I was inspired, positively inspired. You've given me the precise vision for this first segment of the film."

He held up his hands as if framing a headline. "The strength of pure innocence."

"Come again," Rafe said.

"The aliens in this film represent the forces of evil beyond our control. Therefore, man must be heroic and good. Yet, vulnerable. Powerful. Yet, weak as a babe in arms. Dynamic. Yet…"

The wiry young director exuded more energy than Jenna had seen from him thus far in the production. Though she hated to rain on his parade of Hollywood clichés, she couldn't allow Rafe to be misled about the terms of his employment. "Alex, don't you have to check with the producer before hiring or firing anyone?"

"Hugh Montclair has allowed me some small artistic

license in my decision-making," Alex said stiffly. "Rafe will have to work out the money details with our esteemed producer, of course."

And so would Jenna. She had money concerns of her own. "Do you have any idea when Mr. Montclair might be coming to visit the set?"

"Jenna, my dear, I thought you knew. Hugh Montclair is a bit of a recluse. Rafe will have to go to his home."

"I should go along," Jenna said. "It's obvious that you're going to need my animals for longer than specified in my contract. I need to renegotiate terms with Mr. Montclair."

"Careful, Jenna," Alex warned. "You're not Hugh Montclair's favorite person right now. Not after the...the incident, last night."

The incident? "Are you referring to Eddy Benson's death?"

"A nasty bit of business," Alex said. "Our esteemed producer has decided that you need help with your animals. When we spoke on the phone this morning, he said he'd send someone."

"What?" If she'd been doing an unsatisfactory job, the producer was within his rights to fire her. But assigning a helper? "That's not the way I work. Denardo Animal Wranglers has been in business for twenty years and—"

"Fine, fine." Alex flicked his fingers as if waving off the dull business end of filmmaking. "Talk to Hugh about it. My assistant will set up a time for you. Won't you, Dorothy?"

"You bet." Dorothy stepped forward, making a note on her clipboard. This gnomish lady had always worked in the motion picture business and was old enough to claim that her first movie memory as a child was being clasped to the bosom of none other than Mae West. She peered over the reading glasses perched on the tip of her nose and said, "So, Jenna. How's later tonight? Does that work for you?"

"Fine," Jenna said. "After we've finished filming, and I've bedded down the animals, I could leave for a while."

Dorothy turned to Rafe. "What about you?"

"I can be free this evening."

"Okay, kiddo." Dorothy jotted a note on her clipboard. "I'll let Jenna know the time."

Alex gestured to Rafe. "Walk with me. We have a few bits to discuss. Tell me, have you ever worked naked?"

"No, but I wouldn't mind."

Jenna swallowed hard. All other thoughts blanked from her mind. Naked? How would Rafe look in the nude? *Fabulous,* she thought, echoing Alex's assessment.

"Naked, huh?" Dorothy chuckled. "I'd like to see that! Your friend, Rafe, is one great-looking guy."

"Ditto," Jenna replied.

"So, kiddo, are you okay? It must have been a shock for you, finding Eddy like you did."

"I'm going to miss him," Jenna said. "If Eddy had been here, the whole incident with the tiger wouldn't have happened."

"I liked Eddy." Dorothy glanced down at the hen scratchings on her clipboard. "But there were a lot of people who didn't. Like our director."

"Alex?"

"He might look like a namby-pamby, but he's a...what do you call it? A 'seething pot of emotional turmoil.'" Her thin lips grimaced. "That's a line from a movie I worked on. One of those gorgeous costume dramas. I love those things.''

"I thought Alex was fairly new to Hollywood. How has he had time to make enemies?''

"He comes from a theater and movie family. 'Sins of the father,' you know. That's another quote.''

From the Bible, Jenna thought. The greatest of costume dramas. "Did Alex's father know Eddy Benson?''

"His brother,'' Dorothy said. "The brother was seriously injured in a film Eddy was working on a couple of years ago. The poor kid ended up in a wheelchair, lost the use of his legs. Not as bad as Christopher Reeve, but bad.''

Jenna looked toward Alex and Rafe. The two men were standing at the edge of the klieg lights aimed at the Garden of Eden set. Rafe seemed to be glowing, again. "Did Alex blame Eddy for the accident?''

"Sure did.'' Dorothy stood beside her, following her line of sight. "From what I understand, it wasn't really anybody's fault. Alex's brother took a bad fall. People don't realize how dangerous these stunts can be. Anyhow, it was real tragic. Eddy blamed himself.''

Jenna wasn't surprised. Eddy had been extremely responsible in his work—almost to the point of being irritating. He even fussed with her animals. The day before yesterday, he'd informed her that one of her pigs seemed ill, and he'd wanted to take the animal to a vet.

Beside her, Dorothy exhaled a sigh. "That Rafe is something else! Is he single?''

"I don't know. I only met him a few minutes ago.''

"You're single,'' Dorothy pointed out. "If I were you, I'd latch on to him quick. Before our female star gets the chance.''

Latching on had never been one of Jenna's talents. "And how should I do that?"

"Ask him out," Dorothy said. "Don't tell me you've never asked a man out before."

"Sure," Jenna said. In fifth grade, she'd asked Richie Vanderpool to the sock hop. He'd turned her down and stolen her lunch. "It didn't work out too well."

"Dorothy!" came the bellow from Alex. "Where are my stars? I need them on set. Now!"

"Gotta run," she said. "Remember what I told you. Dinah Aaron is coming out here any minute, and I guarantee she's going to have the hots for your stuntman."

Jenna really hadn't considered the possibility of dating anyone involved with this film. Or any other film. Typically, when she was on set, she was too busy with her animals to think about anything else.

But Rafe was different than most movie people. He was different than anyone she'd met before. Supernatural? As he approached her, she had an impending sense that it was now or never. If she didn't act quickly and ask him out, Dinah would be all over him, and there was no way Jenna could compete with the glamorous female star.

Rafe came up beside her and smiled casually. In a low voice, he confided, "You wouldn't believe what Alex has in mind. He wants me to get naked and parade around with the tiger, perhaps pull a thorn from his paw."

"That didn't happen in the Garden of Eden, did it?"

"Not according to any Scripture I've seen. But the idea of aliens landing in Eden isn't biblically accurate, either."

Jenna's lips stretched in a tense grin. In the few minutes he'd been with her, her heartbeat had accelerated, her cheeks felt warm and her palms were sweaty. "How did you get Darius to go along with you?"

"Concentration," he said.

"It was more than that," she said. "It was as if you'd hypnotized him."

"I'm not a sorcerer, Jenna."

"Well, no." Of course not. What had she been thinking? He was just a man. A very good-looking man. "So, Rafe, are you married?"

"No."

"I was thinking, you know, maybe tonight, after we meet with Hugh Montclair, we could kind of go out on a date. Maybe."

Oh God, that was awful! She'd wanted to sound as self-assured as a femme fatale. Instead, she'd been reduced to a stammering klutz.

His eyebrows raised. A slight smile flickered across his well-shaped lips. "Actually, Jenna, I don't date women."

"Oh." Jenna's cheeks flamed. Simultaneously, she felt embarrassed and relieved. He was gay. All the good men were either spoken for or gay. Why hadn't she thought of that? Somebody as delicious as Rafe wouldn't be wandering around unattached.

"Jenna!" Alex bellowed. "I need you. Jenna!"

She went to see what he wanted. "Bye, Rafe. See you later."

"Later," he said.

Rafe watched her hurry toward the director. Her behavior toward him was different than before. She seemed diffident, perhaps hurt. By his refusal to go on a date?

Rafe shrugged. He hadn't meant to injure her pride, but he really couldn't concern himself with the emotional state of this pretty young woman with the wildly curling blond hair. She had little to do with the death of Eddy Benson. Beyond finding the body, Jenna was not a part of this crime. And the murder was the only reason Rafe was here. If Eddy had been infected with a virus, he needed to act quickly.

He turned away from Jenna. A more pressing problem had presented itself. While Alex was talking, Rafe realized that he'd be expected to appear on film. Naked or not, he was fairly certain that his angelic radiance would be evident—if not as an aura, the slight glow that accompanied him might cause the film to distort.

He should have figured that out before he offered himself as a stuntman. It wasn't like him to make a blatant oversight.

Of course, there was a solution, but Rafe wasn't anxious to pursue it. In order to appear on film, he needed to become a mortal.

Though Rafe regularly assumed the human form that most accurately reflected his eternal soul, he was still an angel—a spiritual being made of purest energy. He could fly. He could dematerialize. He could whisper his thoughts into the minds of men without making a physical sound.

Unencumbered by a body, he could taste if he chose to. Yet, he needed no food or drink to survive. He felt neither hunger nor thirst. His beard didn't grow. He didn't sweat.

But if he became human? Not only was the transformation risky, but if he took human substance, Rafe was subject to aches and pains, wheezes and sniffles. As a mortal man, he could die.

The risk didn't frighten him, but the idea that he might fail in this assignment did. He must make no more careless mistakes.

He left the soundstage, needing to begin his investigation of the possible virus. Outside, the Los Angeles skies were a hazy gray. On the movie lot, Rafe could see many other angels, invisible to the human eye, as they enacted their duties as guardians, heralds and special messengers. A delicate female form, complete with pearly wings, lounged atop one of the buildings, casually watching. A guardian shadowed his charge, dogging every step, whispering advice that would be called conscience. Every human had a guardian angel, but these caretakers were not always present.

None of these angels had witnessed Eddy's murder, or else they would have reported to St. Michael. But what had happened to the guardian who should have kept watch over Eddy Benson? Rafe needed to communicate with this individual. On the human side of this investigation, he had already determined that the Los Angeles coroner's office had not yet performed an autopsy on Eddy Benson. His death hadn't even been classified as a murder.

No one knew, except the angels. And Jenna. She had suspicions.

Making sure that no one was observing, Rafe dematerialized, releasing the physical manifestation of himself. He was utterly free, without shape or substance. As pure energy, he soared through the heavens, gliding through beams of light, riding on the wind, seeking truth from a being like himself.

An unassigned guardian angel might be anywhere, but Rafe's essential wisdom guided his flight. He abandoned conscious thought and sensation. His investigative instincts guided him to a small, adobe church near Olvera Street.

Angels were often found in a place of worship. Near

the altar, Rafe identified the former guardian angel of Eddy Benson.

Rafe alighted on a front pew. In an instant, he had resumed an identity, the well-drawn portrait of Rafael. To the being beside him, Rafe posed the silent question: What happened to Eddy Benson?

"I don't know." The angel became solid. He was youthful, a handsome fellow with long blond curls and mournful eyes. "I should have been watching, but it wasn't Eddy's time to die."

"Then he was murdered."

"Yes. I came too late."

"How did he die?" Rafe asked.

"Some sort of poison affected his heart." The young angel shifted uncomfortably. "I'm not a doctor. I don't know exactly what it was."

"Could it have been a virus?"

"I don't know."

Even in the world of the omniscient, there were boundaries to knowledge. All wisdom was available to those who sought such things. However, most thinkers quested for eternal truths, not physical intelligence.

"In Eddy's final days, what was he doing?" Rafe questioned. "Who had he seen?"

"Why do you want to know?"

"I seek to avenge his death. Upon direct orders from Saint Michael."

"You're an avenger? Oh, good." The guardian seemed to lighten with relief. "I'm glad that somebody is taking notice. Eddy Benson wasn't the most important person on earth, but he was a good man."

"My question," Rafe reminded. "Do you suspect anyone of Eddy's murder?"

"Not really. He was working on that stupid movie.

All day, every day, he was involved with those movie people. It really didn't seem like there was anything to worry about.''

''What about Alex Hill?''

''He hated Eddy.'' The guardian considered for a moment. ''Alex Hill is dangerous. And so is that woman.''

''Jenna?''

''No, the beautiful one. Dinah.''

Rafe hadn't yet met her. ''Why do you think she might have something to do with Eddy's murder?''

''I just do,'' the guardian said somewhat petulantly. ''She was always nasty to Eddy, and she isn't the type to offend men, if you know what I mean.''

''Anyone else?''

''It's hard to tell. Everybody in the movies lies and cheats. I hope the next person I get assigned to watch is an accountant or a farmer, maybe. I'd like a farmer.''

''After your negligence with Eddy Benson, you'll be lucky to be guardian to a flea.''

''It happened so fast,'' he whined. ''It wasn't my fault.''

How unfortunate, Rafe thought, that Eddy Benson's guardian angel hadn't been more perceptive. If he had been, Eddy might not have died before his time.

Once again, Rafe took to the skies. Purely for his own pleasure, he assumed the traditional angelic form. Effortlessly, he stroked the air with luminous white wings and sailed above the lingering California smog, reveling in absolute freedom. How could he give this up? Even a brief time as a mortal was an unpleasant prospect.

But it had to be done. He needed to be ready to appear on film while he continued his inquiries.

The transformation was a skill Rafe had discovered during the centuries of his angelic existence. Because he was an avenger at the highest level, it was sometimes necessary to physically confront the forces of evil—dark angels who stood at the shoulder of dictators and sycophants, enticing them with greed and lust for power. If those evil ones had recognized Rafe as an angel, they would have rebuffed him. And so he had learned to take human form to fool them, to turn their attention away from his investigations. Among the angels, humanity was the ultimate deception.

After gliding over the soundstage and determining that everyone was busy on set, he slipped into a private room. It appeared to be a dressing room with a well-lit mirror and a messy makeup table. A woman's clothing, size six, was scattered about carelessly.

Rafe resumed his typical physical manifestation and stood, staring at himself in the mirror. To the mortal eye, he appeared to be one of them. Except for the slight radiance that Jenna had noticed, he had the shape and form of a man.

His eyelids closed as he began his meditation, concentrating upon a void, a nothingness, while exerting the considerable force of his will. A spiral of magnetic energy surrounded him.

"Rafael."

His inner voice whispered to him, calling him from this course, reminding him of the peril. To be trapped in a human body was surely the darkest circle of hell, but he could not allow fear to dissuade him. He must trust in his judgment.

The energy spiral entered at the base of his spine. Coiling upward, it reached his head, the center of idea and thought. Solid matter consumed him. A heavy skeleton weighted him. Human organs formed his new anatomy. His blood, fiery hot, churned along the spinal column, then spread to his limbs. He felt skin beneath his clothing. Flesh, solid flesh.

Fierce pain accompanied every pulsing throb. He suffered the agony of birth, yet he did not lose his concentration. He acknowledged the torture and accepted it. In a labored gasp, he inhaled the first breath of air and felt his lungs crackle and expand. Finally, his angel heart became a heavy, blood-filled organ within his chest.

The change was complete.

Exhausted by the effort, Rafe collapsed into a chair in the dressing room. With his spirit imprisoned in flesh, he could barely move. His arms and legs felt ponderous and heavy. Small aches and twinges made themselves known. He would have to work with this body if he expected to perform as a stuntman.

Slowly, he rose to his feet and looked in the mirror. Physically, he did not appear to be much different than before.

From outside the dressing room, he heard female voices. Though Rafe was not yet recovered enough to face anyone, he must be ready. He jogged his slow-thinking human brain, trying to invent an excuse for being here in a woman's dressing room.

The dressing-room door swung open, framing Jenna and another woman, a brunette with full lips and exquisite makeup.

The brunette stared at him. "Well, hello there."

"Hi," he said. Apparently, that was the best response he could muster with his inferior human brain.

"Most times, I'd be really annoyed to find a man in my dressing room. But you, darling, can stay right where you are."

Who was she? He looked toward Jenna for an answer. Her dark eyes glowered. "Gosh, Rafe, this is an odd place for you to turn up. Especially since you aren't interested in women.''

"Apparently," Dinah said. "He's interested in me. Introduce us, Jenna."

"Dinah Aaron, this is Rafe Santini. He's a stuntman."

"How convenient," Dinah purred as she sidled into the room and approached him. "I have a few stunts in mind."

"Sorry to be here," Rafe said. His voice sounded hoarse, and he cleared his throat, tasting the slick interior of his mouth. "I needed a little privacy. I'll be going now."

"You can stay." Dinah reached up and patted his cheek. "I hope you won't mind if I change clothes."

"You don't need to change," Jenna said in clipped tones. "Alex wanted me to work with you on handling the python."

"But I despise snakes." Her gaze stayed on Rafe. "Don't you?"

"I don't mind reptiles," he said. He considered the snake to be one of the more fascinating creations. "Their method of locomotion is beautiful."

"Slithering? Oh, ick." She lowered her gaze toward his thighs. "I like legs."

"That's...rational." The more he used his voice, the more he become fully ensconced in his human anatomy. He felt stronger, capable of walking.

"Maybe Rafe could help you with the python," Jenna suggested. "He's really good with animals, and—"

"No," Dinah snapped. "I'm not touching your disgusting reptile, and that's final."

"Dinah, if you're going to play Eve in the Garden of Eden, you have to get close to the snake."

"Oh, God, you remind me of poor old Eddy Benson, always trying to tell me what to do and what not to do."

Rafe's ears pricked up. "Did you know Eddy well?"

"Well enough," she said.

"You must be saddened by his death."

"Oh, sure." She gazed into her mirror and touched the corner of her mouth, smoothing her lipstick. "It's always really sad when somebody dies before their time."

How had she known? "Why would you say that? If his death was due to a heart attack, it must have been his time."

"Maybe you're right." Again, she looked at him. "You're deep, aren't you? I like that in a man."

Jenna made a loud, harrumphing noise. "I'm asking for the last time, Dinah, will you come with me so we can—"

"No. For the last time. They're just going to have to rewrite the script or get a double for me in those scenes."

When Jenna turned to leave, Rafe called after her. "Wait. I need to talk with you."

"Stay with me," Dinah said. Clearly, her words were a command. "Right here. Right now."

Whether human or angel, Rafe took orders from no one, except the saints. The human blood flowing through his body warmed. Yet, he must not insult Dinah. The guardian had suggested that she had information about Eddy's death.

Acting upon an instinct that he did not completely comprehend, he caught her manicured hand in his and lifted her fingertips to his lips, lightly brushing her scented skin with a kiss. "If I obeyed you, Dinah, what sort of man would I be?"

"Ooh, Rafe. Very suave." Her greenish eyes shone hard as perfectly matched emeralds. For an instant, he glimpsed a fierce strength behind Dinah's silly posturing. She whispered, "Most men learn to obey me and love it. Don't try to stand up to me. You haven't got a prayer."

Ironically, prayer was the one resource Rafe had in large supply. "It's hard to believe you don't already have a boyfriend."

"Maybe I do." For an instant, he saw honest emotion in her studied, sultry gaze.

"Do you love him?"

She tossed her head. "Leave me, Rafe."

"As you wish."

He exited to the soundstage, scanning with his imperfect human eyes for a sight of Jenna.

She stood beside the catering tables with a piece of chocolate fudge in her hand. As soon as she caught sight of him, she pivoted and stalked toward the room where her animals were housed. Her long, curling hair bounced as she walked. Reflected lights from the set picked out strands of pure gold. Though her torso was hidden beneath the oversized red sweater, her shapely legs were nicely displayed by the fitted black leggings.

Rafe found himself staring at the delicate tapering of her ankles, the enticing swell of her calves and her thighs.

"Jenna," he called to her.

She whirled. Her hair spun behind her. Her complexion blushed pink. When she inhaled, her breasts lifted beneath the sweater.

A work of art, Rafe thought. His admiration for her spirited beauty was similar to the sort of appreciation he had for the works of Michelangelo and Rodin. Yet in his mortal body, he experienced a physical stirring. Beneath his jeans, Rafe felt himself harden in arousal.

Shocked by this response, he was struck motionless, staring at her as she marched back toward him. Her breasts! The slight motion of them caused desire to explode within him.

When she stood in front of him with her fists planted at her waist, outlining the hourglass shape beneath her sweater, he felt weak-kneed and helpless. This was absurd! He was Rafael, an all-powerful Avenging Angel. He was a superior being. He was above such yearnings. And yet his blood hummed through his veins. His mortal body was paralyzed with the desire to make love to this woman.

"I suppose," she snapped, "you think that little performance was cute."

"Cute?"

"First, you tell me that you're gay. Then, you lurk around in Dinah's dressing room."

"Gay," he mumbled dumbly. Had he told her he was gay?

"If you didn't want to go out with me, you could at least have been honest."

"I want to," he said. He wanted to take her in his arms, to feel the softness of her breasts. But how could he begin? What should he say? It had been many lifetimes since he'd engaged in courtship. "Dinner. Can we have dinner?"

When Rafe had been a man, centuries ago, there had been no such preliminaries. The only women he had known, in the biblical sense, had been paid to practice the art of love. Only once had he thought of marriage, but the woman he wished to wed was far too highborn for him, unattainable. He had forgotten all about her...until now.

Jenna glared at him. "Are you asking me out to dinner?"

"Yes. That's what I am doing." Rafe had observed other men as they engaged in this ritual. "It seems appropriate to offer food."

"No, thanks. I don't need a pity date." Her slender shoulders rose and fell in a charming shrug. "Let's just forget this ever happened, okay?"

Should he agree? Should he insist? "Okay."

"Come with me, Rafe. Even if Dinah refuses to spend any time with the animals, you need to get familiar with them."

She pivoted and headed back toward Darius the tiger. Rafe wanted to follow, but his erection made it difficult to walk swiftly. He limped along, despising his all-too-human response to a pretty woman.

He made it to the room full of cages. Unlike the first time he'd encountered her menagerie, the animals gave no sign of recognizing him. Instead of gazing with reverence, the spider monkeys screeched so loudly that the sound hurt his ears.

Jenna informed him, "We have a meeting with Hugh Montclair at eight o'clock. That means we should leave here at about seven-thirty. I'll drive."

"Yes," he said.

He was unable to take his eyes off her. When she leaned into the pen to pick up one of the pot-bellied piglets, her sweater slid up, revealing the curve of her firm, round bottom. The vision was more spectacular than the Sistine Chapel. Rafe groaned.

"What?" Jenna turned toward him. "What's wrong? Are you feeling ill?"

"No." His throat constricted. His voice was hoarse. "I'm all right."

"You look kind of strange." She placed the piglet on the floor.

"Fine," he said. "I'm fine."

"A couple of days ago, Eddy said one of my pigs was sick, but I can't remember which one. I probably shouldn't say this, but they all look pretty much alike to me."

She took another pig from the enclosure. "Anyway, we need to work with herding them. After the success of the movie *Babe,* Alex thinks pigs should have a more prominent role in the Garden of Eden. How's that for logic?"

Rafe's brain had stuck on her mention of Eddy Benson. The murder of Eddy Benson was why he was here, in mortal form. Though it seemed impossible, he had completely forgotten his mission for several minutes.

Jenna picked up another pig. The other two stayed close to her, huddling near her for protection.

Rafe forced himself to speak. "Tell me about Eddy and the sick pig."

"Well, he said he'd take the pig to a veterinarian, and I said that was fine with me, I'd pay for any treatment." She looked up at Rafe. "But he never gave me a bill. I never noticed that one of the pigs was missing."

"Perhaps Eddy changed his mind."

"Must have."

As she reached down for the last of the piglets, Jenna hesitated. A slight frown drew parallel furrows between her eyes. She turned, counted the other four pigs and stared back into the enclosure.

"What's wrong?"

Her eyes widened as she looked toward him. "Rafe, this isn't my pig."

Chapter Three

After twenty minutes on the Garden of Eden set with the eight-foot python draped heavily around her shoulders, Jenna objected, "Alex, it's late, and these lights are too hot for Serena. Are we about done?"

"Who is Serena?"

She held up the snake's delicately patterned body. The graceful almond-shaped head sinuously wove back and forth. Serena was capable of three expressions: tongue flick, mouth open, mouth closed. But it seemed to Jenna that the python was sneering at the director. The snake's apparent disdain was highly justified. This standing-around exercise seemed even more futile than most of the time-wasting nonsense on *Alien Age*.

Jenna explained, "I have to get her out of the lights. It irritates her skin, and prolonged exposure to heat can kill her."

"Come now, Jenna, your creature is little more than a handbag."

Serena flicked her tongue.

"One more moment," Alex said. "Please. I'm on the cusp of an inspiration."

"Time's up," announced a crisp male voice. "Get the snake off set."

Though Jenna was blinded by the glare of lights, she immediately recognized the officious tone and high-handed manner of Taylor Wannamaker. He was a lawyer who policed movie sets for the Society for the Prevention of Cruelty to Animals, and he took his job extremely seriously, even though he knew next to nothing about the creatures he was supposed to protect.

"Well, well, Jenna Denardo," he droned. "I understand you've been having some problems with your pigs."

Alex stepped forward. "All right, Jenna. We're done for the day." He whirled dramatically, confronting Taylor. "Who, may I ask, are you? And what makes you think you can give orders on my set?"

"I'm with the SPCA," Taylor said. "It's my responsibility to make sure none of these animals are mistreated."

"I daresay the snake is not overworked," Alex drawled in his British accent. "All it's done thus far is drape. That's hardly a workout."

"But the lights," Taylor said. "They're too hot."

"She's fine," Jenna assured him. Knowing that Taylor wasn't friendly with snakes, she thrust forward a thick coil of Serena. "Here, you can feel for yourself."

"No, thank you," he said tight-lipped. "It's lucky for both of you that I arrived before any damage was done."

"I resent that implication," Jenna said. "None of my animals have ever been injured on a set."

"I wasn't implying—"

"Yes, you were," she flared. Taylor had been assigned to one other film she had worked on. At that time, he wrongly cited her for improper care. "Now, what's this about my pigs?"

"Would you mind putting the snake down, Jenna?"

She was tempted to do as he asked, dropping Serena to the floor where she would glide among the electrical wires and terrify the crew. But one animal escapee per day was plenty.

"I'll return Serena to her cage," Jenna said. "When I come back, I want a full explanation of your pig comment."

In the separate room where her animals were kept, Jenna lifted the snake from her shoulders and placed her in the soft cotton bag, which she locked inside a wooden box punched with airholes. When she turned, Rafe was standing behind her.

He was so close, she couldn't avoid bumping into him. Off balance, she caught hold of his forearm, feeling solid muscle beneath skin. Unlike the previous time she had touched him, there were no dramatic shock waves. He felt warm and pleasantly furry. When she looked up into his blue eyes, his gaze regarded her with a gentleness she hadn't seen before. "You're not glowing anymore."

"No."

And yet his magnetism increased. She was drawn to him in a way that defied explanation. Even without the glow, Rafe was far from average or plain. "You're a very mysterious person."

"Not really."

"Who are you really? Where did you come from?"

"I've always been here."

"In L.A.?"

"The City of Angels."

The way he subtly emphasized the word "angels" gave her pause. Was that it? Was he an angel, an otherworldly being sent to watch over her?

Jenna shook the thought from her head. Though it

would be lovely to believe in such a heavenly phenomenon, she had no cause to assume that her life was especially protected. She'd had her share of tragedy and sorrow. Besides, if Rafe were an angel, she wouldn't break out in a sweat whenever she saw him. Her stomach wouldn't clench in a knot. She wouldn't feel this ridiculous urge to giggle. She wouldn't feel so...sexual.

Jenna cleared her throat. "About our dinner tonight," she said. "I'm afraid we don't have time to do more than grab a burger. It's already after six, and I've got to take care of the animals before we leave for our eight o'clock appointment with Hugh Montclair."

"Fine," he said. "We'll grab a burger."

"Do you mind if I drive? I have a couple of errands on the way."

"Not at all."

Rafe felt the corners of his mouth stretching into a full grin of amusement. She'd have to drive because he didn't have a car. He hadn't thought that far ahead before he abandoned his angelic powers. Nor did he have a wallet with ready cash.

Though he should have been irritated by his lack of planning, he had a giddy sense of well-being when he was with Jenna. She seemed to brighten the world around her.

He should have been researching the possibility of a virus and investigating the murder. With a vengeance. After all, that was his true identity—Avenging Angel. Instead, he'd contented himself with gossip from the other stuntmen, learning very little. Several mentioned Sean Hill, the brother of Alex, who had been severely injured while Eddy Benson was in charge. If anyone had a motive to murder Eddy, it was Sean.

"See you, Rafe. I need to go back on the set and hammer Taylor Wannamaker."

"Who?"

"He's this obnoxious lawyer who works for the SPCA. The last time I saw Taylor, he filed an SPCA complaint because my goofy little Pekinese got filthy. Unsanitary conditions. That was what Taylor said."

"What really happened?" Rafe couldn't imagine Jenna mistreating any of her menagerie.

"It was in the script that my dog would jump into a mud puddle, and getting messy was far from cruelty for this particular pup who loves to turn her gorgeous, shiny coat into a mass of tangles."

Rafe fell into step beside her. "May I watch you hammer?"

"It won't be pretty."

But he thought it was adorable when Jenna charged up to the tall, well-dressed lawyer and snapped, "What's the problem with my pigs?"

"The first time I came to this set, I saw Eddy Benson with a piglet under his arm. He said he was taking it to the vet."

Jenna nodded. "Did you inspect the pig?"

Taylor looked down his long nose, the only odd feature in an otherwise patrician face. "I'm a lawyer, not a vet. I want to be sure you filed all the proper paperwork about a sick animal."

"As it turned out," Jenna said. "The pig didn't need medical attention. Eddy overreacted."

"He did that a lot, didn't he?"

Alex interrupted, "Shall we not speak ill of the dead?"

"I'm not surprised he had a heart attack." Without taking his eyes off Jenna, he added, "He died near your animals, didn't he? Why was he there? Looking for you, Ms. Denardo?''

Rafe didn't like the way this lawyer focused on her. Though their conversation seemed hostile, he sensed a masculine interest from Taylor. The lawyer liked Jenna. Maybe, he even wanted her.

The realization triggered a clenching in the pit of Rafe's belly. What was this sensation? Jealousy?

"Excuse me," he said, "are you investigating the death of Eddy Benson?"

"Why would I? It was a heart attack." He continued to look at Jenna. "Do you have reason to believe it was something else? We can't be too careful with animals these days. They carry so many diseases."

"Not my animals," Jenna said. "They're all in excellent health."

"Even the tiger?" Taylor paused. He was smirking, not unlike a kid who was about to tattle on his playmates. "I had a report, earlier today, that there was a dangerous situation with a tiger escape. As you know, Jenna, the SPCA cannot condone this sort of irresponsible handling."

"Merely a rehearsal," Alex said smoothly. He linked arms with Taylor, drawing him away from the potential explosion from Jenna. "You're a good-looking young man. Ever worked in film?"

"No."

"I'm shocked, simply appalled. With your strong features, especially that nose, you'd be a perfect romantic lead."

"Really?"

"Oh, yes. Do you act?" Behind his back, Alex signaled Jenna and Rafe to move away.

Under her breath, Jenna said, "That was close. If Taylor had been here when Darius escaped, it might have cost me my license."

"But nothing happened," Rafe said.

"And most of the SPCA people would understand. They're very reasonable and responsible. But Taylor is trying to make a reputation for himself in this town."

"In animal protection?" Rafe scoffed. That seemed an odd, ineffectual route to power. "He'd be better off as an entertainment laywer. Or a divorce lawyer."

"Yes, but that would require intelligence," Jenna said. "Smarts are a quality that Taylor lacks. Let's go feed my animals and get out of here. It's been a long day."

As if she hadn't had enough headaches, a strange young man marched toward her. "Miss Denardo," he said.

"What now?"

His black hair was cut short as a combat Marine's, and he looked as if he was about to salute her as he said, "I was sent by Hugh Montclair to help you. My name is Danny Vincenzo."

"That's very nice, Danny. But I don't need any help."

"I beg to differ, ma'am. You have an appointment with my employer at twenty hundred hours and—"

"When?"

"Eight p.m., ma'am. And you need someone to keep an eye on the animals while you're gone."

She didn't intend to be gone for more than two hours, and there shouldn't be any problems in that brief time. Still, Jenna decided it was easier to accept Danny's assistance and discuss the situation with Hugh at their meeting. Besides, there were a number of unpleasant tasks to perform before the animals were bedded down for the night.

''Fine.'' She led the way back to the menagerie room where she handed Danny a shovel. ''Dig in.''

''Yes, ma'am.''

After they'd fed, cleaned and bedded the animals, Jenna checked her appearance in the privacy of her tiny dressing room. Not as gorgeous as Dinah Aaron, former fashion model. But she looked okay.

Perched on the edge of her sofa bed, Jenna dialed the phone number for the ranch. Technically, she and her mother were partners in Denardo Animal Wranglers, and she needed to tell Kate about the developments on this project.

As Jenna expected, the answering machine picked up. Her mother never answered the phone without screening the calls. After the beep, Jenna began talking. ''Mom, it's me. It seems that I'm going to be running long on this contract. Tonight, I'm going to talk with Hugh Montclair about—''

''Hello, Jenna.'' Her mother's voice was rousing and cheerful. Though she'd buried herself at the ranch after her husband's death, she maintained the illusion that she was bright and optimistic. ''You sound wonderful, honey.''

''No, I don't. I'm tired. And this movie is a disaster.'' Since her mother never watched the news, Jenna filled her in on the death of Eddy Benson and her own part in finding him.

''I'm so sorry,'' Kate said. ''I liked Eddy.''

''So did I.''

''Now, what's this about Hugh?''

''I'll need to be here another week at least.'' And there was more. The incident with Darius had convinced her that she couldn't handle this number and variety of animals all by herself. But she didn't want to enlist the aid of Danny Vincenzo. Allowing Hugh Montclair to call the shots set a bad precedent. "Also, I need to hire another handler to help me out."

"Jenna, honey, that's going to eat up all our profits."

"Not if I can get Hugh Montclair to pay for it."

"That old skinflint? He didn't get to be a wealthy man by spending extra. On his trips to Africa, he was famous for not hiring enough bearers to carry his equipment."

Jenna was puzzled. "Do you know him?"

"It was back in the days when I thought I might become an actress." Her mother's voice took on a dreamy quality. "Gosh, it must have been thirty years ago. Before I met your father, I dated Hugh."

Would wonders never cease! Dating the reclusive Hugh Montclair was akin to having a relationship with the late Howard Hughes.

Her mother continued, "Hugh was the one who got me interested in animals. He's a veterinary anthropologist with lots of other academic degrees. I think he even wrote a book about animal behavior."

"I didn't know."

"He's always been a little sweet on me," she said. "Actually, it was Hugh who called to offer the *Alien Age* job."

"You're amazing, Mom."

"I'm just old, honey. I've done a lot of living."

Jenna had an inspiration. "We wouldn't need to hire another handler if you'd come to the set and help me out."

"Me? Leave the ranch?"

"Sure. Berta and Jim can take care of everything while you're gone. They know the routine."

"I don't think so," Kate said quickly. "One of the mares is about to foal, and I—"

"Darius got out."

"My God, what happened?"

"No one was injured. Darius is fine."

She hadn't planned to tell her mother about the tiger escape, hadn't wanted to worry her needlessly. But Jenna was willing to play that card if Darius's adventure convinced her mother to leave the secluded ranch and get back into the mainstream of living. "Please, Mom. This job is too much for me to manage all by myself. I need you."

A silence hummed through the telephone wires as Kate considered. For the past three years, her mother had barely travelled farther than the local supermarket. Too often, she never even left her bed. Or she didn't sleep at all. She forgot to eat. Sometimes, she would spend hours wandering among the twenty-six orange trees she'd planted—one tree for each year she'd been married to Jenna's father.

"All right," Kate said. "I'll be there in the morning. And, please, tell Hugh that I will be participating. We'll need more compensation."

"You got it." Jenna would have paid out of her own small savings for her mother to begin living again. "I'll see you in the morning. Nine o'clock?"

"Earlier. You know how little I sleep." She sighed. "I hope I'm not making a mistake."

"Definitely not."

As soon as Jenna hung up the phone, she did a little happy dance in the limited space of her living quarters. Maybe *Alien Age* wasn't such a huge disaster, after all.

There was a tap on the door, and she heard Rafe's voice. "Jenna? Are you all right?"

She flung the door wide. "Everything is great!"

"Uh-huh." He nodded. "I heard you talking. Is there someone in here with you?"

"Don't worry, Rafe. I'm not losing my mind. I'm just happy. Come on, I'll explain on the way."

Unlike most men, he was a good listener. As they drove toward the Beverly Hills estate of Hugh Montclair, Rafe paid thoughtful attention as she explained about her father's death and her mother's self-imposed seclusion.

"If it wasn't so tragic," Jenna said, "I'd think it was romantic for my mother to be pining away over the one true love of her life."

"It sounds like your parents had a special sort of love."

"A perfect love. Warm and affectionate, but not goopy. They had a grand passion. Even when they disagreed, they were never cruel to each other."

When she was growing up, she never realized how remarkable their relationship was—not until she started dating and discovering the complexities of relating to a man. "Maybe that's why I'm not married. My parents' perfect love convinced me that I wasn't willing to settle for less."

"You deserve as much," he said.

"Well, thanks. But you hardly know me. I'm lousy at relationships. It's always been easier for me to relate to animals than to human males."

"Some people would say they were one and the same—the human male and the beast."

It was the second time he'd made a disparaging remark about humanity. "You don't seem to hold our species in high regard."

"I've seen too much," he said. "Man is, by far, the cruelest animal."

His words were heavy, and she wondered what could

possibly have caused such sorrow. "Tell me about your-self, Rafe. I've hardly given you a chance to talk."

"Right now," he said, "I'm very hungry."

His physical hunger, Rafe thought, must be the reason for this gnawing emptiness he felt inside. Physical dis-comfort was part of being mortal, and he needed to be aware of the needs of this body that was so foreign to him.

"We can't stop, Rafe. We're running late." She dug into the glove compartment and pulled out two candy bars, offering one to him. "Chocolate?"

He accepted the morsel. Though he was more accus-tomed to gourmet dining, the sweet taste aroused his human taste buds. Apparently, he was less discerning as a mortal.

She handed him the map Dorothy had drawn for them. "The turnoff is around here somewhere. Help me look for it."

As an angel, he could have flown to this estate in the blink of an eye. Being mortal required more patience. He studied the map and directed her along winding road-ways that climbed one hill and descended another. The foliage in this part of the world was dull, ordinary shrub-bery, prone to the devastating, southern California fires that scorched the landscape. The homes in this exclusive territory were set back from the road.

At the final turn, Rafe experienced foreboding. How did humans cope with these constant sensations? A tin-gling crawled across his scalp and shivered down his spine. When the carved stone gateway leading to Hugh Montclair's estate loomed into sight, he was aware of a gathering turmoil within him.

"Wow!" Jenna said. "It looks like Count Dracula's castle."

There were angels here. Rafe couldn't see them in his human body, but he sensed the nearness of dark angels, fallen creatures who thrived upon destruction and despair. It was most fortunate, he thought, that he had assumed a mortal disguise. They wouldn't recognize him for what he was.

He looked up at the stone gargoyles that hunched in grotesque poses on either end of the gateway above a heavy, wrought iron scrawl that spelled "Montclair." The iron bars across the gateway were narrowly spaced to keep intruders out—or to confine the evil within.

Here, Rafe knew, he would find the solution to Eddy Benson's murder.

When Jenna pulled up to the intercom and announced their presence, a dark-skinned man came from a gatehouse to unlock the bars and wave them inside. Though his hair was longer and his attitude more pleasant, he resembled Danny Vincenzo.

"Thank you," Jenna called out.

"You might want to roll up your windows," he advised. "At nightfall, the bats come out."

Jenna rolled up her window and whispered, "What did I tell you? Count Dracula."

They followed an asphalt road, lit by mushroom lamps, as it wound through a forest that seemed to have been imported from all around the world. As well as palm trees, there were maple, birch and fruit-bearing trees. There was wildlife as well. A fat furry animal darted away from the headlights. Rafe spied a lemur among the high branches of an elm.

They parked in front of a sprawling stucco villa, covered with vines and topped with a bell tower and a red tile roof. At the carved mahogany doors, they were greeted by a man who looked like a clone of the gate-keeper. He introduced himself as Nick as he showed them into a spacious living room, which was furnished in a light, modern, airy style with panoramic windows offering a view of the grounds.

"This is lovely," Jenna said. "Somehow, I'd expected antiques."

"Dr. Montclair will be with you in a moment," Nick said. "In the meantime, may I offer refreshment?"

"Water for me," Jenna said.

Nick turned to Rafe. "And you, sir? We have an excellent wine cellar."

In his angelic existence, Rafe had savored many fine wines without the ill effects of intoxication. His human taste buds were aroused by the mention of wine. What would it be like? Would he appreciate the flavor and bouquet? Would he merely taste the alcohol? "A merlot."

"Certainly."

After Nick left to fetch their drinks, Rafe wandered through the room, studying the furnishings. This room seemed bland, designed purely for social occasions, except for a display of artifacts on open glass shelves. Most of the objects were talismans from Africa, and one was remarkable. It was a small, stone Venus with drooping breasts. Though she stood only a few inches tall, the statue exuded power. She was a graven image, the recipient of many heathen prayers.

From the picture window, Jenna beckoned to him. "Take a look at this landscape. Down there, at the bottom of the hill, that huge building looks like a barn. This place is incredible. I wish it was daylight, so we could see better."

As he looked into the trees, Rafe saw a furtive movement among the shadows. The resident deer? Or something more sinister?

"Good evening."

Hugh Montclair made his entrance. Impressive, Rafe thought, and he wondered why the wealthy producer would bother to strut for them. Montclair's khaki bush jacket and trousers showed excellent tailoring. His mustache was thick but trimmed. Though he must have been in his sixties, his tall, muscular frame gave the appearance of youth, and he was confident enough not to hide the fact that his short-trimmed gray hair had thinned to near baldness.

The aura of wealth and power was unmistakable. Rafe had been acquainted with many men like Hugh Montclair. Too often, they had been adversaries.

"Jenna Denardo," Hugh said warmly, "you're as lovely as your mother. Seeing you takes me back to a more innocent time."

Rafe crossed the room and exchanged a firm handshake. "Rafe Santini," he said as introduction.

"And you're looking for a job as a stuntman. Alex Hill seems impressed with you. Did you really tame a tiger simply by looking in his eye?"

"It's a trick I learned in Africa," Rafe said carefully. "I'm glad it worked."

"So am I. This film has enough bad publicity with Eddy Benson's death."

"Did you know Eddy?"

"Very well, indeed." Hugh gave nothing away. He didn't express a liking or a dislike for Eddy. "Tell me where you've been in Africa."

As they chatted, Nick returned with Jenna's water and Rafe's wine. He uncorked a full bottle and poured the sparkling ruby liquid into a crystal glass.

Rafe's first sip awakened astounding sensations in his mouth. His tongue came alive. His nostrils twitched with the fragrance. He nodded to Nick. "Delicious."

"It's from a vineyard up the coast," Hugh said. "It was founded and run by my dearest friend, Paolo Vincenzo. He was Nick's father."

Recognizing the sadness that shaded Nick's brown eyes, Rafe assumed that his father's death was recent. He held up his glass. "Your father's memory lives in his artistry."

"Paolo's memory lives in many ways," Hugh said. He turned to Jenna. "Tell me about your mother."

As Jenna spoke about the ranch and her mother, Rafe studied Nick Vincenzo. Though the young man moved with the silent unobtrusive air of a perfect butler, his posture was not that of a servant. The lining of his navy blue sports jacket was scarlet silk. Likewise, there was a surprising strength in his manner.

After carefully measuring Hugh's drink, Nick didn't leave the room. Nor did he stand at attention, awaiting orders. He seated himself at a small desk, opened a drawer and calmly perused a leather-bound booklet—not intruding on their conversation, but overseeing.

Jenna concluded, "Anyway, Mom will be joining me tomorrow to work on the film."

"Kate will be coming here?" Hugh brightened.

"Yes, sir. That is, of course, if you agree to the monetary changes in our contract."

"Name your price. I'll make the necessary contractual adjustments immediately."

She turned toward Rafe. "And will you be hiring Rafe? He's very good with the animals."

"Certainly. I trust your judgment implicitly, Jenna." He glanced toward Nick. "Would you run off the contracts for me? Standard union scale for Rafe Santini. Double the existing amount for Jenna and her mother.''

"Thank you," Jenna said. "That's most generous."

He clapped his powerful hands together and rubbed the palms. "The pleasure is mine."

"My mother mentioned that you were responsible for her interest in animals."

"I merely aroused her natural talents," he said. "She accompanied me on a trip to Brazil. It was the first time she'd seen Rio. Through her eyes, I experienced a beauty I had not known."

As Hugh reminisced, Rafe finished the wine in his glass and poured himself another. A subtle warmth had spread through his body, relaxing his limbs. Perhaps the apprehension he'd felt earlier was due to thirst. He would have to remember to drink more liquids when he was in human form. Even his vision seemed sharper.

Suddenly, it occurred to him that he was ignoring his social manners. Introspection in the company of others was considered rudeness. "Your landscaping," he said to Hugh. "It's unusual."

From the surprised expressions on the faces of Hugh and Jenna, Rafe deduced that he had blurted. He hadn't been following their conversation.

"Yes," Hugh said. "All the planting was supervised by Paolo. We were quite a team. He was the expert in plant life, and I specialized in animals."

"My mother tells me that you have several academic degrees," Jenna said.

"Biology, anthropology, chemistry, veterinary science."

"And Paolo?" Rafe asked.

"He was a genius." Hugh's tone and facial expression were tinged with a darkness, an anger. He continued, "The man who opened the gate for you is another of his sons. Though he modestly calls himself a gardener, he has an advanced degree in botany."

"And Danny Vincenzo," Jenna said. "He's another son, isn't he?"

"A good boy. Possibly not as bright as his brothers, but Danny is a good worker and has his uses."

"I'd like to dismiss him as soon as I return to the set," Jenna said. "It's nothing personal. You understand."

"For tonight, Jenna. Danny will stay near you."

"I don't need a bodyguard."

Hugh nodded toward Rafe. "Apparently not, but I insist."

Rafe knew he should respond, but his tongue felt pleasantly lazy and his brain couldn't come up with the words. He took another sip of wine.

"You seem to be a man who enjoys the finer things," Hugh said. "Would you care for a cigar, Rafe? I am privileged to have a supply of Cubans."

Rafe exhaled a blissful sigh. "That would be heaven."

Jenna piped up, "So would I."

"You smoke cigars?" Rafe asked.

"My father always said that special occasions should always be celebrated with a fine cigar."

"He advised you to smoke?"

"I have two younger brothers," she explained. "After any noteworthy achievement, my father used to take them into his study, and they'd all smoke cigars. One time, my mother and I decided we shouldn't be excluded."

Rafe's gaze lingered upon her. Her thick mass of blond curls framed the loveliest face he'd seen on earth or in heaven. And she smoked cigars! Truly, Jenna was the perfect woman.

As they savored excellent Cuban cigars, Rafe couldn't take his eyes off her. He admired the perfect "O" of her mouth as she puffed on her cigar. The cylinder of brown tobacco looked huge in her small, graceful hand. She conversed with vivacious energy, gesturing frequently. Her entire body was involved as she talked.

Then, Rafe heard the name "Eddy Benson," and he remembered why he was here, in human form. He was investigating. His job as an avenger was to find who killed the old man who coordinated stunts for the movies.

"I understand that you found Eddy," said Hugh. "Is that right, Jenna?"

"He was dying," she said.

"That must have been difficult for you. Do you have any idea why he was with your animals?" He leaned forward, showing great interest. "Did Eddy have a chance to explain?"

"He couldn't talk." Jenna sighed. "Maybe he was with the animals because he'd been concerned about one of my pigs. That worries me."

"And why is that?"

She frowned at the glowing tip of her cigar. "This afternoon, I discovered that one of my pigs is missing. There was a substitute."

Nick, who had returned to the room with a sheaf of papers in his hand, said, "About the pig. May I explain, sir?"

"Please do."

"Eddy brought your pig here. Dr. Montclair is a veterinarian, and he thought we might be able to help. I gave him a substitute pig from the barn so you wouldn't be inconvenienced while your animal was being examined.''

''And is my pig all right?''

''He's fine.''

''Your animal was a good match,'' Jenna said. ''I didn't even notice the substitution until today.''

''We have several piglets to choose from.'' Nick placed the papers on the coffee table. ''Here are the contracts.''

Hugh signed the papers without looking at them, leaving Nick to separate the documents for Rafe and Jenna.

''Why,'' Jenna asked, ''do you have so many pigs? Do you raise them?''

''They're good breeders,'' Nick explained. ''We've been giving them away so they won't overpopulate the barn.''

She looked toward Hugh. ''What was wrong with my pig? What did your examination show?''

Again, Nick did the talking. ''He's well. Eddy overreacted.''

''When can I have him back?''

''I'll take care of it, Jenna.''

In the back of his sluggish mind, Rafe had the distinct impression that Nick had given them important information. Eddy had been at the Montclair estate before he died. If he'd been infected with a virus, this might be the point of origin.

Rafe should try to see as much as possible of this place. Struggling to be alert, he said, ''You've got a lot of animals. Maybe you can give us a tour of your barns.''

''Another time,'' Hugh said.

Jenna concurred. ''It's late. I really ought to get back to the movie lot.''

"So responsible," Hugh said. "Like your mother."

When Jenna rose to her feet, Rafe knew he should do likewise. But his legs felt rubbery. Concentrating with all his might, he managed to stand. The room seemed to be slowly spinning. On sheer willpower, he maneuvered across the carpet and out the door. The bracing night air revived him enough that he managed to climb into the passenger side of the truck without stumbling.

Hugh stood on the veranda, waving good-bye as Jenna turned the key in the ignition and threw the truck into gear.

"Honestly, Rafe," she said. "I can't believe you got drunk."

Drunk? That explained the way he was feeling. Wine was, of course, intoxicating. More so because he hadn't been drunk in centuries. A distant memory awakened—not in his mind, which was befogged with the fine merlot, but in the very cells of this human body. He'd been drunk before. When he was a sinful man, he had often partaken of strong drink.

"You can hardly stand," Jenna said. "I didn't think you had that much."

"Haven't had wine in a long time."

"It shows. If I were you, I wouldn't have wine again."

Rafael took orders from no one. "Are you telling me what to do?"

"By advising you not to make an ass of yourself? That doesn't seem too pushy. You can file it under the category of Good Advice."

"Pull over," he said. There was a human need festering in his mind. He had to do this now, before he could consider the consequences. "Do as I say, Jenna."

She glided to a stop at the edge of the winding road that led to the stucco villa. "What?"

He reached toward her. His fingers tangled in the silky texture of her hair.

"What are you doing, Rafe?"

"I'm going to kiss you." He pulled her closer.

"Not here," she objected. "Not like this."

"This may be the only chance." The only time when his inhibitions were low enough to exceed his wisdom. "Please, Jenna."

Their lips met.

Chapter Four

Jenna hardly knew Rafe Santini, and he had been weird since the first time she laid eyes on him. That eerie glow. Taming Darius. There was the electricity when she'd touched him, and a personality that vacillated between arrogance and the deepest empathy she'd ever known in a man. He'd gotten sloppy drunk on two and a half glasses of wine. Now, he was kissing her.

Whatever he was, it sure wasn't gay. His tongue lightly probed, and, in that instant, Jenna forgot each and every one of her reasons to be wary of him. His mouth was warm and sexy. He tasted pleasantly of wine.

He ended the kiss and leaned away from her. What was going on here? She peered into his breathtaking blue eyes. In his gaze, she saw longing and arousal. Why had he stopped with one tender kiss?

For such a confident man, Rafe seemed as awkward as a kid, stealing a forbidden pleasure for the first time. His grin was sheepishly guilty. Seeming not to know what to do with his hands, he gestured clumsily. But his eyes told a different story. In his gaze, she recognized a wordless appeal that she couldn't resist.

His voice was husky. "I shouldn't have—"

Jenna held his face between her hands and kissed him

hard. Her mouth consumed his. When her tongue tentatively explored the shape and texture of his lips, Rafe came alive in her arms.

With a burst of ravaging passion, he grasped her so tightly that she was lifted from the seat behind the steering wheel. Her body molded against his, and their combined heat ignited a flame in her heart. Roughly, he caressed her, searching until he felt the softness of her breast. His desire raged, consuming her, drawing her closer, compelling her response.

This was the kiss she'd been waiting for all her life. When it ended, Jenna was both satisfied and unfulfilled, because she wanted more.

This time, when she studied his expression, the youthful innocence was gone. Instead, she recognized a man who was ready to make love.

With a groan, he fell back in his seat. "Let's get out of here."

She restarted the truck. Boldly, Jenna asked, "My place or yours?"

"I won't lie down with you," he said. His voice was rough around the edges, serrated like a knife. "It would be wrong."

"You're joking."

"I've never been more serious."

"Excuse me, Rafe, but I don't see what's so wrong about it. We're consenting adults. I want to spend tonight with you, and I think you feel the same about me. Don't you want to make love?"

"There are reasons...I can't."

Once again, he was rejecting her advances. He was toying with her. "Damn you, Rafe."

"That may very well be."

She paused at the gate for Paolo's son to open the

matched iron bars. She then thanked him and proceeded down the road, trying to ignore the masculine presence of Rafe Santini. Once again, he had embarrassed her. How could she have been so trusting, so foolish! Her aroused passions became outrage, a hot anger that burned painfully.

"Try to understand," he said. "I'm not like other men."

"I should say not. Other men don't reject me. Other men don't tame tigers." Her voice rose to a shout. "Other men don't glow in the dark!"

"I can explain."

"Don't bother. Where should I drop you off?"

"Here."

"What are you saying? That you'll walk from here? Oh, please, don't be childish. I'll take you to your car."

"It's best if you let me out here. Now."

If that was what he wanted, fine! How dare he kiss her as if he meant it, then refuse her when she offered herself to him. At the bottom of the secluded hillside, she parked. "Good-bye, Rafe."

He opened the car door. "If you'll listen for five minutes, I'll explain everything."

"I don't care," she said, faking a breezy attitude. "I'm sure there's a reason for your behavior, I just don't care to hear it."

After he was out of the car, she gunned the engine and aimed toward the R.I.P. movie lot. There were a couple of errands she had intended to run, but she couldn't recall what they were. All she wanted was quiet—a solitude to cuddle her like a warm blanket and soothe this cold humiliation.

In her rearview mirror, she noticed a set of headlights that stayed precisely two car-lengths behind her. Before she had time to worry that she was being followed, she dismissed her suspicion. Someone trailing her? Why? More likely, this was coincidence. It was only ten o'clock, and there was plenty of traffic about—especially when she reached the dismal, urban streets near the studio.

Her headlights cut through heavy shadows in this run-down section of greater Los Angeles. City of Angels? Hah! The sidewalks were littered with the homeless, the hookers and the hustlers.

Waiting for a red light, Jenna stared into the eyes of a young girl who was crossing the street. She couldn't have been older than thirteen, half Jenna's age, but already this young creature had discarded poignant innocence. She waggled her skinny pelvis. Her hair snaked in tangles down her back. The girl's face, beneath layered makeup, was lit by a green neon sign, and she sneered ghoulishly at Jenna's beat-up truck.

Aching with regret, Jenna looked away. She wanted to help the girl, but knew she couldn't. Human relations were too complicated. No wonder she preferred the company of animals.

She had covered the distance to the movie lot in twenty-six minutes. No doubt, it was record time, but not fast enough for Jenna. She wanted to be as far away from Rafe as possible, and she wouldn't waste one moment's guilt on worrying about how he would get back to town from the desolate hills. A long walk would do him good. He could sober up.

She drove carefully through the movie lot, between the three-story soundstage buildings. During the day, this two-lane alley was crowded with actors, technicians and related movie people. At night, when the motion picture magic was absent, there was an uneasy silence, a sense of waiting. Except for the night watchmen making their occasional patrols, no one was here.

"Perfect," Jenna muttered as she parked by Soundstage 7. Desertion suited her. She slammed the door to the truck with a resounding thud.

"Jenna."

What was that? She thought she'd heard Rafe's voice, calling to her. But that was impossible. He had to be somewhere in the hills beyond Hollywood, hiking back to town.

"Jenna, listen."

She whirled and saw him. A faint glow burnished his shoulders. "How did you get here?"

"I flew," he said.

Panic raced through her. A loud gasp choked in her throat as she stared at the impossible vision. She must be going crazy. Turning, she ran from him toward the door to the soundstage.

Blocking her way, he appeared in front of her. "Listen to me," he said.

"You don't exist. I'm imagining you. There's no way you could cover that distance and get here first. No way."

He caught her arms in his grasp, and she felt a tremor of powerful electricity in his touch. She must be going mad, having a nervous breakdown. The stress of working on this film and having Eddy die in her arms had caught up with her.

"Look at me, Jenna."

Helplessly, she gazed into his face. He radiated energy. It sparked from his long hair. His blue eyes glistened like butane flames.

"Jenna, I told you that I was not like other men, and I'm not. I'm not a mortal man at all."

"What?"

"You sensed it the first time we met. You saw a nimbus of light surrounding me. Very few people have your sensitivity." He paused. "I'm an angel."

Jenna blinked hard, hoping that when she opened her eyes again he would be gone. But he stood before her, holding her upper arms and shimmering as brightly as a fallen star.

More gently, he asked, "Don't you believe in angels, Jenna?"

"Not like you."

"I suppose you think all angels have flowing white robes, wings and harps."

She shook her head, not knowing what to believe. This couldn't be happening.

He released his grip on her arms. "I'm not a choir angel, nor a cherub, nor a guardian angel. I'm an Avenging Angel. It's my duty to investigate the wrongs that are done by men and to exact vengeance. I'm here to solve the murder of Eddy Benson."

"He died of a heart attack," she said weakly.

"You know better than that. Eddy was poisoned. It wasn't his time to die."

"Poisoned? How? I don't understand."

"You don't need to. It's unnecessary for you to consider Eddy's murder. That's my problem, and it doesn't concern you."

"Now wait a minute." She dug in her heels. Jenna didn't care who or what Rafe was, she didn't like being treated in such a condescending manner. "If Eddy was murdered, I want to know who did it."

"I didn't come here to talk about Eddy. I need to explain something to you. Are you ready to listen?"

"I don't think I like your attitude." What was she

doing? Talking back to a celestial being? That had to be some unforgivable form of heresy, but Jenna didn't consider the consequences. All she knew was that Rafe Santini—man or angel—had no right to order her around. "I cared about Eddy. If he was murdered, I'm going to do everything I can to make sure his killer comes to justice."

"That's my job," he said. "And I'm very good at it."

"What kind of angel are you? You kissed me. And you got drunk. How can an angel get sloshed?"

He sighed. "To appear on film, I need to take human form. To become mortal."

Jenna shook her head. This was too much! "So, you were a man, but you're not anymore."

"That's correct. At this moment, I'm an angel. When we kissed, I was mortal." He paced away from her, then back again. "I wish I could say that I regret losing control. But I don't. The taste of your lips on mine was…" He touched his mouth. "It will never happen again. Obviously, there can never be any sort of relationship between us. Do you understand me, Jenna?"

"How can this be true?"

"It's simple," he said. "I never lie."

"Of course not." A slightly hysterical giggle bubbled up in her throat. "An angel can't sin, and lying would be a sin."

"I don't want to hurt you."

She looked up at him. Her eyes mated with his. "Too late, Rafe."

Like a sudden gust of wind, he vanished.

She stepped away from the flat white wall of the soundstage building. He was gone. There was no one

else in sight. Her gaze lifted heavenward, and she saw
the stars, dimmed by city lights.

An angel?

Confused, Jenna fitted her key in the lock and entered
Soundstage 7. Her head tilted down. She shuffled across
the concrete floor. The vast hollow space was spooky,
but Jenna didn't care. Rafe's unbelievable identity was
beginning to sink into her brain. He was an angel.

She released a huge sigh. An angel. She could never
love him—not in the way she longed to love him.

Somewhere on the soundstage, Danny Vincenzo, another of Paolo's many sons, was probably lurking, but
she didn't see him and she didn't go looking. The last
thing she wanted right now was a conversation. She'd
heard too much already. Too many questions were spinning in her head.

After a brief check on her slumbering animals, Jenna
went into her tiny dressing room, pulled the sofa into a
bed and collapsed onto it. She barely had time to kick
off her shoes before she succumbed to sleep.

Hours later—or perhaps only a few moments—she
came half awake. Jenna felt herself rising, slowly,
weightlessly. Like a deep-sea diver ascending from the
depths, she floated toward the light of consciousness.

Had there been a sound?

Gradually, her eyelids opened to slits. The room was
mostly dark, but she didn't remember turning off the
overhead light before she went to bed. Oh well, she must
have done so.

Trying to get comfortable, she rolled onto her back.
She was under the down quilt she'd brought from the
ranch. Beneath the covers, she was naked, except for her
bra and panties.

That couldn't be right. Jenna knew she hadn't bothered to undress herself last night. She'd been so mentally and emotionally exhausted that she'd fallen asleep as soon as her body flopped onto the lumpy mattress.

Turning her head ever so slightly, she became aware of light spilling from the room where her animals slept. She peered through barely opened eyes. Framed in the doorway, she saw the silhouette of a broad-shouldered man. Backlit, his features were hidden. He towered above her.

Her breath caught. She froze like a scared rabbit in high brush, praying that she would be invisible, that the predator would leave her unharmed. Every sinew in her body went taut.

In a horrifying way, she'd almost expected the arrival of this unknown person. The threat had been there, waiting at the edge of her consciousness like the shadowy presence on the soundstage the night Eddy had died, like the feeling she'd had earlier tonight when headlights followed her.

He wanted something from her.

She lay still, waiting for him to speak. But he was silent. And she realized that her animals had not made a sound. Who was this man?

She waited for him to act, but he didn't move. Why was he here?

Jenna had to know. Even if confrontation was dangerous, she had to catch hold of this dark spectre and force him to become solid before he slid inside her mind, haunting her. Beneath her pillow, she had her gun. If she screamed for help, Danny Vincenzo might come to her aid. She needed to do something.

Before she could decide, the figure in the doorway came toward her. Swiftly, he clamped a damp cloth over her nostrils, suffocating her. A musty odor engulfed her.

As soon as she inhaled, she felt a helpless lethargy. She tried to struggle, but her arms and legs would not move.

Her eyes closed. Who was he? What was happening to her?

The darkness of sleep silenced her questions.

THE NEXT MORNING, Jenna wakened with a start. Last night there had been a man right here in her room. He'd undressed her, watched her. He had drugged her with some powerful sedative.

And yet she felt perfectly normal, alert as she ever was in the early morning. Had it really happened? Was she hallucinating? My God, what was wrong with her?

Her mother stood over her. "Honey? It's almost eight o'clock. Time to rise and shine. Are you awake?"

"Now I am. Hi, Mom."

Jenna rubbed her eyes and pressed her lips together, keeping her panic inside. She sure as hell wasn't going to tell her mother about last night. Everything needed to go smoothly for Kate. Jenna wanted this to be a good experience. She needed to convince her mother that life was worth living.

"You looked so peaceful," her mother said. "Were you having a nice dream?"

"Oh, Mom. I'm so glad you're here."

If she were a child again, she'd turn all these complex problems over to her mother. Mama could chase away the goblins with a kiss on the forehead and a whispered lullaby.

"I hate to rush you," Kate prodded, "but the actors and technicians are already on set. And that director? Alex? He's had some sort of brainstorm and wants to see you right away."

"Give me a minute," Jenna said. She needed to quell

the fears, to transform last night's confusion into a plan of action. "Let me wake up."

"I'll get some coffee from the catering table." Kate Denardo straightened to her full height of five feet, three inches. She tucked a tendril of her short, honey-blond hair behind her ear and regarded her daughter with an expression of concern. "Are you all right?"

"I'm fine."

"And did you talk to Hugh last night?"

Jenna forced herself to smile. "He likes you a lot. And he agreed to pay double our usual fee for the duration of this job."

"I hope you didn't take advantage of him," her mother chided. "It wouldn't be fair to use our old friendship."

"He offered. I accepted."

"Very well." Kate regarded her with a critical eye. "My advice to you, young lady, is to clean yourself up and put on some makeup. It's a brand new day, and time's a-wastin'."

When her mother left, Jenna closed her eyes and tried to understand what had happened last night. She'd seen a man, a stranger, watching her. But it couldn't have been a stranger or else her animals would have reacted. He'd drugged her with something like chloroform. But he couldn't have! She would have experienced some sort of physical reaction, and she truly felt fine. She must have been dreaming last night. And yet, under the comforter, she wore only her bra and panties. She knew she hadn't undressed before going to bed. Oh, God, what was going on?

She hurried through her shower and pulled her hair back in a thick ponytail. By the time Kate returned with her coffee, Jenna was dressed in Levi's and a gray sweatshirt that reflected her mood—a cloudy gray, hazy and confused.

Though it would take more than a quick dose of caffeine for Jenna to be fully prepared to face another day, fraught with potential disaster, she slipped into her shoes and headed toward the soundstage. Her only consolation was that today couldn't possibly be worse than yesterday or the day before. "Okay, Mom. Let's see what Alex wants."

They didn't have to look far to find the wiry director in his typical black outfit. Jenna and her mother could have located Alex by decibel level alone. He was standing between the two stars, Dinah Aaron and Jason Kendall. Alex's modulated British tones trembled at the edge of a screech. "You are Adam and Eve. Symbolically. Don't you understand?"

Dinah glanced up from a bored study of her fingernails, tightened the sash on her terry cloth robe and nodded. "I get it, Alex. Gawd!"

Behind her, a hairdresser fussed with an astoundingly realistic wig of shining, chestnut hair that cascaded almost to the back of Dinah's knees.

Alex turned to the male star, who was frowning thoughtfully. "And you, Jason? Do you understand?"

"I just don't know why we always have to relate to the traditional Judeo-Christian thing. I mean, why can't we be Isis and Osiris? Or something Zen?"

"The image," Alex said, "is innocence. It matters very little to me whether you imagine yourselves as Bonnie and Clyde as long as you perform as I direct."

"Okay," Jason said. "I can do innocent. But why no dialogue? I thought this was supposed to be an action movie. I don't like this whole Eden thing."

Alex clapped his hand over his mouth, obviously

holding back a torrent of explanation. When he dropped his hand, a stiff smile curled inside his goatee. "Because I don't want you to speak. Now, do you both remember your directions?"

"I do," Dinah said. Without hesitation, she untied the sash of her robe and slipped out of it. "First, we get naked."

Though she was wearing a body stocking and a thick layer of flesh-tone paint, she appeared to be as nude as Venus rising from the sea. The effect was stunning. Every man within fifty feet gaped, slack-jawed.

Except for one, Jenna noticed. Rafe totally ignored the nearly naked movie goddess as he came toward Jenna with a cup of coffee in his hand. Glowing again, he seemed to walk in a spotlight.

In spite of everything that had happened between them, Jenna was relieved to see him. He was on her side.

His lips didn't seem to move as he gently inquired, "Are you all right?"

A dozen explanations jammed in her throat. She wanted to tell him about last night, about the silhouette of the man and the drug that made her sleep, and her deeper terror that none of it had really happened and she was going crazy.

"Jenna?"

"Rafe Santini, I'd like you to meet my mother, Kate."

As they shook hands, Kate wasted no time in making her opinion known. "Dorothy tells me that you and my daughter are dating, Rafe. Now, I try not to be an interfering mother, but I'll say one thing: Jenna can't cook worth beans, but she's a good person and a hard worker."

Jenna groaned. "Gosh, Mom. Aren't you going to tell him that I have good teeth, too?"

Indulgently, Kate grinned at Rafe. "Only four cavities in her whole life."

As the discussion between the director and his two stars heated up, Taylor Wannamaker came toward them. Accompanying him was Danny Vincenzo, who stopped dead in his tracks when he saw Dinah in the almost nude.

Alex shouted, "Jenna! Rafe! Please, help me out!"

She and Rafe formed a huddle with the others.

"All right," Alex said. "In the simplest possible terms, here is my vision. There will be no dialogue in the Garden scene. The camera will catch the man and woman, unawares. Their nudity is utterly selfless. Their attitude is childlike. Adam's state of innocence allows him to soothe the savage beast, as it were."

"Excuse me," Jason said. "Could you be a little more specific?"

"I want you to walk, naked, with the tiger. Think of the huge cat as your companion."

Jason was shaking his head. "No way. I've got a rep for doing my own stunts, but we're talking about motorcycles, car crashes and kung fu fighting. That big cat looks mean."

Alex turned to Jenna. "Is it possible to guarantee Jason's safety?"

"We'll need to block out the action carefully, but we can manage to create the illusion that he and the tiger are buddies."

"What about me?" Dinah whined.

"You," said Alex, "will be wearing the python."

"Unless you're talking about snakeskin pumps and a matching belt, forget it." Dinah fluffed her wig. "I have a medical reason for not handling the snake."

Jenna could hardly wait to hear this feeble excuse. "And what is that?"

"My shrink says I have an illness. I have severe herpetophobia. That's fear of reptiles." Triumphantly, she glared at Alex. "You'll have to get a double for me in the python scenes."

"I'm with her," Jason said. "I thought we were supposed to be fighting aliens, not playing tiger bait."

"You both want doubles?"

The two stars nodded.

For a moment, Jenna almost felt sorry for Alex. The leading man and leading lady, for whatever reason, were pulling a power play. They banded together, acting within the terms of their contracts, which surely called for doubles and stuntpersons when requested. Alex was losing control of the production. His effectiveness as a director was being compromised.

Surprisingly, he said, "Very well."

Jason cleared his throat and asked, "Does this mean we're going to scratch the Eden sequence?"

"It means that Rafe will double for you in the scene." He looked to Jenna, "And I would very much appreciate if you would be Eve with python."

"I can't," she said quickly. "I'm not an actress."

"There's no dialogue. Surely, you've appeared on screen before with your animals."

"Briefly," she conceded. With a nod toward the seminude Dinah, she added, "But I was always fully dressed."

Jenna would not even consider the possibility of parading around wearing nothing but a wig and an almost nonexistent body stocking. The very idea was absurd. She couldn't double for Dinah. She wouldn't.

Further discussion was cut short by the arrival of Hugh Montclair and Nick. As soon as he was recognized, excitement buzzed through the soundstage. In a business that thrived on gossip, the reclusive movie producer had attained legendary status. He was wealthy, volatile and eccentric. In Hollywood, Hugh Montclair was royalty.

He ignored all others and approached Kate Denardo. Gallantly, he shook her hand. Gently, he kissed her cheek.

As he turned toward Alex, Hugh's expression transformed to sheer dominance. "Why aren't we filming?"

"Excellent question," Alex said. "Perhaps we could adjourn to more private quarters and discuss our small dilemma."

Following in the wake of Hugh Montclair were two men who were far less imposing. Both wore suits, white shirts and unremarkable neckties. Compared to the colorful, flamboyant movie crowd, they were as dull as field mice.

The taller of the two stepped forward. "Who's in charge here?"

"Now what?" Alex demanded.

"I'm Detective Metz from the LAPD." He held out a badge for inspection. "Homicide division. We're investigating the murder of Eddy Benson."

"Murder?" Alex questioned. "He died of a stroke."

"He was poisoned," Jenna blurted out, remembering her conversation with Rafe.

As soon as she spoke, she knew she'd made a mistake. All eyes focused upon her. She felt Rafe move closer to her, and she was glad of his protection. Otherwise, she was very much on her own.

Detective Metz asked, "What's your name, Miss?"

"Jenna Denardo."

There must be something she could do to deflect this unwanted attention, but Jenna didn't feel capable of a glib wisecrack. Her empty stomach wrenched. She was frightened.

The detective said, "You discovered the body. Correct?"

"Not exactly. Eddy wasn't dead. I called the ambulance."

From a distance, she heard the monkeys chattering in their cages. Jenna wished she could be with them, tending to them. She longed for her familiar backstage safety.

"And why do you think Eddy Benson was poisoned?"

Helplessly, she looked toward Rafe. He'd told her. And Rafe never lied.

"Miss Denardo, did Eddy say anything to you before he died?"

"Yes." Jenna nodded. "He said—"

"Don't tell me yet," the detective said. He turned to Alex. "I'll need a room for questioning, and I want to start with Miss Denardo."

As she gazed from face to face, Jenna saw hostility on every countenance. Why had she spoken? She'd made a dreadful mistake. If Eddy Benson had been killed, it was a distinct possibility that someone in this circle was a murderer.

Chapter Five

After a brief conference with Alex and Hugh, the detectives commandeered an office at the rear of the soundstage. Metz ushered Jenna into the room, closed the door behind her and arranged himself behind a functional metal desk. "Please sit down, Miss Denardo."

She perched at the edge of the straight-backed wooden chair on the applicant's side of the desk. This interview wouldn't be simple. Jenna liked to think of herself as a woman who had nothing to hide. But how much could she tell these two clean-cut representatives of the law?

If she said she was drugged last night by a mysterious stranger who used some bizarre sedative with no aftereffect, would they think she was imagining things? Of course they would! Jenna hardly believed it herself. And she definitely didn't want to start explaining about how she thought her pig had been stolen.

Metz got right to the point. "Miss Denardo, why do you think Eddy Benson was poisoned?"

Jenna hesitated. She'd heard it from Rafe, and he couldn't lie. Common sense warned her: Don't take that road. Metz would probably call for a straitjacket.

"Poison is a logical answer," she said, carefully avoiding an actual deception.

"How so?"

"It's like this, Detective. I was with Eddy when he died, and I didn't see any evidence of bludgeoning, beating, shooting or stabbing. He didn't drown, and he wasn't pushed off the top of a tall building." As she spoke, her natural defenses fell into place. Her spine straightened. In a calm voice, she concluded, "Therefore, the murder weapon had to be poison."

"Very logical." Unsmiling, Metz studied her. "I hope you're taking this situation seriously, Miss Denardo."

"Yes, sir. I am. I liked Eddy, and I want to see his murderer brought to justice."

"Good. Now, tell me—in detail—what happened on the night Eddy Benson died."

Jenna complied, running through the description she'd repeated many times before. "And then the paramedics came."

"You said that he'd spoken to you."

"He said one word: *Francis.*"

"Are you sure? Maybe he said *branches.* Or *cancers.*"

"It was Francis. I heard him very clearly. Unfortunately, I have no idea what it means. I don't know anybody named Francis, except for Francis the Talking Mule, and it really doesn't seem like—"

"Let's go back to your comment about poison. What kind of poison killed Eddy Benson?"

"I don't know."

"Think carefully. In your work as an animal handler, do you deal with unusual substances that might be harmful to humans?"

"Occasionally," Jenna admitted. "Some of the antibiotics we use in treating infections might have a negative effect on humans. And, of course, some people are allergic.''

''What exactly are these substances?''

''I can give you a list of everything I have in my first-aid kit, but I really don't think it'll do any good.''

''I'll be the judge of that, miss.'' He laced his fingers together, not taking any notes at all, and asked, ''Why did he come here?''

''I don't know.'' She recalled her sense that there had been someone else on Soundstage 7. ''Maybe he was running from someone.''

Metz said nothing.

''Or else,'' Jenna said, ''he might have been looking for someone. Or something.''

''Uh-huh. Tell me again about that night. Don't leave anything out.''

She repeated her story. Then repeated it again, with a rising sense of frustration. It almost seemed like Detective Metz suspected her.

Finally he was ready to move on. ''When did your mother arrive on set?''

''Leave my mother out of this,'' she said. Today marked Kate Denardo's first venture into real life after three years of seclusion. She didn't need to be hassled by the LAPD. ''She got here only an hour ago.''

''Why?''

''I needed her help.''

''Miss Denardo, it sounds like you're protecting your mother. Why?''

Her cheeks felt hot. Her rear molars ground together.

Metz probed like a dentist poking at a painful abscess. ''What are you protecting her from?''

Accusations. For the past three years, family and friends kept telling Jenna that her mother was depressed, seriously depressed, clinically depressed. Kate's mourning had gone on too long. Many people suggested mood-altering drugs.

And Jenna had tried to get her to a counselor or a psychiatrist. Kate refused. Her healing, she claimed, would take time. And she'd been right. She was a hundred times better now than she'd been three years ago.

Metz wouldn't back off. "What's wrong with your mom?"

"Why are you asking?"

"Hugh Montclair said I shouldn't talk to her. I wondered why. I mean, she doesn't seem to have anything physically wrong with her."

"What are you saying? That she's crazy?"

"I didn't say it." He spread his hands wide. "You did."

"This is absurd. My mother was back home at the ranch when Eddy was murdered. You have no reason to pester her."

His gaze was level and cool. "Is there anything else you want to tell me, Miss Denardo?"

"Nothing," she said. Any thought of confiding in the police or asking for their protection vanished.

Metz escorted her back to the soundstage and signaled to Alex that he was ready for the next witness. Then, the detective turned to Jenna and placed a business card in her hand. "Don't leave town without notifying my office."

She felt like shredding his card and throwing the pieces in the air. His suspicions outraged her. As she stalked toward the menagerie room, Jenna felt like steam must be blasting out of her ears.

Rafe materialized beside her. "Are you all right?"

"It's okay. I'll be fine."

"How much did he tell you about Eddy's death?"

"I did all the talking."

Under his breath, Rafe said, "Metz should have said something. He should have told you."

"About what?"

"Come with me, Jenna. I've already informed your mother that you have a few errands."

"But I can't leave her alone. One of these people might be a murderer."

"I don't want to alarm you, Jenna, but there is an urgency. I need to talk with you. Immediately."

Jenna looked toward the catering table, where Kate Denardo was engaged in a conversation with Dorothy, Alex's assistant. Her mother seemed fine. She waved to Jenna, shooing her out the door.

Conflicting emotions tore at Jenna's heart. She didn't want to spend the rest of her life watching over Kate, but her mother needed her. Didn't she?

Rafe leaned close to her ear. "She'll be okay. Her guardian angel is with her."

"Really? How can you tell?"

"I can see her. Your mother's guardian is strong and courageous."

"And mine? Do I have a guardian with me?"

"Not right now," he said. "I dismissed him."

Jenna couldn't believe she was having this conversation. "How can you do that?"

"I pulled rank." He gestured toward the exit. "Let's go."

Outside, it was a sunny day for September. A few high clouds scooted across the eggshell-blue skies, but the temperature was balmy. At midmorning, the R.I.P. movie lot was crowded with an assortment of business-people, technicians and actors in costumes ranging from high fashion to alien makeup. Just another ordinary day in the City of Angels—blessed with beautiful weather and populated by odd people. "All right, Rafe. What is it that Metz should have told me?"

"This will take some explanation." He circled a sleek, black convertible and held open the passenger door for her.

"Nice wheels," she commented. "An Infiniti?"

"New model. The Eternity."

"I thought an avenging angel would ride in a fiery chariot."

"Consider this the nineties version."

He slipped behind the steering wheel of the car that looked like it had been designed especially for him. With his long black hair, incredible build and classic features, Rafe was the archetype of southern California glamour. Though he claimed to be an angel, he blended with the other wealthy and powerful people of Hollywood. She could easily imagine him shopping on Rodeo Drive, attending high-powered cocktail parties, playing golf with moguls.

She stared at his profile, trying to discover whether he was glowing or not. In the sunlight, she couldn't tell. "Are you an angel right now, or a mortal?"

"It doesn't matter."

"Actually, it does," she said. "Because if you're an angel, you've probably got some superpowers. Right?"

He shrugged. "I'm not Batman."

"But this car looks like the Batmobile. And, last night, you said you could fly. Can you make yourself invisible? Do you have super strength? Can you read minds?"

"My business is serious, Jenna."

"But if you're an angel, why don't you already have

all the answers? Why don't you know who killed Eddy?''

"I have certain skills and abilities that make it easier for me to discover the facts, but I have to go through the same deductive process as any street detective.''

"So, you're not all-knowing?''

"No.''

"You'll have to forgive me, Rafe, but I'm finding it hard to be casual about your secret identity. I've never met an angel before.''

"Are you sure?''

"Absolutely.'' At last, this was something she could be certain about. "I've never before met anyone like you.''

Being with him eased some of her confusion. She enjoyed watching him as he glided through traffic, hitting every green light. His finesse made the most boring, mundane task seem masterful.

"I have information from the coroner's office,'' he said.

"Autopsy information? How did you find out about that?''

"I have my ways.''

"Okay, what's the news?''

"Basically, the coroner who performed the autopsy is stumped. He discovered a substance in Eddy's blood that couldn't be explained. At first, he didn't consider poison. Then, he found a fresh needle mark on Eddy's arm.''

That seemed to gel with her observations. Eddy hadn't been bludgeoned, stabbed or shot. Therefore, poison was a logical answer.

Rafe continued, "He was injected sometime within the last two days before he died. This isn't any kind of standard poison. So far, the analysis indicates an unknown virus or bacteria.''

''A virus? Is it contagious?''

''The coroner doesn't know. He's called in specialists to stand over the microscope beside him.''

''My God, I was exposed to whatever Eddy had. And so were my animals.''

''Exactly. That's why Metz should have told you about it. Have you experienced any unusual physical symptoms in the past few days?''

''Like what?''

''Fever,'' he suggested. ''Aching in the joints. Something like a flu.''

Hallucinations? Had her brain been infected? Jenna stared at the license plate on the car in front of them. Her vision was clear. ''I don't think there's anything wrong with me. How is the virus passed? Is it airborne?''

''Right now, the assumption is that the illness is passed through bodily fluids.'' He glanced over at her. ''If we further assume that Eddy contracted this deadly virus by injection, the incubation period is short, probably only forty-eight hours. Since you're showing no signs of illness, you're probably safe. But I'm not so sure about your animals.''

''Why?''

''In addition to the puncture wound, the coroner found a laceration. It looks like an animal bite.''

''If one of my animals bit Eddy, they'd be infected.'' And the illness could pass from one species to another. ''Is there some kind of blood test we can do?''

''I'd think so,'' he said. ''Metz should have suggested it.''

Rafe turned onto a residential street and pulled into

the driveway of a modern, stucco house. The thick land-scaping hid most of the windows.

"What are you doing?" Jenna demanded. "I need to get back to the soundstage and get these tests under way. Did the coroner have any idea which animal bit Eddy?"

"It was a pig."

Pigs could be aggressive animals. She'd heard stories about farm pigs who had a tendency to attack, slashing with their tusks. They were known to kill more people than dogs. And pigs ate their victims. But Jenna's animals were as sweet-tempered as *Babe*. At the very most, they might butt somebody out of the way. But to bite?

"Where was the bite?"

Rafe illustrated by holding up his own well-formed hand. "On the edge. Just below the little finger."

"That sounds like Eddy stuck his hand into the pig's mouth. But why would he do that?"

Layers of puzzlement piled one on top of the other until the final answer was hidden behind an impenetrable shield. Jenna shook her head, trying to clear it as she stared at the attractive suburban house. "What are we doing here?"

"I wanted you to know the location of this house." He got out of the car and came around to her door. "If you need a safe haven, come here."

"Am I in danger?" She almost hoped the answer was yes. If someone was after her, it would explain her midnight intruder.

"I'm not sure," Rafe said. "It never hurts to be prepared."

"Do you live here?"

"For now I do."

She followed him from the carport to the entrance. "I thought angels lived...somewhere else."

"In Heaven?"

"Something like that. I like to think my dad is an angel in Heaven. And I hope it's more than fluffy white clouds. He'd be bored with that. What's it like, Rafe?"

"Some things are too complex for explanation."

"Is there a place? Is it a state of being?"

When he gazed down at her, his blue eyes seemed fond and warm, far too warm for an angel. "Think of infinity. Infinite possibilities spread beyond anyone's comprehension, even mine. That's where Heaven lies."

"Have you always been an angel?"

"I was human once, but it was so long ago I've lost count of the years." He turned the doorknob and pushed the door open. "You don't need a key. This house will always be open for you and for your mother. No one else can enter."

"How does that work?"

"It just does. There's high tech, and there's a technology that comes from on high."

"I hope Bill Gates never finds out about that."

Inside, the house was attractively furnished with a fawn leather sectional sofa and chairs. An entertainment center featured television, CD and stereo. In the spacious kitchen, he showed her fully stocked cupboards and a packed refrigerator. Jenna had the impression that someone could live here, very comfortably, for several days.

"Rafe, I don't understand. Why did you bring me here?"

"I wanted you to know of this sanctuary, close to the movie lot. If you come here, you'll be protected." He frowned slightly. "And so will I."

"But why do we need protection?"

He turned away from her. "You're probably hungry. Help yourself from the refrigerator."

Frowning, she opened the refrigerator door. There was a brand of bagel that she liked and a hazelnut spread that tasted almost as good as chocolate. And a six-pack of her favorite soda pop. "Very nice, Rafe. And can I get anything for you? Toast? A glass of milk? Or can I get something from you, like a straightforward explanation of what's going on?"

She glanced over at him as he leaned against the white tiled countertop with his arms folded across his broad chest. "You don't need food," she said. "When you're an angel, you don't need to eat or drink, do you?"

"It's not necessary to feed my celestial body," he said. "When I'm mortal, it's a different story. As you saw last night, I get drunk when I have alcohol. Human flesh requires nourishment. That's one of the reasons I arranged for this house. It might be necessary for me to take human form during much of this investigation. I'll need a place to sleep, food and a car."

"So, you conjured this place up?"

"In a sense."

"Another unexplained mystery," she said sardonically. "Up until now, my life has been fairly simple. Feed the animals, clean up after them, train them and show up for work on time. All of a sudden, I've gone through the looking glass into a world where everything is innuendo and puzzlement. It's making my brain hurt."

"If it's any consolation, I'm also confused."

He thought of the many complicated situations in the past that had required his intelligence. There had been wars. There had been devastation. He'd seen empires topple and watched others, even more corrupt, arise to take their place.

Yet this murder of a Hollywood stuntman boggled his mind.

"Just tell me one thing, Rafe. Am I in danger?"

"I fear that you are. It's this virus, Jenna. It could be a simple poison—like food poisoning. Or it might be more devastating than the plague. And if the virus is synthetic, man-made, it was purposely developed."

"For chemical warfare?"

"There could be international implications. Widespread death. Possibly, Eddy was murdered because he got in the way."

"And I might be in the way, too."

He nodded. "I don't want to frighten you, but—"

"It's almost a relief," she said.

What was she talking about? "Explain."

"When Eddy came crashing onto the soundstage, I had a feeling that somebody else was there. I didn't see anyone, but there was a sense—a prickly feeling on the back of my neck."

"He might have been followed," Rafe concluded. "Or pursued. Why didn't you mention this before?"

"For one thing, you told me that this investigation was none of my business." She busied herself with spreading creamy hazelnut on her bagel. "For another thing, I just wasn't sure. It might have been my imagination."

"Is there more?" he asked.

"Last night, after I dropped you off, I had the impression that another car was following me. Again, it wasn't anything definite."

"Yet you said nothing. Jenna, you need to trust your intuition. It's highly accurate."

"What makes you think so?"

"You noticed my aura," he said. "That indicates a high level of perception."

"I've never thought of myself like that. I was always

considered to be too trusting, too naive, not a very good judge of people.''

Innocence, he thought, was the wisest judge. That was why children could see things that were not apparent to adults. Somehow, Jenna had evaded the decadence of Hollywood and remained clear-sighted enough to see the truth. "How have you stayed so untouched?"

"I grew up on the ranch," she said. "We were kind of secluded. I didn't have many friends. It always seemed like I was an outsider, but I wasn't unhappy. The opposite, in fact. My life was good. I liked my family. We were close."

He saw pain in her eyes. "Were you?"

"I guess I was a little separate from them, too. I mean, my parents had each other. And my little brothers played together." She lifted her chin. "They never tried to make me feel excluded. But I was, somehow, different."

Rafe wanted to hold her, to comfort her. He would offer himself to be kindred to her, bonded forever. But he carefully held back. There could never be a true relationship between Jenna, a mortal woman, and himself.

"There's something else," she continued. "Last night, I was exhausted. I fell into bed, fully dressed. When I woke up during the night, I was under the covers, wearing only my bra and panties."

"You don't remember taking off your clothes?"

"No." She shook her head, and her long curling hair rippled. "I'm about to tell you something that sounds impossible and crazy. Promise you won't laugh?"

"I promise."

"I was lying in bed. It was dark, except for the light coming through the open doorway. I looked over and saw the silhouette of a man. He scared me. I was half-asleep. I didn't know what to do. Before I could react, he came at me and put some kind of cloth over my nose. There was a musty odor, and I fell back to sleep immediately."

As an angel, Rafe was forbidden to use profane language, but the urge to swear had never been so strong. Rage burst explosively within him. Vengeance was his life. At this moment, he wished to wield his sword of flame and smite down the terror that had dared to menace this innocent woman.

"Do you believe me?" she asked. "I mean, it doesn't make logical sense. I'm not familiar with chloroform, but I regularly need to sedate or tranquilize the animals, so I know something about drugs. I can hardly believe that I was drugged and don't feel any aftereffect."

He reined in his temper, focusing upon her question, engaging his mind. "Think of this, Jenna. We're dealing with a person who is clever enough to create a chemical virus. This individual might also have developed a new type of anesthetic."

"But why?" she said. "Why would they bother with me? I don't know anything. And if I was a threat, why wouldn't they just kill me? Why bother with anesthetic?"

"I don't know."

"Rafe, is somebody after me?"

"Let's assume that they are."

"Why?"

"You were with Eddy when he died. He might have told you something or given you a piece of evidence that you don't realize is important. Perhaps last night when you were drugged, the murderer was searching for a clue that you might have in your possession."

"I don't have anything."

"The killer doesn't know that," he reminded her.

"Today on the soundstage, you announced to everyone that Eddy had spoken to you before he died."

She groaned. "I can't believe I did that."

"Out of curiosity," Rafe said, "what were Eddy Benson's dying words?"

"It was a strange thing to say, but I'm sure I heard him correctly." She looked up at him. "Before he died, Eddy said one word. 'Francis.'"

A smile twitched the corners of Rafe's mouth. He knew exactly what Eddy was talking about. "Makes perfect sense to me."

"Is it a clue?"

"Eddy Benson spoke the single word that brought me to you," Rafe said. "When I was given this case, I was told that the assignment had come from the highest authority. With his dying breath, Eddy called upon Saint Francis of Assisi, patron saint of animals."

Chapter Six

When they returned to the soundstage, the *Alien Age* cameras were rolling. Both the on-set visit of Hugh Montclair and Detective Metz's investigation had solidified Alex Hill's loose inspirations more quickly than red wine stains silk. The director had finally taken charge.

There were no long discussions of motivation or script changes while Alex put the lovely Dinah and handsome Jason through their paces. In their revealing bodysuits, the two stars frolicked in the Garden of Eden. Jenna plunged into work immediately, helping her mother set up a shot with cockatoos, a peacock and both llamas.

With filming under way, Kate backed off the set. Her shoulders sagged wearily. In these few hours, she'd engaged in more social interaction than she had in the past three years.

"Are you okay, Mom?"

"Very well." But her determined optimism sounded weak.

"Did you talk to Detective Metz?"

"Just for a moment. I really had nothing to add."

"And Hugh?"

"It's always pleasant to see old friends. We're going out to dinner tonight."

That revelation worried Jenna on a couple of different levels. She didn't want her mother to be overtired. And she wasn't sure how much she trusted Hugh Montclair. The pig substitution and the fact that Eddy had visited him at his home gave her cause for concern. "Are you sure that you should go out tonight?"

"Hey, who's the mother here, anyway?" Kate smiled. "Actually, I'd rather stay here and get to bed early, but I felt so sorry for Hugh. The death of his friend, Paolo Vincenzo, was terribly hard on him."

Jenna gave her a little hug. "Hugh's a big boy. He can take care of himself."

"I know that, honey. It's been a long time since I thought about anyone but myself. It feels good."

"You're not tired?" Jenna asked. "It's not necessary to make up for three years in one day."

"Don't worry about me. I can keep up."

And the pace Alex set definitely kept them busy. Jenna's wrangling work was complicated by the fact that Rafe had decided to protect her. Every time she turned around, he was there, hovering. The concept of having an angel on her shoulder was far more pleasant than the reality of a tall, husky angel who was behaving more like a Secret Service bodyguard for the U.S. President than a motion picture stuntman.

After she and the artistic director arranged the branches of a fig tree to hide the cockatoo's perch, she stepped back out of the shot and bumped into Rafe. Exasperated, Jenna said, "Would you please give me some room?"

He scanned in both directions. Without moving his lips, he seemed to speak to her. "We can't be too careful. One of these people could be a murderer."

"How do you *do* that?" she asked. "I can hear you talking, but you aren't really saying anything out loud."

"It's like a thought bubble," he explained without making a sound. "I think the words and send them to you. By the way, you're the only one who can hear what I'm saying."

Teasing, she whispered, "So, you could be talking dirty, and nobody would know."

"I never talk dirty."

In spite of his rigid morality, he was undeniably, amazingly sexy. From the wide span of his shoulders to his narrow hips, his body was perfectly proportioned. She liked the firm line of his jaw and the enticing bit of chest hair revealed at the unbuttoned collar of his blue Oxford cloth shirt. Even his protective manner was endearing.

She grinned up at him. "Much as I enjoy having your protection, isn't it counterproductive?"

"What do you mean?" he asked directly, not in thought bubble.

"Whoever killed Eddy isn't likely to approach me while you're standing guard."

He scoffed. "If you're offering yourself as a decoy to draw out the murderer, forget it. I'm a professional, Jenna. And I don't put civilians in danger while I'm doing my job."

A professional angel. A bodyguard. An avenger. Rafe was truly remarkable. Yet all she could think about when she looked into his intense blue eyes was how his mouth had felt when he'd kissed her, how strong he'd been when he'd pulled her into his embrace.

"Jenna!" Alex bellowed. "I want three piglets in the foreground for this shot."

She turned to Rafe. "Might as well make yourself useful. Do you mind carrying a pig?"

"No problem."

They met Kate in the animal room where she was counting piglets. Unlike Jenna, her mother had quickly located the alien pig. She pointed. "Who is he?"

"A loaner from Hugh," Jenna said. "I'll explain later."

On set, they rehearsed twice, trying to run the piglets from Jenna to Kate and keep them in the shot. Though pigs are fairly intelligent, these little creatures were confused by the number of technicians milling around, the lights and the equipment. One of them had discovered a fondness for nibbling the fronds of a bird-of-paradise flower.

Dinah, standing and waiting in her skimpy body stocking, stamped her foot. "What's wrong with your stupid animals? I'm freezing to death."

An attentive wardrobe person dashed toward her with a bathrobe.

Dinah raged, "I have goose bumps!"

Jenna turned to Rafe. Remembering his skill with Darius the tiger, she figured a couple of pigs would be a snap for him to control. Quietly, she asked, "Can you help me out here?"

"Certainly."

Rafe cast a thought toward the three little piglets. *Stillness.*

As one, they turned toward him, gazing up with total reverence on their porcine faces.

Come to me.

The pigs waddled toward him and gathered at his feet. If he'd ever felt this assignment was beneath his level of skill as an avenger, this was the moment. He, who had matched wits with kings and princes, was performing a mind meld with piglets.

"You're wonderful," Jenna said.

And when she spoke, he felt that it was so. Her sweet approval validated his actions. A sense of rightness swelled within him. There was nowhere else he wished to be.

"I'll go across the set with the pigs," she said, "then you call them. Okay?"

"Yes."

She herded her little troop of professional pigs to the opposite side of the set. On cue, she unleashed them, and they trotted obediently to Rafe. Several times they repeated this act, while their human counterparts in the scene goofed their actions.

Finally, Alex shouted, "Cut. That was perfect. One more scene for today. Actors only. Jenna, we're done with the animals for the day."

With Rafe's help, Jenna and her mother managed to round up the pigs and the several birds that had been on set. By four o'clock, they were all safely back in their cages.

"We're lucky," Kate said. "At least, there's no dialogue in this sequence, and we don't have to worry about noise from the animals."

"Very lucky," Jenna agreed. It was fulfilling to see her mother at work, facing practical concerns instead of sunk in the depths of an unshakable depression. "You've been great, Mom."

"Haven't lost my touch, have I?" Kate smoothed the snowy feathers of a greater sulfur-crested cockatoo and cooed to him, "You were such a good boy."

"Are you tired, Mom?"

"A bit. But I'm looking forward to my dinner with

Hugh. I'm afraid none of the clothes I brought with me will be fancy enough for an exclusive restaurant in Malibu, but I'll simply have to cope."

She headed toward the small dressing room that they were now sharing. "I'll be busy in here for a good long while, Jenna. At my age, it takes a little bit longer to clean up."

"Take all the time you need, Mom."

"If it would help," Rafe offered, "I have a house nearby."

"I couldn't impose," Kate said. Firmly, she added, "This is where I need to be. Working again."

As she watched her mother close the door to the tiny dressing room, Jenna's eyes welled with happy tears. After three years of mourning, Kate had waded back into the mainstream of life. Thus far, she'd just gotten her toes wet. Her dinner date tonight might take her knee-deep.

Jenna wiped at her eyelids. "She seems to be doing well."

"Yes," Rafe said, "very well."

"Do you think it's safe for her to go out with Hugh? Could he be involved in Eddy Benson's murder?"

Slowly, Rafe nodded. "Everyone on this set is involved in some way. Each of them has a piece of the answer."

"But Hugh isn't dangerous or anything," she said. "Is he?"

"You were the one who was reminded of Count Dracula," he said.

She'd been joking, of course, about the scary-looking entry gate to his estate and the warning from the gate-keeper about bats. But there was something about Hugh that made her nervous. Not that she could imagine the wealthy, powerful Hugh Montclair lurking around her dressing room at night to drug her. That wasn't his style.

She looked up to see one of the Vincenzo boys enter the animal room with a piglet under his arm.

"Hello, Jenna," he said.

Jenna hesitated before putting the name with this face. All three brothers looked very much alike. Average height, black hair, swarthy complexion and strong features. Danny, who had been sent to help Jenna at work, was younger and had a short, military haircut. The gate-keeper/gardener seemed casual and easygoing. The neatly groomed man who stood before her was Nick Vincenzo. He was cooler than his brothers, almost chilly.

"Hi, Nick," Jenna said. "I see you've brought my pig."

"Good as new," he said.

"Then Eddy was wrong in his diagnosis," Rafe said. "The pig wasn't sick, after all."

"Not a bit."

"Didn't you tell us last night that you were in charge of finding new homes for them?"

"That's correct," Nick said. "Where should I put him?"

Jenna led the way to the enclosure. "The next time you start getting rid of pigs, I might want a couple. Would you let me know?"

"They aren't for sale." He placed Jenna's pig down on the straw. When he straightened, he fastidiously re-aligned his double-breasted suit jacket. "I give away the pigs as a tax write-off."

"You handle a lot of Hugh's business," Rafe said. "Are you an accountant?"

"I hire the accountants," Nick informed him. "Running Dr. Montclair's estate and correspondence is a full-time job.''

"I can imagine," Jenna said. She wanted more information about Montclair without seeming to pry. "As far as I know, Hugh produces movies, writes scholarly books, takes field trips to Africa and...what else?"

"He's a busy man." Nick smiled. His white teeth were perfect, an orthodontist's dream. Smoothly, he changed the subject. "I'm pleased that your mother is going out with Dr. Montclair. He's happier than I've seen him in years."

Quietly, Jenna confided, "My mother feels the same. My father's death, three years ago, was hard on her."

"It's much the same with us," Nick said.

"When did your father die?" Rafe asked.

"He passed away eight months ago." Nick's dark eyes turned inward. "He had a long, painful sickness. Since we knew the end was coming, it wasn't so hard for my younger brothers and me to let go. We believed his death would reunite him with our beloved mother, and it was a mercy for his suffering to end."

"But Hugh didn't feel that way," Rafe surmised.

"He fought my father's illness until the very end. So many medicines and treatments and experts."

"What did your father die of?"

"Does it matter?" Nick said. "He's gone."

His abrupt statement rang cold and hollow. Nick Vincenzo had cultivated a perfect appearance. No doubt, he was utterly efficient, but Jenna couldn't help wondering about the condition of his soul.

"Something puzzles me," Rafe said. "Why would Hugh raise Vietnamese potbellied pigs? They're runts by nature. Surely, you don't use them for their meat."

"I don't question Dr. Montclair's decisions." He

turned to Jenna. "It would be good if the doctor and your mother found happiness with each other. If you'll excuse me, I need to be on my way."

But Rafe had another question. "When Eddy brought this pig for treatment, do you remember what happened?"

"I don't recall. Probably they took saliva samples and blood samples." He scooped Hugh's pig from the pen. "It was nice to see you both."

After he left, Jenna turned toward Rafe. There was something odd about Nick, but she couldn't quite place it. Before she could say anything, he placed a finger across his lips, indicating that she should be silent.

"Why?" she demanded in a whisper.

He nodded toward the doorway where a long shadow eased across the door frame.

"Who's there?" Jenna asked.

Taylor Wannamaker stepped through the door frame. "Jenna, I thought I might find you here."

"And how long did you need to eavesdrop before you were sure you'd found me?"

"Eavesdrop?" His long nose wrinkled in disdain. "As usual, you've overestimated your own importance. What could you possibly say that might be worth listening to?"

"What do you want?" Jenna demanded.

"According to Detective Metz, Eddy Benson was bitten by one of your animals."

"What? You don't know that! How can you come in here and accuse my animals?"

"It's a supposition, and a rather valid one since the only animals Eddy would have come in contact with were right here in this room. In any case, I'm ordering a quarantine."

"You can't do that," Jenna sputtered. "We're in the middle of a shoot."

"But I can," Taylor said. "It's within my authority. If I believe the animals are a danger, I can restrict their use."

"Dangerous?" She erupted. "Look at those piglets! Do they look vicious to you?"

"They might be carrying a disease," he said.

"Of all the vindictive, ludicrous, obnoxious—"

"Jenna," Rafe said gently. "May I offer a suggestion?"

Not unless it had something to do with disemboweling Taylor Wannamaker. "What?"

"Why don't we check for disease? Jenna can take blood samples from the animals and submit them to the coroner's office for testing."

Taylor frowned. "Seems like a lot of work."

"You're right," Rafe said. "It would require special effort on your part, Taylor. You'd have to negotiate with the highest authorities in the LAPD and the coroner's office."

"I would, indeed."

Jenna saw the transparent ruse that Rafe had offered. He was offering Taylor a chance to look important and to talk with important people. Though it went against her grain to be nice to Taylor in any way, she said, "I'd cooperate. What do you say, Taylor?"

"I'd have to negotiate everything, wouldn't I?"

"Absolutely," Rafe said. "You'd be responsible for enforcing the policies of the SPCA, while building a reputation as someone who's friendly to the motion picture industry."

"That's not a bad reputation to have." His frown became a self-satisfied smirk. "All right, Jenna. I suggest you start taking blood samples immediately."

"I'll do it tonight," she said.

"Tomorrow morning, bright and early, I'll deal with it," he said. Turning on his heel, he strode toward the door. "Oh, and I'll tell Alex Hill myself. I'm sure he'll appreciate being able to continue filming without interruption."

Jenna glared at his retreating form. She went to the door and slammed it behind him. "Nice job, Rafe. You made that pompous jerk think the blood samples were his own idea."

"Thank you." Bending Taylor's overblown ego to do his bidding had been child's play, but Rafe felt a rush of pride. Jenna's opinion was absurdly important to him.

"I have a request," she said.

"Name it."

"I want you to follow my mother and Hugh tonight. She's still fragile, and I don't want her to be hurt."

"And you suspect Hugh might harm her?"

"I don't know. But what if he does?" Her dark eyes pleaded, "I'm scared for her. Please, Rafe, watch over my mother."

"Her guardian angel should be enough."

"Please."

"I'll do it on one condition. You promise to stay here, lock the door and keep your pistol handy."

"Thank you."

She reached toward him, wanting to confirm his words with a physical touch. Then, it seemed, she remembered that he was an angel, and she pulled her hand back. Her slight gesture caused a sharp twinge of regret within him. If he'd been mortal, she would be in his arms right now. He would be holding her, stroking her silken hair and feeling the softness of her breasts crushed against his chest. They would kiss. Excitement would race through him, arousing every nerve ending, wakening desires.

But that was not to be. Not now. Not ever.

INVISIBLE, RAFE WAITED until Jenna had her evening's work under way. He watched as she checked the syringes and vials she'd obtained from a veterinary supply store. Handling the equipment efficiently, she had obviously done this type of procedure before.

Humming softly, Jenna knelt on the floor and cradled one of the piglets in her arms. Her hands were gentle. Though she'd pulled her hair back in a loose ponytail, a golden strand escaped and fell across her cheek. Swift as an unseen breeze, he whisked the tendril back into place and stepped back.

He admired her grace as if she were a work of art. The delicate crook of her arm pleased his esthetic sensibility. Her neck inclined, swanlike. Thick lashes obscured her dark, beautiful eyes.

She hesitated for an instant, then looked up. Though she couldn't see him, there was recognition in her gaze. A subtle smile curved her lips.

Rafe had never seen such loveliness.

Jenna's guardian angel made his presence known, and they conversed in unspoken thought.

"She's very pretty," Rafe said without speaking.

"And sweet," the other agreed. "I'm fortunate."

"Stay with her. Warn her of danger."

"I'll do my best."

Rafe floated aloft, taking to the skies. If he'd calculated the timing correctly, Hugh Montclair and Kate Denardo should already have arrived in Malibu.

The restaurant, named Plata D'Or, offered a spectac-

ular view of the Pacific sunset, and Hugh had obtained
a table beside the floor-to-ceiling windows. Though Rafe
had not been to this particular eatery, he recognized the
accoutrements of fine dining. Tablecloths were white
linen. The place settings featured heavy silver. The lighting mixed the glow of candles with track lights focused
on original oil paintings.

Still invisible, Rafe tuned his sense of smell to the
savory aromas that wafted from the kitchen. The menu
was sophisticated. Presentation was excellent. But Rafe
was unconcerned with the setting. He'd often come in
contact with the finer things in mortal life. Tonight, he
was more interested in observing the courtship ritual.
Hugh Montclair was a sophisticated man, attracted to
Kate Denardo, and Rafe wanted to see how well he succeeded in pleasing her.

Hugh was studying the wine list.

"I'll just have coffee," Kate said. "But you go right
ahead."

"I prefer to share coffee with you," Hugh said gallantly. To the wine steward, he said, "Sumatran."

Kate gazed through the window, remarked on the
view, and Hugh took her comment as a cue to mention
his travels. His anecdotes conveyed the image of an impressive life-style. Still, Kate's attention seemed to wander.

If Rafe had been offering a critique of the date, he
would have given Hugh a "ten" for class and a "four"
for sensitivity. He fell another point in Rafe's estimation
when he ordered for Kate, and she corrected him.

"I can't have lobster. Don't you remember? I'm allergic to shellfish."

"Veal?"

"Oh, I don't eat veal on principle. I hate the way the

calves are raised. Something with chicken would be fine for me.''

Rafe was about to dub this date "Portrait of a Man Striking Out." But Hugh must have had the same sense. He changed the topic. "Tell me about your children."

Kate spoke in a pleasant and amusing fashion about her two boys, then she moved on to Jenna. "She needs to have a life of her own. To meet a man, fall in love, get married and have children. I'm afraid I've held her back."

"Nonsense, Kate." He reached across the table and patted her hand. "You're a perfect mother."

"Perfectly selfish," she said. "When I saw Jenna leaving the building with Rafe this morning, I was happy for her. And sad at the same time."

"Why?" Hugh asked.

Silently, Rafe echoed that thought.

Her mother said, "I think Rafe might be the man she's been waiting for. I see how she looks at him. It's the same way I used to look at her father."

Again, Hugh spoke the words that Rafe was thinking. "And why does this make you sad?"

"To love so deeply..." Kate sighed. "In the end, it can only hurt her. No love can last forever."

Though Rafael had no physical body, he felt as if Jenna's mother had plunged a dagger into his heart. His intention was not to hurt Jenna, not ever, not in the slightest way. He couldn't allow her to love him.

Most urgently, he needed to conclude this investigation and leave her. Before it was too late.

JENNA FINISHED taking blood samples from all the animals except the tiger, and she'd already decided that

Rafe should handle that task with his angelic powers. That way she wouldn't have to sedate Darius.

When she stored the carefully labeled specimens in the refrigerator in her dressing room, she had a strange sense that she could hear someone shouting her name as if from the bottom of a well, warning her, telling her to hide.

But she should have been alone on the soundstage.

Next door, the monkeys shrieked. Jenna heard them running around their cages. Then, the birds began to squawk.

A distinctly human voice said, "Settle down, you ridiculous creatures."

The accent was unmistakable. "Alex?" she called.

"Do come out here, Jenna. Your menagerie is behaving badly."

She stepped through the doorway. Though she didn't think she had anything to fear from him, Jenna knew her handgun was nearby.

He stood beside the llamas. His eyes were hard. "If you don't mind, I'd prefer chatting in another place. After a day of shouting at actors, I don't fancy hollering to be heard over a crew of cockatoos."

"First, let me get them bedded down." She checked the water in each of the separate birdcages before placing a cover over the top. "What are you doing here?"

"I've just checked the rushes for today's work. Quite beautiful, really. And I thought we might take advantage of this quiet time to discuss the scene tomorrow morning."

"What scene?"

"I simply cannot get Dinah to hold the snake. And it's rather necessary, you know, for Eve to communicate with the snake in the Garden of Eden. I'm afraid you'll have to play Eve."

"Naked? No way!"

"You won't really be nude. It's an illusion, costuming."

"I'm not an actress," she pointed out. "And I'm definitely not a body double for Dinah."

"Rafe has already agreed to his part with the tiger in this scene."

"Good for Rafe," she said. "I'm still not interested."

"I thought you might have hesitations. That's why I've come tonight to convince you."

She was beginning to have a very bad feeling about this conversation. With his dark goatee, dressed all in black, Alex looked like the very devil.

But Jenna remained nonchalant. "It doesn't matter if we talk tonight, tomorrow or next week. I'm not going to do it."

"I know how very interested you are in Eddy Benson's death," Alex said smoothly. "Unless I miss my guess, your friend Rafe is somehow investigating."

Jenna said nothing. She wasn't a good liar, and she definitely wasn't in the same league as Alex when it came to manipulation and slyness. She tossed the last cover over the birdcages and led the way out of the room, too far from her gun if she needed protection.

In the quiet of the outer soundstage, she said, "What are you getting at, Alex?"

"I have a bit of information," he said. "And I would be willing to share if you would agree to do this brief scene for me tomorrow morning. Say yes, Jenna. We'll film early in the morning with a minimal crew and no embarrassment whatsoever."

"Are you trying to blackmail me? That doesn't make any sense. I don't have anything to hide."

"But you have people to protect, don't you? What if I told you that Hugh Montclair isn't the great hero he pretends to be? I think, perhaps, you owe it to your mother to find out all you can about the man."

That had to be the most twisted logic in the world, and yet it was effective. Jenna would do anything to protect her mother. "What do you know, Alex?"

"A bit about chemistry." His manner intensified. "A thing or two about poisons. Murder."

"Tell me."

"Not so fast, my dear. I'll want your promise that you will do the scene with the snake in the morning."

"Why is it so important that I do it?"

"This isn't a big-budget film, Jenna. If I hire an actress, I'd have to work with the girl and get her to handle the snake. Really, dear, wouldn't you be more comfortable taking care of your own python?"

She conceded the point. "Possibly."

"It's one small, simple scene. Not worth the trouble of hiring another actress, but integral to my vision for Eden."

"You can't hold back information about a murder."

He laughed, and the sound was magnified by echo. "I don't have to tell a soul. Not unless directly questioned. Even then, I'm rather clever with words. Besides, I never cared a damn for Eddy Benson. His incompetence crippled my brother."

"Did you hate him?"

His penetrating gaze stared right through her defenses. "Surely you know about my brother, the former stunt-man who lost the use of his legs because Eddy Benson was negligent. Everyone knows how thoroughly I hated Eddy.''

"Why did you hire him?''

"I didn't. Eddy was Hugh's idea.''

An ugly sneer distorted his lips. His hatred had festered within him for a long time. Jenna braced herself to run. "Did you kill him?''

"I might have wished him dead, but I would never harm my own production with a murder on set.''

"All right, Alex, tell me what you know.''

"And you'll agree to that tiny scene in the morning?''

"Yes.''

Now that he'd won, Alex breathed more easily. "Thank you, Jenna. You shan't regret this.''

That remained to be seen. "Tell me.''

"Hugh's dearest friend, Paolo Vincenzo, died of AIDS. Apparently, he was infected while in South America doing some sort of business for Hugh.''

That wasn't much of a secret. Though Nick had avoided mentioning the cause of his father's death earlier today, she could have found out.

Alex continued, "But here's the really interesting part. It seems that Hugh has become obsessed with finding a cure.''

"A cure for AIDS?''

"One of his degrees is in chemistry, you know. And he set up a regular research center on his estate. He does his testing and experimentation on pigs.''

And Eddy had been bitten by a pig. The viral infection that killed him must have come from the pig.

Alex gave a little wave of his hand. "Good night, Jenna. I'll see you in the morning.''

Chapter Seven

Jenna had set her alarm for half past four in the morning, but she awakened before the buzzer went off. The uncomfortable sofa bed was made almost uninhabitable by the fact that Jenna and her mother were both scrunched beneath the goose-down comforter. The Denardos were small women, but both were accustomed to sleeping alone. The night had been a silent battle for space and covers.

Jenna's lower back ached and her eyelids felt scratchy. In a few short hours, she'd promised to appear in front of a movie camera, wearing little more than a smile and a python. She needed to report to makeup by five o'clock so they could slather her naked skin with paint. Before that, she had just enough time for a shower and recrimination.

In the tiny shower stall, she rinsed her body with steaming hot water. Why, oh why, had she allowed Alex to talk her into this? And where was Rafe? She'd expected him to return here after her mother's date, but Jenna hadn't wanted to look like she was waiting up for either of them. When she went to bed to fake sleep, her ruse worked too well. She was sleeping soundly before either of them returned.

Out of the shower, she shrugged into a worn, red plaid flannel robe and wrapped a towel around her wet hair. When she shuffled into the animals' room, which was lit by a single bulb, she caught sight of Rafe's incandescent glow. Shadows fell across his face, highlighting his high cheekbones and chiseled jaw. He looked tall, dark and handsome. Perfect, as usual.

"I've got news for you," she said. "But first, how did Mom's date go last night?"

"It was...nice."

She waited for him to say more, but he was silent. Apparently, he didn't understand the various stages of dating, all the subtle clues that marked a date as "friendly," "more than friends" or "Wow!" "Candlelight?" she asked. "Expensive restaurant? Did they stay for dessert?"

"Yes. Yes. And yes."

"Any physical contact?"

Rafe considered for a moment. "He might have reached across the table once or twice and squeezed her hand."

Here was the clincher. "Did they kiss good-night? If so, what kind of kiss?"

"On the cheek," Rafe said.

Jenna nodded, satisfied. Kate and Hugh were friends, nothing more. "I'm relieved. I don't really like Hugh."

"You said you had information."

She told him about her conversation with Alex. The idea of testing fatal serum on animals disgusted her. In Jenna's mind, it was murder. Good reason to dislike Hugh Montclair.

On the other hand, taken in the context of what Alex said had happened, Eddy's death could be considered an accident.

She concluded, "He was bitten by the infected pig. I figure the bite might have happened when he was getting a saliva sample for the physical examination."

"Very neat," Rafe said.

"Very," she agreed.

"Except for one thing. Eddy Benson was murdered. At the end, he realized what had happened to him, and he called upon Saint Francis to avenge his death."

"How could anybody know the pig was going to bite Eddy? Or that the infection would be passed through the bite? Maybe Eddy called upon Saint Francis for a different reason. Maybe to protect the pigs."

"He was murdered," Rafe repeated. "If Eddy was infected with a bite, it must have been one of Hugh's pigs that bit him."

"Right," she said.

"Why would he be taking saliva samples from Hugh's livestock?"

Jenna groaned. Of course, Rafe was right. They were back to zero. Alex's information was worthless. "I can't believe I promised Alex that I'd do the seminude scene with the snake."

"I'll be there." Rafe grinned. "For support."

"Darn right, you will. Alex said he'd talked to you, and you're playing Adam to my Eve."

"I am?"

"He wants you to do something with Darius."

"That's a problem," he said. "I can't do this scene as an angel. The film will pick up my aura."

With a jolt, she realized their dilemma. "If you're a mortal, you won't have any control over the tiger."

"Exactly."

"We'll have to use conventional methods for handling him. That's all."

But she wasn't pleased about this turn of events. Working with the tiger was always difficult, and Alex was under the impression that Rafe was able to communicate with the big cat on a special magical level.

"The transformation," Rafe said, "is difficult. I haven't prepared myself. I had hoped to use the house for my meditation prior to the change."

"There isn't time," she said. "The makeup people are going to need both of us as soon as possible."

"Makeup?"

"Even if you have a terrific suntan, the bright lights on the set wash out all color. We'll both need tons of body paint."

He hooked his thumbs in the pockets of his Levi's and paced rapidly back and forth. His slight aura seemed to follow him like the tail of a comet.

"What's the matter?" she asked. "I had the impression that you kind of liked being human."

"I'm an angel, Jenna. I don't like to haul around a thick body of human flesh. The effects are unpredictable. And I'm vulnerable. If you cut me, I'll bleed."

"If I cut you right now," she said, "what would happen?"

"You wouldn't," he said.

Very true, and she pitied anyone who would try to attack him. As an angel, Rafe was cloaked in invulnerability. With a fierce glance, he could dispel any threat.

"All right," he said, "this can't be helped. I'll have to transform right here. Right now. Keep watch for me, Jenna. There must be no interruption. Whatever happens, you must not touch me and, please, try to maintain quiet."

He sat on the floor in a lotus position. His eyes closed. Jenna watched in utter fascination. From nowhere, a wind stirred the air in the room. A sparkling energy field surrounded Rafe, swirling around him like a luminous tornado.

A slight vibration hummed through him, and she heard a distant whir that came closer and closer. Rafe seemed to rise several inches off the floor.

His breathing became labored. He was shivering, yet heat radiated from him in waves.

Jenna wanted to go to him, to hold him, to comfort him in what appeared to be a most strenuous effort. But he'd warned her about physical contact. She knotted her hands helplessly.

Suddenly, he blinked. He seemed to settle into himself. In a hoarse voice, he said, "It's done."

"Are you all right?"

He nodded. His broad chest heaved with each new breath. The simple movement of his head seemed like an effort.

"Is it okay?" She knelt beside him. "Are you all right?"

His blue eyes seemed to have difficulty focusing as he gazed at her. "I'll be fine."

"You seem hot. Should I get you a glass of water or something?"

Clumsily, his hand rested on her shoulder. "Help me stand. It takes a moment to gain my strength."

"Then maybe you should remain sitting. There's no reason to rush. Not really. The makeup can wait."

"Jenna!" His deep voice was strong. "I don't wish to sit here like a lump of clay."

In her struggle to help him rise to his feet, the towel fell from her hair. Her flannel robe gaped, and she clutched it together to cover herself.

On his feet, Rafe stared down at her. With slow deliberate motions, he embraced her. His hands radiated warmth as he caressed her. "Soft," he whispered. "Your skin is like satin."

Her robe came apart, but Jenna didn't care. She was caught in the intensity of the moment, unable to consider beyond the taste of his mouth upon hers. As he kissed her, she melted against him.

When Rafe stepped away from her, she was trembling.

"I'm sorry," he said. "I had no right to kiss you."

"Don't apologize."

"You understand, don't you? There can never be a relationship between us."

"I understand." He was her ephemeral lover. His existence was only for a moment, while he was mortal. Then he would be an angel again—distant, untouchable. "I'll take any kisses I can get."

"There's a problem," he said.

"What's that?"

He shuffled his feet, and she realized that when he was an angel, she never heard him walking. "As a mortal man, I lack control," he said. "Especially, um, below the waist."

Jenna glanced down. There was a sexy bulge in his jeans. "Personally, I think it's very attractive."

"How am I going to walk around in a body stocking with this hanging out?"

She grinned. "I'm told that men think of other things to control *that*. Think of something unsexual." Helpfully, she continued, "Think of wading across a river. It's cold, ice cold. Fast moving current…"

"Sunlight reflecting, like the sparkle in your eyes. My body tingling, alive." He shook his head. "Not water. Water is sensual."

"How about sports?" she suggested. "Football."

"I'd think of what you would look like in a cheer-leader uniform. The Dallas Cowboy cheerleaders, I know, have very attractive outfits."

"Forget sports," Jenna said. "An old boyfriend once told me that when he got turned on, he did mathematical equations in his head."

"Logic," Rafe said, "requires total concentration. Yes, that might be effective and relevant, since I need to concentrate on the facts of the murder."

"I guess logic is a good antidote to sex."

"And murder," Rafe said. "When I think of injustice, my human body reacts. There's no room for another emotion." He looked at her. "How do you suppose Alex got his information about Hugh?"

"Because he wanted me to do this scene." But that explanation was too simple. Had he wanted to confuse her? Why did he tell Jenna? How did he think she was involved? "Do you think Alex killed Eddy?"

"Alex should be considered as a suspect. Keep in mind that in addition to the bite, there was the mark of a hypodermic needle."

Pondering these clues, Jenna and Rafe reported to the makeup area where Dorothy, the director's assistant, gave orders to three other women.

"Body makeup from head to toe," Dorothy said. "They're supposed to look naked. Jenna and Rafe, you just sit there, okay? Wardrobe! Where is that woman?"

These people were professionals. There was very little giggling and silliness as they did their jobs, treating Jenna and Rafe with the impersonality of a couple of sides of beef.

After they were fitted in filmy body stockings—a one-piece bathing suit for Jenna and briefs for Rafe—the makeup artists set to work with makeup that covered every imperfection. Jenna watched the scar on her knee from a horseback riding accident disappear. Tan lines vanished.

With Rafe, the makeup ladies complained about the thick body hair on his arms and chest.

"You're lucky," Dorothy said to him. "Jason has a lot of hair, too. If he didn't, we'd need to shave you."

"Forget it," Rafe said.

"You're really in much better shape than Jason."

"Is that a problem?"

"Not for you." Dorothy grinned. "Not at all."

After they'd been coated with a goo that seemed to clog every pore, the hairstylists descended. It was a struggle to get Jenna's thick hair tucked under the Eve wig that fell almost to her knees. After being stabbed by dozens of bobby pins, she felt as if her scalp was a pincushion.

Rafe was outfitted with a far less elaborate wig, one that matched Jason's chestnut-brown hair.

When they were finished, Rafe and Jenna stood side by side, studying themselves in a full-length mirror. She shouldn't have wasted a second's worry about being too undressed. With the bodysuit and the thick makeup, Jenna realized she'd often been more scantily clad at the beach.

Rafe, however, was gorgeous. His shoulder span was impressive. The muscles in his stomach were taut. And he had the straightest, most well-developed legs she'd ever seen on a man.

Jenna tore her gaze away from him before she could succumb to the urge to climb his body like a jungle gym. She couldn't allow her mind to wander down that particular path. Working with the snake and the tiger was going to be complicated, and she needed to be sharp.

"You're adorable," Dorothy said. "You look like Ken and Barbie."

"Who?" Rafe asked.

Jenna explained, "With this makeup spackled all over, we look like plastic dolls. Unfortunately, I don't have Barbie's legs."

"You've got great legs," he said. "Great everything…not that I'm looking."

"I certainly hope not," she retorted. "Remember your little problem."

"Not so little," he said.

Alex swept into the room and eyed them critically.

"Not bad," Dorothy said. "They're not identical to Dinah and Jason. For one thing, Jenna's too short. But they'll be okay as long as you don't do close-ups."

"Right," Alex said briskly. "Come along, you two. Let's get this scene shot before the rest of the crew arrives."

"Good idea," Jenna said. "While we're working with Darius, I want the soundstage doors locked. Only necessary personnel should be present. We need to avoid distractions."

"But I was under the impression that Rafe was able to coax the tiger through hoops."

"Not today," Rafe informed him. "The thing that happened the other day was pure luck. It probably won't happen again."

"Very well."

As Alex explained his vision of Rafe playing with the tiger, coming in direct physical contact, Jenna added her own instructions. "Under no circumstance should Rafe be on the ground, lower than the tiger. As long as Darius doesn't think he's lunch, we ought to be okay. Also, we'll have to keep the tiger on a restraint leash."

With careful maneuvering, Jenna and her mother set up the scenes with Darius, putting the tiger through his paces. The cameras were filming when Rafe stepped onto the set.

Though he was now mortal, Rafe was clearly the dominant animal. Respectfully, he approached the huge cat and circled him. One step at a time, he approached until, finally, he reached out to stroke the gleaming fur of Darius's striped coat.

The tiger tossed his head. With his giant paw, fortunately declawed, he smacked Rafe's muscled thigh. But Rafe stood firm.

The tiger took a step toward him.

"Darius, sit!" Jenna shouted.

He took another stalking step.

Instead of getting out of the way, Rafe strode into danger, into Darius's range. He reached out, quick as a whip, and slapped the tiger's ear.

Darius threw back his head and roared.

Jenna held her breath. She knew that Rafe was vulnerable. With fierce teeth, Darius could shred his human flesh. But the tiger did not attack. He and Rafe eyed each other curiously.

There seemed to be an understanding between them. As if they shared a secret joke. When they played with each other, Rafe's strength in handling Darius was a pleasure to watch. They were two beautiful animals.

Jenna had to admit that Alex's vision had been brilliant. This scene between man and tiger would play very well on film.

When they concluded, Darius was lying down and Rafe sat behind him.

"Cut and print," Alex said. "Fabulous! That was fabulous."

As soon as Jenna and her mother had returned Darius to his cage, the director called for her. "Jenna, I want you to do much the same with the snake as Rafe did with the tiger. Just enjoy yourself. Don't worry about continuity, we'll cut together the images that work."

Feeling stiff and self-conscious, Jenna allowed Serena to dangle from her arm and glide through the tangled wig. "There," she said. "Is that enough?"

Alex approached her. He spoke softly so only she could hear. "Think of a dance, Jenna. You are the embodiment of femininity. You are Eve. And the snake is your partner."

He turned back toward the cameras. "Could we have some music please? Classical, I should think."

"Dancing?" Jenna said. Beyond the lights, she could see her mother watching. "Like a belly dance? I don't know how to do that."

"You're not a stripper, Jenna. This shouldn't be an exotic-dancer thing with sexy poses. It's innocent. Do whatever you feel like doing and I won't interrupt you again."

The sounds of Tchaikovsky's *Swan Lake* issued from a boom box, and Jenna returned to the set. She felt ridiculously clumsy at first, but after a moment, the sinuous grace of the python gave her a feeling of movement. Though she did not for one instant forget that the camera was running and people were watching her, she managed a sort of dancing rhythm.

"Fabulous!" Alex shouted. "Keep the music going. Rafe, you enter the scene with her. Jenna, pass the snake to him."

The bright lights focused on the set seemed to create a separate world. As Rafe came toward her, nearly nude,

Jenna's heart leapt. If only this could be real. Just the two of them, naked and innocent in the garden.

Violins serenaded them. Rafe stretched out his arm toward her. As she clasped his fingers, she arranged the python to twine around their joined hands.

They moved together, finding a special dance that was theirs alone. His eyes spoke to her. His body fitted with hers, then separated. Seductively, she drew him back to her.

He lifted her above his head, and she glided—graceful as the python around her shoulders—down his body.

"Cut and print," Alex shouted.

There was a round of applause from the people who had gathered around the set.

"Rafe and Jenna, that was marvelous! I believe the temperature in this building has risen by several degrees. If you two would please step off set, we can hose you down."

She lifted Serena the python from her shoulders. "Back to business," she said. "Thank goodness that's over."

Quietly, Rafe said, "I think we've just begun."

Together they went to the animal room where Kate was waiting. She beamed at them. "Very pretty, you two. If I were Alex, I'd want you to be Adam and Eve. You look wonderful together."

"Gosh, Mom. Thanks." This was her mother. What else could she say? Jenna held out the snake. "Would you mind cleaning Serena off? She's got makeup goop all over her."

There was a tap on the outer door, and they heard Dorothy call out, "Have you got the snake put away?"

"She won't hurt you," Jenna said. "Come on in."

Dorothy kept her distance, standing in the doorway. "I need the wig, Jenna."

"Good! I can't wait to get this thing off." She yanked out bobby pins. "This hair must weigh ten pounds."

"You guys did real good," Dorothy said. "Alex loved it, and so did everybody else. There ain't nothing like young love."

"We're not in love," Jenna said as she removed the long wig from her head and held it toward Dorothy.

"Then you're the best actress since Sarah Bernhardt." Dorothy took the wig and checked her clipboard. "Get yourself cleaned up, then I'm going to need three monkeys and a llama on set."

"Monkeys and a llama." Jenna exhaled a huge sigh. "That's more like it."

"Agreed," Rafe said. "I'm going to get my clothes from makeup, and I'll pick up your robe. May I use your shower when you're done?"

"Why not save water," Dorothy said.

"Good idea," Kate teased. "Shower together."

Jenna glanced between the two women who grinned good-naturedly. In their eyes, she and Rafe were a young couple, falling in love. Kate and Dorothy didn't know the complexities of the situation, and if Jenna tried to explain, they would surely call her crazy.

Rafe was an angel. She couldn't allow herself to love him because he was not of this earth. Might as well fall in love with the summer sun when September came to take it away.

"I'll bathe alone," she said.

After she'd scrubbed and dressed, Jenna felt like she'd already done a full day's work even though it was barely ten o'clock in the morning. As far as she was concerned, being an actress was a less desirable occupation than swabbing toilets with a toothbrush. And it was devastatingly hard to be with Rafe, especially when he was a mortal man with natural desires.

No wonder she was tired. Her stress level couldn't rise much higher. When she heard hostile voices from the animals' room beyond her dressing room, she charged forth, ready to tear somebody's head off.

"It's really none of your business." Taylor Wannamaker sneered. "You're only a stuntman."

"I'll come with you to deliver the blood samples," Rafe said. "I want to make sure they're handled correctly."

Though he'd slipped into his Levi's, he hadn't yet put on his shirt. Bare-chested, with his long, black hair tied in a ponytail and his complexion darkened with makeup, he looked savage compared to Taylor in his Brooks Brothers suit.

"I told you," Taylor said. "It's not your job."

"You're taking these samples to the coroner's office, aren't you?"

"I don't have to put up with this." Taylor lifted his long snout in the air. "When Jenna comes out, tell her I'm waiting."

She stepped into the room. "I'm here. What's going on?"

Taylor rushed toward her, spewing his explanation. "I came for the blood samples so they can be tested. It's no big deal, except that your boyfriend doesn't trust me."

"Neither do I," Jenna said.

"Well, maybe I'm not taking the samples to the coroner's office, but I'm in contact with a reputable veterinarian who is a specialist in animal disease, and he's going to do the tests in his own lab."

"Why not the coroner?" Jenna asked. "He has Eddy's blood samples to compare with these."

"It's like this. When I talked with the coroner, he said this much lab work would probably take a whole week. The vet can do it overnight." Taylor whined, "My way is best. I need to know, right away, if your animals are sick."

"Look around the room, Taylor. Do any of these animals appear to be ill?"

"How would I know?"

"Exactly. And how would you know if a vet is reputable or not?"

"Of course he's reputable. I'm talking about Hugh Montclair."

Jenna's blood began to boil. Taylor was willing to risk the health of her animals for a chance to score brownie points with Hugh. "How could you?"

"He deserves to know what's going on with his own movie," Taylor said. "He really is a very well-known vet."

"The sort of vet who might help your career?"

When Taylor stiffened his spine and planted his fists on his hips, his gawky frame looked like an umbrella snapping into shape. "Listen, Jenna, you'd better do as I say."

Smoothly, Rafe interrupted, "Here's what we'll do, Taylor. Jenna and I were planning to visit Hugh this afternoon, anyway."

"You were?"

"That's right," Jenna snapped. "And the samples won't be ready until later anyway. I still need to do the tiger."

Rafe continued, "We'll take the blood samples and save you a trip. Since you're in such a hurry."

Peevishly, Taylor grumbled, "How do I know you won't cheat?"

"I never cheat. I don't lie. I'm so squeaky-clean that filth like you just slides right off." Rafe took one stride toward him. "I'll take care of the blood samples."

Taylor backed up quickly, then tidied his necktie and smoothed his hair. "I'll be in touch with Hugh."

When he was gone, Rafe turned to Jenna. "Looks like Taylor is doing us a favor for a change. I wanted a reason to visit Hugh and have a look at his operation. To investigate."

She nodded. Hugh Montclair looked suspicious. He was experimenting with viruses, and Eddy had been there two days before he died.

"When we were there before," Rafe said, "I sensed a presence."

"I don't understand," she said. "What kind of presence?"

"It was evil, Jenna. Pure evil."

Chapter Eight

Just after two o'clock in the afternoon, Rafe packed the marked blood samples from Jenna's animals in a rented refrigerated case, stowed the case in the trunk of his convertible and set out for the Montclair estate. On this visit, Rafe planned to be more alert. No wine. No cigar. No distractions.

Ironically, the murder of Eddy Benson was turning into the most unusual case in Rafe's career as an avenger. He'd been drunk. He'd led three little piglets across a fake Garden of Eden. He'd been half naked, dancing with a python. And he had twice kissed Jenna.

He drove slowly along the narrow lane between soundstages where pedestrian traffic was heavy. He'd definitely been behaving in an un-angelic manner. If Rafe had been less experienced, less senior in his job, he would've been reprimanded for the liberties he'd taken. But Saint Michael trusted him.

Focus, Rafe told himself. He needed to focus on the problem at hand. Most likely, Eddy had discovered Hugh's use of pigs for testing and had been murdered—by injection of a fatal virus—before he could report Montclair to the authorities. But Rafe also needed to consider the more ominous view of the murder. A dangerous virus had been developed and was spreading—either by carelessness or design.

This afternoon he would find answers at Hugh Montclair's estate.

In the parking lot beside the front gate of the R.I.P. movie lot, Jenna flagged him down and hopped into the passenger seat. "Okay, let's go."

"I'm not taking you with me. This confrontation might be dangerous."

"As opposed to confronting Alex?" Her fine eyebrows lifted in a high arch. "Or dealing with Taylor?"

He scoffed. "Taylor? We have nothing to fear from Taylor. A field mouse has nothing to fear from—"

"Don't be so sure. Taylor might have killed Eddy so he could meet Hugh and advance his stupid career."

What was she talking about? There was no logic whatsoever to her thinking. "That's not a reason for murder."

His gut instinct told him that Hugh was the murderer. He had created a virus that could kill within forty-eight hours. He had been with Eddy during the relevant time frame.

"I'm not staying here," Jenna said. "Every time you leave me here, something scary happens. I'd rather be with you."

"If you're frightened, I can take you to the safe house."

"I'm coming with you, Rafe. Whether you're willing to admit it or not, you need me."

On a certain level, Rafe couldn't argue with that. His need for her was undeniable, almost debilitating. He couldn't rid his mind of her image. Jenna gave vibrant life to fantasies he wasn't even aware of having. The sound of her voice thrilled him. The clean fragrance of her honey-blond hair made him weak in the knees. Oh yes, he needed her. But not for protection.

He gazed toward her. It really wouldn't hurt to have Jenna along. He wasn't planning any guerrilla tactics, and her presence was a diversion that might cause Hugh to be less guarded.

"Please, Rafe." She touched his arm, sending a sensual quiver through his body. "I want to be with you."

With a resigned sigh, he fired up the engine of his powerful car and drove through the R.I.P. gates into the streets of Los Angeles. On the movie lot, the atmosphere was light, airy, magical. On the streets, hard reality surrounded them, painted in harsh shadows. Discordant noise came from strained throats, car horns, slamming doors.

In the deepest core of his being, Rafe empathized with the miserable souls who inhabited these streets. They were his legacy, his kin. A part of him would always be with them. From their suffering came the chance for great redemption. His life as a man and as an angel was proof.

"It seems dismal here," Jenna said. "Like the sun never shines on these streets."

"You'd be surprised."

"How so?"

"Which is more beautiful?" he asked. "Acres of bountiful roses tended by gardeners. Or a dandelion that grows in the crack of a sidewalk and brings a smile to the lips of a child who has never seen a rose."

"The dandelion," she said without hesitation.

"Those who seek the sun will find their own light."

As he had done.

Within a mile, they had left the urban blight. Rafe made a slight detour to remind her, again, of the location of the safe house, then he proceeded toward Hugh's bountiful acres.

"I'm glad you let me come with you," she said. "You need somebody to watch your back."

"That sounds like a line from a movie."

"Why do you think police officers travel in twos? When entering a dangerous situation, it's safer if you have two sets of eyes and ears."

"And how do you intend to overwhelm the bad guys, Jenna?"

She patted her purse. "I'm carrying my gun, and my Dad taught me how to shoot."

"Your father was an interesting man. Taught you to shoot and to smoke cigars."

"And to ride," she said with a soft, nostalgic smile. "He was more than interesting, Rafe. My father taught me what a real man should be."

"And your mother?"

"She showed me how to be a woman."

He envied her family ties. After all these years, Rafe couldn't remember what his mother looked like. If he had ever known his father, he'd forgotten. For as long as he could clearly recall, Rafael Santini had been alone.

Until he met Jenna, he hadn't felt a lack.

"Rafe? What did you mean when you said there was evil at Hugh's house?"

"Evil," he said. "Cruelty, corruption, avarice. You know what evil means."

"But how can it be in one place?"

"Evil generates its own energy, and there are those who encourage it. If they knew I was an angel, they might force the action."

"Bad angels?"

That explanation was far too simplistic, as was the

metaphor of *Alien Age* where creatures from another planet came to annihilate the Garden of Eden. Yet he nodded. "Yes."

"Have you ever fought against one of them?"

"It's forbidden. Our battles are within the hearts and souls of men and women."

He was uncomfortable with the course of this conversation. Ethical questions were generally too complex to discuss with mortals. And, to be truthful, Rafe couldn't explain many of the hows and whys. He was a man of action, not words. An unerring internal compass directed him toward justice and revenge.

Though they were uninvited visitors at the Montclair estate, it took only a few minutes for the gatekeeper to respond to their summons. Though he was as young as his brothers, he seemed winded by the effort of latching the electronically controlled iron gates. Despite the warm weather, he wore a heavy leather jacket, zipped to the collar.

From the passenger seat, Jenna peered across Rafe to look at the young man. "Are you feeling sick?"

"A touch of the chills," he said, dragging himself toward the car to stand beside Rafe. "It's nothing."

"You're Nick and Danny's brother, aren't you?"

"That's right. I'm Frank."

"Is that a nickname?"

"My real name is Francis, but I never use it. Sounds too sissy."

Francis? Rafe wished that he had the more acute perception of an angel as he studied the features of the young man who stood beside the car. Had he been wrong to assume that Eddy Benson had called upon Saint Francis with his dying breath? Was he referring to this young man named Francis? "How well did you know Eddy Benson?"

"We weren't buddies or anything." Frank slowly closed his eyes and opened them again. He seemed to grow paler by the minute. "When I first came here, I wanted to be in movies. I worked with Eddy on a motorcycle flick. I liked him."

"Are you all right?" Jenna asked. "You look like you're going to faint."

"Kind of dizzy," he said.

Jenna climbed out of the car and went to him. "You look terrible. Get in the car. We'll take you to the house."

Though unsteady on his feet, he resisted. "I'm fine, really. Just need some rest."

"I insist," Jenna said.

Rafe agreed with her diagnosis. He joined her, taking Frank by the arm and guiding him into the narrow back seat of the sporty car. This young man was about to collapse before their eyes.

"How long have you been ill?" Rafe asked. He was thinking of the forty-eight hours, counting backwards. Two days ago, he and Jenna had been here, and Frank had seemed perfectly healthy.

"It just started this morning," Frank said. "First, I get chilly, then really hot. It's just a flu bug, I'm sure."

Jenna's eyes were worried as she gazed at Rafe. "I hope that's all it is."

Rafe had one more question as they drove toward the front entryway of the sprawling stucco mansion. "Have you ever met Alex Hill?"

"I know his brother real well. Sean Hill. We're supposed to get together tonight." He gasped. "I met Sean on that movie where Eddy Benson was the stunt coordinator. Sean got injured."

"Tell me about Sean."

"He's a great guy. Lost the use of his legs, but it hasn't slowed him down a bit. He has a beautiful girlfriend, used to be a model."

At the front door, Rafe helped Frank from the car. The young man was so weak that he could barely walk.

Jenna hurried ahead of them. She rang the bell and knocked at the same time.

When Nick appeared and saw his brother, he ran to him. "Frank, what's wrong? What happened?"

"I'm really okay. Just need some rest."

Together, Nick and Rafe carried the ailing Frank into the house and up a staircase to a bedroom. As soon as they had him lying down on the bed, Nick excused himself, "I think I know what he needs. I'll find Dr. Montclair."

Frank's breathing was labored. His forehead glistened with sweat. He reached weakly for the zipper on his leather jacket. "Hot," he said, "I'm so hot."

Rafe unfastened the zipper and eased him out of the jacket. Only a moment ago, Frank had been shivering. Now, he was on fire, sweating.

Hugh strode into the room with Nick, took one look at Frank and opened a black doctor's bag that he had brought with him. "I think I know what he has. We've had an outbreak of flu around here. One of the stablehands had it last week."

"Sir," Nick said, "let me handle this."

"Of course."

Nick peeled off his suit jacket. He took a hypodermic from the case and filled it with a blue liquid from a small vial.

"What is that?" Rafe asked.

"The antidote," Hugh said.

Expertly, Nick found the vein in his brother's arm, inserted the needle and depressed the plunger. "Frankie, you'll be all right. You have to be all right."

Hugh stepped toward the door. "Make him comfortable and keep an eye on him. If he gets worse, call me."

Nick Vincenzo fired a tense glare in the direction of his employer. "I'll take care of my brother."

Hugh ushered Rafe from the room toward the stairs. "It's a good thing that you found him before he was too ill to move. The Vincenzo men think of themselves as being indestructible. Foolish machismo. That's what killed their father."

"I thought it was AIDS."

Hugh's eyes narrowed. "He went untreated too long. If I'd known earlier about his disease, I might have been able to cure him."

Rafe didn't argue, but he thought Hugh's claim was exceedingly strange. How could this part-time chemist expect to find a cure? Brilliant scientists all around the world had been working night and day on the virus. They had not yet succeeded. Hugh's ego was as inflated as a balloon in the Macy's Thanksgiving Day parade.

He greeted Jenna in the living room and reassured her about Frank's condition. "To what do I owe the honor of this surprise visit?"

"I thought you'd be expecting us," Jenna said. "Taylor Wannamaker said he'd arranged with you to test blood samples from my animals."

"Oh, yes." Hugh went toward the kitchen, motioning for them to follow. "Can I offer you something to eat or drink?"

Remembering the disaster with the wine, Rafe refused, but Jenna accepted bottled water from the refrigerator.

Nonchalant, Hugh said, "I'm not quite clear about why I'm doing these blood samples. Taylor had said he would explain when he got here. There was something about the coroner's office."

Rafe had the sense that Hugh was baiting him, playing a game of cat and mouse. To win, Rafe had to throw him off guard. But how? "Of course you know that Eddy Benson was poisoned."

"Yes," Hugh said. "I know."

"The coroner's office suspects that this poison is viral in nature. When they were performing the autopsy, they discovered a bite mark from an animal, probably a pig, on Eddy's hand."

"I knew that, too. Eddy was with me when the accident occurred."

"What happened?" Jenna asked.

"Eddy brought over your pig from the soundstage. He said the animal looked sick to him, and I agreed to examine it. Eddy was assisting me, getting a saliva sample with a swab, when he was bitten."

"It was my pig?" Jenna asked. "The one he'd picked up at the studio?"

"Yes."

"Oh, dear," Jenna said softly. Her eyes downcast, she appeared to be on the verge of tears.

Rafe almost applauded. Her sadness was exactly the sort of diversion that might confuse Hugh. As Rafe observed, the smug expression slid from the older man's face. Nervously, he touched his thick, white mustache.

"I don't understand," Hugh murmured. "What's wrong, Jenna?"

She crossed the room and sank into a chair at the kitchen table. "My pig killed Eddy."

"Now, Jenna, I'm sure that's not what happened."

"What else could it be? And if my pig is sick with this terrible illness, he could infect other people. My other animals could be dying. They might have to be put down, all of them."

"Why don't you wait until I've done the testing?" Hugh offered. "I'm sure we won't find this disease among your animals."

"Why not? What else could it be?" Rafe asked, deliberately repeating her question.

"Let's not make rash assumptions." Hugh frowned at both of them. "We should proceed scientifically."

"Identification and containment," Rafe said. "Isn't that the rule with a virus?"

"Indeed, and we'll start with the pigs."

Why not with the virus? With the antidote? "Is it possible for a pig to pass an illness to a man?"

"Oh, yes. The metabolisms of pigs and humans are very similar. That's why pigs are often used for experimental testing."

"Is that what you did?" Rafe inquired with mock innocence. "When you were working to find an AIDS cure, did you use the pigs for experimentation?"

"Of course not," Hugh said. "That's illegal. The SPCA would close down my barns. I'd find myself in the courts with some bleeding-heart animal-rights activist telling me that animal experiments are inhumane."

"Such experimentation is inhumane," Rafe said.

"What do you know about it?" Hugh puffed out his chest. His mustache was twitching. "Listen here, young man, I've spent my whole life studying animal behavior. I've lived in the rain forests and the outback and the

African veldt, and I can tell you one thing. Animals were put here on this earth to serve mankind. That's their function, their only function. They have no higher purpose. They have no emotions."

Rafe glanced toward Jenna. Her sadness quickly turned into a hard, angry glare. In the first few moments after he met her, she'd told him that she believed her monkeys were capable of mischief and emotion.

Now, however, was not the time for her to launch this opinion at Hugh Montclair. He was off guard, on the verge of divulging an even more damaging confession.

"Following that logic," Rafe said, "there might also be humans not worthy of saving. A lower breed of humanity that was put on this earth to serve."

"Let me pose the question," Hugh said. "If humanity could be spared from a devastating disease, wouldn't the solution be worth the death of a few others?"

Had he used Eddy Benson for experimentation?

Hugh Montclair's logic chilled Rafe to the bone. When a man began to believe that he had the power to decide who should live and who should die, the consequence was unnatural disaster.

Though Rafe was unable to see the cold, skeletal fist of evil, he sensed the presence of dark angels who counselled Hugh Montclair. More than ever, he was convinced that the death of Eddy Benson was only the beginning of the terror that Hugh Montclair might release on the world.

"When Paolo died," Hugh said, "it changed my thinking about so many things."

Rafe stayed quiet, waiting for him to continue.

"The world seemed chaotic, unfair." His jaw clenched. His eyes blazed like hot coals, silently expressing the powerful emotions that churned within him. "It wasn't right for Paolo to die."

Rafe could see the fierce strength of his obsession, but could only guess at the form it had taken. Why had Hugh infected Eddy Benson with the virus?

Hugh clapped his hands together, shattering the mood. "Well, now. Let's get those samples from your car, and I'll start my lab work. The sooner I'm done, the sooner your worries will be alleviated, Jenna."

Energetically, he strode away from the kitchen. At the front entry, he paused. "I'll run upstairs quickly and check on Frank. Wait for me."

When Hugh was at the top of the stairs, Rafe whispered to Jenna, "Acting like you were upset was brilliant. You really got him talking."

"I wasn't pretending." She slung her purse over her shoulder and took a sip from her water bottle. "I'm scared, Rafe. What if my animals are sick?"

"It's not your pig. This is some weird virus that Hugh concocted. How could your pig have caught the illness?"

"Eddy was bitten by my pig. What else could it be?"

"The injection," he whispered.

Hugh was coming down the stairs. "Frank is resting more comfortably. Nick says he'll be fine."

"That's some wonder drug you used on him," Rafe said. "What was it?"

"An anti-infection serum. Like penicillin." He opened the front door. "Shall we?"

Rafe carried the refrigerated case that was about the size of a picnic cooler into the house. Following Hugh, they climbed the stairs again and proceeded all the way down the hallway, turning once into the west wing of the house.

The laboratory was a corner room, lined with windows on two sides. White floors, walls and countertops contrasted with a black desk and file cabinets. Lab equipment, ranging from simple microscopes to a four-foot-tall robotic-looking machine, was neatly arrayed. A bank of computers sat near the window, flashing colorful screen-saver designs.

Hugh opened a shiny black door. "This is the refrigerator. Put the blood samples in here, so they'll be safe."

Inside, the room was cool, but not freezing. A long counter stretched along one wall. On the wall opposite, there were two stainless steel doors, both fitted with elaborate locking systems.

Rafe placed the cooler on the countertop. "You're the only one who uses this lab, right?"

"Only Nick and myself."

"Is Nick a chemist?"

"He developed an interest while we were working on a cure for his father. Nick is untrained, but actually quite brilliant."

"Why do you need so much security?"

"It's a safety precaution," he said. "I have a regular staff of twelve people, some of whom might think my laboratory refrigerator was a good place to store their lunch. I wouldn't want anyone locked in here by accident."

Jenna shivered, "Let's get out of here."

Rafe suspected that the virus was stored in one of these walk-in refrigerators, behind the steel doors. He wanted a look inside but seriously doubted that Hugh would comply. And even if he did, he wouldn't have rows of vials labelled Deadly Virus—Do Not Touch.

"This is fascinating," Rafe said, returning to the main lab.

"Are you familiar with chemistry?"

"A little."

"Unusual for a stuntman," Hugh commented.

"But my real fascination is this," Rafe said as he strode toward the computers.

Over the years in dealing with international crime, Rafe had become skilled at computer work. Given ten minutes, he might be able to locate and download a file that proved Hugh was using animals in experimentation. If he notified the SPCA, they could stop Hugh from further experimentation. But that didn't solve the question of Eddy Benson's murder.

Rafe gazed longingly at the computers. "What do you use these for?"

"Everything ranging from genetics research to medical records for my employees. When I first studied chemistry, my tools were pencil and paper. Now, the most difficult computations are accomplished at the touch of a button. With no possibility of human error. This is the future."

"And what does the future hold?"

"Precision," he said.

Lightly, Hugh touched Jenna's shoulder and directed her away from the lab. "If you two will leave me alone, I'll get started on those samples. I might be able to give Jenna's animals a clean bill of health by tomorrow morning."

Rafe was reluctant to leave. The laboratory was Hugh's innermost cave of secrets. If Rafe had been an angel, surveillance would have been simple. He could turn invisible and explore. His best chance as a human was to download computer files so he could study them later.

On their way through the house, Jenna asked, "Could

we check on Frank before we go? I'm still worried about him."

"He's probably sleeping," Hugh said, "but we can look in."

Quietly, Hugh opened the door to the bedroom. Frank was sitting up in the bed. Though he was still wan, his breathing was steady and he seemed comfortable.

Across the room from him, Nick leaned against the dresser. His arms folded across his chest and his eyebrows were drawn into a scowl. Rafe had the impression that the two brothers had been arguing.

"What do you want?" Nick snapped.

Jenna answered, "We came to see how Frank was doing." She sat on the bed beside him. "How are you feeling now?"

"I'm okay."

"I can take care of my brother," Nick said. "I've taken care of Frank and Danny and my brother, who runs the winery up the coast, since they were children and our mother died."

"Are you the oldest?" she asked.

Nick adjusted his necktie, as if pulling his clothing together made him more responsible. "This isn't your business. I want you both to leave so my brother can rest."

"Knock it off," Frank said. "I'm not a kid anymore."

"That's how you behave. Like a careless child." Nick turned on his heel and left the room. "Don't you get out of bed. Not for a minute."

The door slammed behind him, and Frank smiled weakly. "He means well. Nick has worked hard to keep the family together, especially after Papa died."

And Nick must know all about Hugh Montclair's virus, Rafe thought. So how could Frank have been infected? He was the botanical expert; he worked with plants, not animals. The likelihood of his being bitten was remote. Nor would Hugh purposely infect the son of his dearest friend.

How was the virus passed from one person to another? Was it airborne? If that were the case, it would spread like lightning. But Jenna had been exposed to Eddy when he was dying, and she didn't seem to be suffering from any ill effects.

She patted Frank on the hand. "Is there anything we can do for you?"

"As a matter of fact," he said, "I was supposed to get together with Sean Hill tonight, but I'm not going to make it. Would you pass that message along to his girlfriend?"

"Sure," Jenna said. "What's her name and phone number?"

"You'll be seeing her later. She's the star of *Alien Age*. Dinah Aaron."

Chapter Nine

On the drive back toward the R.I.P. movie lot, Jenna tried to make sense of the clues they'd discovered at the Montclair estate. The interconnections among the people involved seemed like a spiderweb radiating outward, with Eddy Benson at the center.

She mused aloud, "Dinah Aaron, the star of *Alien Age,* is dating Sean Hill, the stuntman who was injured while Eddy Benson was in charge. And Hugh Montclair connects to Sean Hill through Frank Vincenzo and, of course, through Alex Hill, who is also connected to Dinah."

Rafe nodded. "Your point?"

"Motives," she said. "People who might have wanted to kill Eddy to avenge what had happened to Sean are Dinah, Alex, Frank and Sean himself."

"But the virus that killed Eddy belongs to Hugh. His death couldn't have occurred without Hugh."

"He talks like a murderer," Jenna said. "Did you hear his disgusting philosophy about animals? Not to mention lesser humans. I really don't care for Hugh Montclair."

Which brought up another whole other set of problems. What if her mother was interested in Hugh? What if she was—heaven forbid!—falling in love with him? After three years of seeing her mother's spirit suppressed by grief, Jenna didn't want to thwart Kate's chance for happiness.

"I don't know what to do, Rafe. What if Hugh killed Eddy? I can't let my mother associate with that man."

Paused at a stoplight, he glanced toward her. "Give your mother some credit. If she was wise enough to find perfect love with your father, I doubt that she'll fall for a murderer."

"If he's a murderer."

"For the present," he said, "let's not worry too much about *who* killed Eddy. Let's think about *how* it was done."

"Pig bite or injection," she said.

"Then *how* was Frank Vincenzo infected?"

Jenna went silent as she considered the question that loomed at the forefront of his mind. *How* was the virus spread? And *how* could it be destroyed before anyone else died?

Rafe began to formulate a plan. If the virus was stored in the walk-in refrigerators beside Hugh's lab, it might be destroyed by heat. If the electrical power to Hugh's estate was disrupted, the death serum could be ruined.

"I'm taking you to the safe house," he said.

"But I need to be back on set," she objected. "It's not fair to leave my mother with all the work. Besides, I'm worried about her. I know she appears to be okay to everyone around her, but she's still fragile."

"You're in greater danger, Jenna. You saw Eddy die. You came with me to talk with Hugh, and the man is no fool. He knows we suspect something."

"Hugh would never hurt me. Not while he's so infatuated with my mother."

Rafe smiled. Because Jenna was a good person, nefarious motives did not occur to her. She didn't realize that Hugh might be delighted to have her out of the way. Without Jenna, her mother would be bereft, and Hugh Montclair could step in to fill the void.

He glided the car to a stop outside the safe house. "This won't take too long, Jenna. I promise."

"What are you going to do?"

"I need my angelic abilities."

"I thought you couldn't be an angel when you were at Hugh's estate."

"To short out the electric power, I don't need to enter his estate."

Rafe left the car and entered the house with Jenna chasing after him, nipping at his heels like a determined terrier.

"Electrical power?" she asked. "What do you mean?"

"It's not necessary for you to know."

This was something he needed to do alone. He'd kill the electricity for the Montclair estate, thereby killing the virus. Finally, he had a clear, direct course of action. Rafe felt vital and strong. His human form was charged with energy.

"Rafe," she called to him.

He turned and gazed at her. The curtains were drawn in the house he had procured for a safe haven. In the lamplight, Jenna's blond hair shimmered like precious gold. Though her beautiful, dark eyes were clouded with confusion, she was lovely.

"I want to help," she said.

"There's nothing you can do. Trust me."

"I do," she said simply. "I believe in you."

Her faith bolstered him in a way that he'd never experienced before. Rafe didn't consider himself to be a hero, but the trust in Jenna's eyes made him feel valorous.

"There must be something I can do," she said.

"Not this time."

"I care about you." The sincerity in her voice resonated like a prayer. "I don't want anything bad to happen to you, Rafe. Please be careful."

Soon he would be an angel, and there was very little that could harm him. Still, her concern touched him. As she came toward him, her graceful stride aroused feelings of warm appreciation. His eyes were drawn to the fullness of her hips, the motion of her breasts beneath her oversized sweater.

His desire for her might have been foolish, destined to remain unfulfilled, but he couldn't stop the flood of mortal emotion she awakened as she came near to him.

"I can't love you, Rafe. I know that. But I care for you. These moments we've shared are precious to me. I won't forget you."

Never before in his centuries of existence had he longed so deeply. He wanted to accept and encourage her love, her impossible love. He wanted to be with her, the way a man can be with a woman. He yearned with every fiber of his mortal body to make love to her.

"Please be careful, my angel. Come back to me."

"In a way, Jenna, I will always be with you."

If the decision were up to him, Rafe would stay with her forever. He would experience this forbidden joy he had never known, the pure love of a woman. But that could never happen. He was not of this earth. Not like other men.

Alone in the bedroom, he struggled to blank his mind for the necessary meditation before he returned to his angelic form. His deep concentration warred with emotion—human emotion. He needed clarity, but his mind churned with other possibilities. The love of a woman? What would it feel like? His mortal body ached with physical need.

During his angelic existence, Jenna was only the third human to whom he had revealed his true identity. Before, when he had identified himself, the indiscretion resulted in immediate contact from Saint Michael. Rafe had been called on the carpet and roundly chastised. Where was Michael now?

"Enough," Rafe said aloud. He could not allow himself to be drawn from his higher purpose. The virus must be destroyed.

Forcibly, he thrust Jenna from his mind. He had a job to do.

Every muscle of his human body strained as he concentrated on returning to his angelic form. His exertion was more intense than ever before. Beads of sweat broke across his forehead. His rear molars clenched together. He was holding his breath, fighting for the change. But there seemed to be a tether, an invisible strand that restrained his metamorphosis.

He curled into a fetal position. His muscles were on the verge of breaking. His back throbbed as wings ripped through the frail human flesh. The pain was almost more than he could stand. Energy swirled around him. His human senses exploded in a flash of blinding light.

Then there was stillness. Rafe opened his arms. He was free from earthly restraints. Slowly, the power of angels animated his naked form. His wings spread. The span was almost too wide for the bedroom.

When his eyelids lifted, he saw two forms. Saint Michael sat in the corner of the room. Jenna stood in the doorway.

"I'm sorry," she said. "I heard noises in here, and I was afraid."

But she didn't appear to be frightened. Her generous lips smiled. "Oh, Rafe. I never dreamed that anything could be so magnificent. May I touch your wings?"

His voice was firm, but gentle. "Leave me, Jenna."

"Okay, sure. I'll be waiting out here."

As she closed the door behind her, he modified his shape to the more acceptable human form. Usually this change could be accomplished in a wink. This time, it took fierce concentration and effort.

"Problems?" Michael asked.

When Rafe turned to face him, his wings were gone. He appeared—as Michael did—to be human. "Nothing I can't handle."

"Don't be so sure," Saint Michael advised. "This time, your arrogance might lead you into an impossible situation."

"Can you explain?"

"You're one of the few angels who can become fully human. You needed to learn this skill for your work as an avenger. As I recall, the first time you did this, the fate of humanity hung in the balance. The danger, of course, is succumbing to the pleasures of the flesh."

"Pleasure?" Rafe thought of being drunk. That had not been a positive experience. And yet, it was different than anything he'd known as an angel. His mind had been empty. His awareness dulled. When he was human, food tasted different—not necessarily better, but different. Water was marvelous because it slaked a thirst he did not know as an angel. "I'm not sure that *pleasure* is the right word, Mike."

"Don't deny it," Michael interrupted. "You know what I'm talking about. The woman."

Even in his angel body, these attributes of the flesh were imprinted on his mind. Too readily, he remembered how he felt when he kissed her, the almost unbearable pleasure of holding her, the longing he felt, the human love.

"Poor Rafael," Michael said with deep sincerity. "It was more difficult, this time, to become an angel. Correct?"

"Yes."

"I fear that you're being seduced into human form. You might fall victim to love."

"Is that wrong?"

"Lust is a sin. You know that."

But the way Rafe felt about Jenna wasn't lust. He felt a pure, sacred connection to her. He wanted to be with her forever, to fulfill her every desire, to make her his own and to belong completely to her. "And love? Is love wrong?"

"Well, of course not." Michael rolled his eyes. "It astonishes me that an angel can live for centuries and still not comprehend the simplest equations. Surely, you've seen what love looks like."

"Seldom," Rafe said. "As a warrior, I generally don't come into contact with lovers."

"Then you've been deaf, dumb and blind."

Quietly, Rafe said, "As an angel, I have no ears to hear the words being spoken. No human lips to speak of such things. My vision is consumed with battle and danger. I'm an angel, Mike. How can I know human emotion?"

"It's part of being mortal. The human heart and soul aren't fully developed without love. And that includes the physical act of lovemaking. That's the practical side, the need to perpetuate the species.''

"Do all mortals experience love?"

"It's always there for them. The mother with a babe at the breast. Newlyweds. A gray-haired couple, holding hands and watching the sunset. Quite a wonderful accomplishment.''

"Could I experience—"

"No,'' Michael said. "You cannot love Jenna as a man and still be an angel.''

Aching sadness tightened within him, constricting his spirit. Not to be an angel? Not to be a warrior? He couldn't live such an empty existence.

Michael warned, "If you fall in love with her, you'll lose your angelic attributes. To be frank with you, Rafe, we can't afford to have that happen. In working this case, you've discovered an evil that might destroy humanity.''

"The virus?"

"You need every bit of your angelic power to combat it.'' Michael leaned back in his chair and sighed. The nimbus of light that surrounded him expanded to fill the room. "Thus far, the evil at the Montclair estate has not been alerted to our presence. Fortunately, you haven't visited Hugh Montclair in angelic form.''

Not fortunate, Rafe thought. As soon as he'd recognized the presence of evil, he'd known that he could not show himself as an angel. "My actions have been purposeful.''

"There you go again,'' Michael said. "Arrogance. With you, it's always pride.''

"Tell me what I must do.''

"Destroy every trace of this virus. No matter what the sacrifice. You have to kill this disease before it escapes and runs rampant across the earth, leaving death and devastation.''

''I have a plan,'' Rafe said. ''I'm going to knock out the electrical power to the estate, disabling the refrigerators.''

''Are you sure that's where the virus is kept?''

''How can I be sure, Mike? I've only been able to explore the place as a man. I can't see through walls. I can't become invisible and seek out the hiding place. I hate these limitations. Being human makes it nearly impossible to do my job.''

Saint Michael rose from his chair and came toward him. ''You must succeed, Rafe. Do whatever you need to do. Use great speed. It must be done.''

Michael held up his hand in blessing. Then he was gone.

Rafe felt the absence of Saint Michael. There was a sense of bereavement, as if he might never gaze upon the countenance of the warrior archangel again. Not to be an angel? Was that the necessary sacrifice?

Such contemplation was too fearsome to imagine, and Rafe wasn't a thinker. He was an avenger, a warrior. He needed to be strong. Right now, he needed to destroy this terrible threat.

With renewed vigor, he strode into the outer room where Jenna sat waiting. As he gazed upon her, he felt warm desire, similar to his longing as a mortal. At the core of his being, there was a softness. Was it love? A love that was more powerful than his centuries of battle? Clearly, he couldn't succumb to these gentle feelings. Now more than ever, he needed the full range of his powers.

''Stay here, Jenna.''

"Where are you going? What are you doing?"

"You must stay here and be safe. I'll be back."

THERE WAS ABSOLUTELY no way Jenna could obey Rafe's instructions to "stay here and be safe." Especially not after he'd told her that approaching the Montclair estate as an angel was dangerous.

Maybe he didn't think he needed her, but he did. She could help him. She could protect his back.

Grabbing her purse with the handgun inside, she dashed out the door and slid behind the steering wheel of his sleek, black convertible. She wasn't too surprised to find the keys in the ignition. Since Rafe changed form as quickly as most people changed socks, he really couldn't be carrying car keys and a wallet in his back pocket. When he was an angel...

Jenna's thoughts trailed off and she sighed. When he was an angel, Rafe was pure magnificence. The vision of him, winged and naked before her, consumed her memory. His body was as perfect as any Michelangelo sculpture. The incandescent glow fired her senses. And the wings! They were huge! Somewhere in the back of her mind, she must have known that—according to the physics of flight—an angel's wingspan would have to be extra large in order to lift their human-sized physical form. Still, she hadn't been prepared for the overwhelming fan of pearly white feathers that had filled the bedroom.

How could he be the same man who had kissed her? Not a man, she reminded herself. Rafe was an angel, not a poor earthbound being who would suffer and die. The wonder of him was eternal.

And he was in danger. She turned the key in the ignition and revved the powerful engine. In some unexplainable way, she felt the threat to him as surely as if somebody had aimed a loaded pistol at the direct center of her forehead.

Driving the Infiniti was far different from chugging around in her beat-up truck, and Jenna reveled in the surge of speed that came with a light tap on the accelerator. As she glided through traffic on the way to the Montclair estate, the wind whipped through her hair and cooled her flushed cheeks.

Overhead, the skies hung heavy with dark rainclouds that obscured the late afternoon sunlight. There seemed to be turbulence in the heavens, and she wondered if Rafe had the power to affect the weather. A few days ago, she wouldn't have believed that any being could turn the sun to rain. But now? She wouldn't be the least bit surprised if Rafe could transform dawn to dusk and cause the winds to blow.

A bolt of lightning zigzagged through the skies. Angel fire?

Though she wasn't sure what she was looking for, Jenna remembered that he'd mentioned cutting off the electrical power to the Montclair estate, causing the refrigerated units to quit working.

In her mind, shorting out the power meant hitting the source. Since Rafe wouldn't want to black out all of Los Angeles, he'd probably damage the generator nearest the Montclair mansion. As she neared the hills, she scanned for power lines.

More lightning sliced through the roiling clouds. Thunder exploded like cannon fire. A few raindrops splattered the windshield.

At a high point on the twisting hillside road, Jenna pulled over and touched a button on the dashboard. Mechanically, the convertible's roof rose. As soon as she'd latched the top into place, she realized that she wouldn't be able to scan for power lines with the top up.

With her purse strapped across her chest, she left the car and started walking. The Montclair estate, she knew from traversing this route so many times before, was just around the next curve.

Leaving the road, she hiked to a vantage point. To the left she could see the stone gargoyles at the front entry to Hugh Montclair's acreage. Because of the stormy darkness, the lamps on either side of the gates were lit.

Her gaze followed the overhead cables down the hill to her right. They led to several towers and a generator complex, surrounded by a chain-link fence to keep the curious at bay. An ugly modern sculpture of steel and wire, the towers and generators formed a hub.

Despite the ominous clouds, the rainfall was light. Moisture hung in the air, but it wasn't pouring. And the lightning continued in ferocious bursts.

Jenna gazed beyond the false seclusion of these hills. Through a gap, she saw the City of Angels. The sprawl of streets and houses, headlights and neon, stretched as far as the eye could see. Teeming millions trod upon those pavements and steered along those highways. Inside houses, stores and buildings, they peered through windows. She imagined that most of them were looking up, as she was, cursing the unexpected storm.

Jenna crouched down beside a scrub juniper and waited. She knew better than to seek shelter beneath a tree. When she was a little girl, a tall cottonwood at the ranch had been struck by lightning and had become a pillar of flame. Jenna had been frightened, and her mother had soothed her, telling her that lightning was one of nature's wonders, as beautiful as the birth of a foal.

Staring at the generators, she waited and watched, not knowing what to expect. An explosion? Or merely a subtle flicker and a blanking out of lights? Anticipation built within her. Jenna felt like a spectator at a Fourth of July celebration, waiting for the fireworks to begin.

When the clouds parted above the generators, a gasp caught in her throat. She saw a pale lavender light, shimmering as if the sun were struggling to break through the storm. Then she saw him! Her heart swelled at the vision. Outlined in shadow against the light, a winged man swooped down from the heavens, soaring with incredible grace. His wings were not gossamer, but powerful appendages of glistening white.

As he neared the towers, electricity cracked and fizzed. Waves of blue static rippled the atmosphere. Magnetically, the fingers of light arced toward him, and he gathered the strands around him. He swirled high, caught in the vortex of a luminescent tornado. With a sudden pitch of his body, he tore himself free of the electricity, which crashed back to earth. The generator tower flared with brilliant illumination. It sputtered, and all the lights died.

Like thick curtains, the clouds drew closed. Rafe shot upwards through the space, rocketing to invisible heights.

When Jenna looked back toward the Montclair estate, the lamps beside the gate were dark.

He'd succeeded! Miraculously, Rafe had shut down the electricity. The refrigerated units in Hugh Montclair's laboratory would lose all power. The virus would die.

It was incredible. Unbelievable! With a sharp intake of breath, Jenna clutched her hand to her breast. Her heart fluttered like a captive butterfly. If she lived to be a thousand, she would never experience such a sight again. Truly, she was in the presence of the fantastic.

The rain came more steadily, but she didn't move. She couldn't. She was rooted to the spot by the sheer power of what she'd seen. No one would believe her if she told this tale. No one would know that Rafael Santini, an avenging angel, had saved the world from terrible devastation.

Her gaze turned back toward the gates of the Montclair estate. To her utter amazement, the stone gargoyles and heavy iron bars were suddenly lit again.

"Oh, no," she whispered.

She blinked, but the light was still there. Hugh Montclair must have a back-up generator on his property. His electricity was back on. All of Rafe's astounding pyrotechnics had been for nothing.

Jenna sensed Rafe beside her before she turned her head and saw him. He was clad in a flowing garment. His wings were tucked behind him.

"You'll catch your death of cold," he said, "sitting out here without a jacket."

"Could you make the rain stop?"

"That's not really acceptable." He sat beside her on the hillside. One of his wings unfurled and formed a snowy white umbrella over her head. "It wouldn't be right for me to change the weather because my friend Jenna doesn't have the sense to seek shelter from the rain."

She leaned close to him without touching his raiment. Beneath his wing, she felt safe and warm. She gazed at him through misted eyes. "I watched you."

"I know."

"You were so beautiful."

"But my attempt was worthless," he said. "The

power is back on. Hugh must have a generator on the property. I should have known.''

''What will we do next?''

''I'll take human form and slip inside.''

''To disable the electrical equipment?'' she asked.

''I'm not sure. There might be a more direct way to destroy the virus. Once I'm in there, I'll look around.''

''I'm coming with you, Rafe. You'll be mortal. You could get hurt.''

Lightly, he stroked a damp strand of hair from her forehead. ''So could you. No, Jenna. This is my battle.''

His battle? She could have argued that if he failed, her world would be destroyed. She could have told him that she'd be careful and wouldn't take risks. But his blue eyes had hardened like tempered steel. The muscles in his arms were taut, sculpted in ridges like polished teak. His determination convinced her, without words, that he wasn't about to listen to reason.

He stood beside her. ''Go back to the safe house, Jenna. Wait for me there.''

With a whoosh, he was gone, vanished into thin air.

Under her breath, she muttered, ''Like heck I will.''

Darting through the underbrush, Jenna made her way toward the tall stucco wall that surrounded the Montclair estate. The rain was already beginning to abate. The last rays of afternoon sunshine crept past the clouds.

She reached the wall and leaned against it. About six feet in height and smooth, it offered no footholds; there was no way to scale the surface. Not without flying, she thought, but that was Rafe's province.

Jenna traversed the walled boundary until she found an elm tree with overhanging branches. For a former tomboy like herself, it was easy to climb up and over the wall. She dropped soundlessly to the soft earth on the other side.

Carefully, she took note of her position. On the Montclair side of the wall, the foliage was thick and green. Several trees were close to the wall. Escape from this side would be simple.

Unless she was pursued. Were there guards? Hugh had mentioned several employees. Were any of them armed and dangerous? And what about the animals? Guard dogs?

Careful to avoid attracting attention to herself, she moved slowly, keeping herself hidden. She also removed the gun from her purse and held it ready.

She hadn't gone far when she spotted Rafe about fifty yards from her. Dressed in a black shirt and trousers, he eased like a shadow from tree to tree.

So far, so good. Apparently, no one had noticed his approach.

Then she heard a shout.

"Hey, you! What do you think you're doing?"

A man with a black cowboy hat stood in the center of a clearing. He wore a leather jacket. On a shoulder strap, he carried an AK-47 machine gun.

Rafe raised his hands above his head. "I'm unarmed," he said.

"Yeah?" The cowboy came close and patted Rafe down. "What the hell are you doing in here, mister?"

"I wanted to get out of the rain."

"Bull," the cowboy snapped. "You don't look like a homeless person trying to keep warm."

"I won't be a problem. I'll leave."

Jenna crept nearer, keeping herself well hidden behind the unusual foliage of fern and shrub.

The cowboy set down his gun. "You'll leave, all

right. But first, I'm going to teach you a lesson about breaking in where you're not wanted.''

They were close to the same height. Both men were powerfully built.

The cowboy chuckled. ''I'm going to kick your sorry butt.''

He took the first swing. Though Rafe feinted out of the way, the blow connected with his shoulder and spun him around.

Jenna feared that the cowboy had the advantage. The many transformations in form had taken their toll on Rafe. Though he stood his ground, he seemed weary, barely able to hold his arms up.

The cowboy took another poke at him.

This time, Rafe dodged successfully and landed a hard right jab in the other man's face. He followed with another jab.

The cowboy danced backward. ''You want to play rough?''

''No,'' Rafe said. ''I want to leave peacefully.''

''Too late for that.'' His next assault was a flying kick that landed in Rafe's midsection, doubling him over. He followed with a second kick to the face.

Rafe was suddenly flat on his back. He'd been injured. His face was marked with blood, but he was still game. With the cowboy standing over him, Rafe struggled to his feet.

This had to stop. Jenna had to stop it.

But how? She couldn't take a chance at shooting the cowboy, nor did she want to. Kneeling on the ground, she searched for something else to use as a weapon. A fallen tree branch, looking heavy as a club, caught her eye.

She grabbed it and moved closer to the fight.

Rafe had managed to retaliate. He caught the next kick and flipped the cowboy onto his back. Rafe tried to pin the other arm but failed.

The cowboy went for his AK-47. He aimed the muzzle at Rafe's middle. "We're going up to the house, mister. And I'm calling the cops."

Jenna was directly behind him.

She lifted the branch over her head and, with all her strength, she hammered the armed man over the head. He crumpled to the ground, tried to rise, then collapsed in a heap.

Rafe wasn't in much better shape. She ran to his side. "What are you doing here?" he asked.

"Saving your mortal butt," she said. "Come with me."

"Got to make it to the house."

He took two steps in that direction and halted. He was weaving clumsily. Rough abrasions marked the side of his forehead and face. A trickle of blood dribbled from the corner of his mouth. His right arm clutched his stomach.

"Come on, Rafe. Let's get out of here. We need a better plan." When she caught hold of him, he leaned heavily against her. "Come on, now. Can you walk?"

His eyes wavered, unfocused. Had he sustained a concussion? If so, how was he staying on his feet? "Damn it, Rafe. You're either the bravest or the dumbest man I've ever met."

"Not a man." His brave smile tugged at her heart. "I'm an angel."

"Your halo is crooked, Rafe. Let's go."

Chapter Ten

By the time they'd reached the stucco wall that surrounded the Montclair property, Rafe was able to stand
without Jenna's support, but he hadn't regained his
strength. Stumbling and falling, every step was an or-
deal. His ears droned with the noise of a hundred angry
hornets. He was dizzy, confused. His human brain was
scrambled. All he wanted was to sleep—to close his eyes
and give himself over to silent rest.

"We're almost there," Jenna encouraged. "Only a
little farther."

"Leave me," he said hopefully. She was a rugged
taskmaster, driving him onward.

"Don't quit now, Rafe. All you have to do is climb
over the wall."

"Is that all?"

Scaling a six foot wall should have been nothing to
him. Routinely, he soared at high altitudes. As an angel,
he could have dematerialized and walked through the
wall. But he wasn't an angel now. He was a man who
had been in a brutal fistfight with a professional bodyguard. Rafe Santini was a mortal man who was learning
what it was to suffer pain.

He lowered his head and closed his eyes, hoping to

clear his blurred vision. The bruises on his forehead and face throbbed. Worse than the hurting was the overwhelming weakness.

"Let's go." Jenna nudged his arm. "We have to hurry. That cowboy is going to wake up. Others will come looking for us. We have to get out of here."

She pushed him toward the thick trunk of an elm tree. Roughly, she grabbed his forearms and placed his hands on a chest-high branch. "Climb, Rafe. You can do it."

His skull felt like it had been split in two. The roaring in his ears, ceaseless as the Pacific surf, obscured the sound of her voice. "What?"

"Try, Rafe! Hurry!"

Her head whipped around. He saw the swift motion in a series of stop-action frames. He wanted to help her instead of being a burden. But his eyelids were too heavy. His arms fell helplessly to his sides.

"Someone's coming," she said. "Get down. Stay very still."

His instincts told him to rise up and protect her, to rescue Jenna and himself. So many times before, he'd defended the innocent, hefted his mighty sword of flame and smote the wrongdoers. He'd been Rafael, Avenging Angel.

Now he was human. His body would not obey his will.

"Get down," she said.

Gratefully, he sank to the earth, closed his eyes and fell into a deep slumber.

"Don't move," she whispered.

Even as she spoke, Jenna knew her instruction was unnecessary. Rafe was out cold. He wasn't going anywhere. Their only hope for escape was to avoid notice.

Then, somehow, she'd rouse him, get him to a doctor. He needed medical attention.

Crouched beside him at the trunk of the elm tree, she was grateful for the lush shrubbery of the Montclair gardens. A prickly bush, thick with ripe chokecherries, hid them from view.

The cowboy she'd clunked must have awakened and alerted the others, because she could hear a search getting under way. Deep, strong voices shouted to each other. How many of them were there? The leaves rustled and the earth seemed to quiver beneath her feet as unseen men moved among the trees and bushes.

Peering through the branches, she recognized Danny, the Vincenzo brother who had been sent to help her with the animals at R.I.P. studios. He wore a camouflage jacket and crept stealthily through the greenery.

His presence made sense to her. In the organization of the Montclair estate, it seemed that each of the brothers had his own domain. Nick took care of the Montclair business. Frank was the gardener. Danny must be in charge of security.

Though Danny didn't appear to be armed, she assumed that he probably had a handgun somewhere on him. Her own pistol was inside her backpack-sized purse. Did she dare to lift the flap, reach inside and take it out? Would the movement attract his attention?

Danny's dark-eyed gaze scanned the stucco wall. For a moment, he appeared to stare directly at them.

She froze, not moving, not even breathing. Her own heartbeat resounded loudly in her ears.

Then he pivoted and moved away.

Jenna exhaled a sigh of relief. They were safe for the moment. If she could get Rafe onto his feet and moving, they might be able to escape.

When she tried to lift his head, he groaned.

It wasn't a loud sound, but the noise was enough. Danny was immediately alert. At a trot, he came toward them.

Before Jenna had a chance to retrieve her pistol, he yanked aside the bushes. "Say nothing," he ordered quietly.

"Are you going to help us?"

"Damn it, I said be quiet. Yes, I'll help."

He took two steps away from her and shouted, "Nothing over here."

"Why, Danny? Why would you help us?"

"Because you're trying to stop Hugh Montclair, and that's what I want." He motioned with the flat of his hand. "Stay down. I'll be right back."

Could she trust him? "What have you got against Hugh?"

"My brother, Frank, is dead."

Danny marched off through the trees, leaving her to absorb the shock of his words. *Frank was dead.* Frank, like Eddy, had fallen victim to the lethal virus. Despite the antidote and his apparent recovery, he had succumbed.

His death angered her. Earlier this afternoon, Frank had seemed to be on the road to recovery. He'd been hopeful. He'd given her a message for Sean Hill. How could this tragedy have happened?

Surely Frank's death was accidental. Hugh wouldn't have deliberately killed one of the sons of his great friend, Paolo Vincenzo. Therefore, it stood to reason that Hugh didn't have complete control over the virus. Was it possible that the disease could spread randomly?

If so, why had she been spared? Jenna wondered. She'd been with Eddy when he died. She'd held him in her arms. She'd wiped the sweat from his brow. Her close contact seemed to make her a number one candidate for the virus. Yet she didn't feel ill. No symptoms had appeared. Was she safe, or would she be the next to die?

Danny returned to her side. He stared down at Rafe. "What happened to him?"

"He was in a fight and got kicked in the head. He might have a concussion."

"How were you planning to get him out of here?"

"The same way I came in," she said. "Over the wall. I have a car parked down the road."

"Bring your car over here," Danny said. "I'll get him over the wall."

She hesitated, not wanting to leave Rafe in the care of this man whom she wasn't sure she could trust. But there was no alternative. By herself, Jenna wasn't strong enough to lift Rafe.

"Go ahead," Danny said. "If Hugh finds you here, there'll be hell to pay."

Boosted by adrenaline, she clambered up the tree and over the wall. She hit the ground running on the other side. Dodging through scrub oak and juniper, she raced across the hillside. An intuition warned her against using the road. There could be people watching, waiting for her.

Panting heavily, her lungs clogged with the moist air, she stumbled, tripped and rose again. Her legs felt stiff, but she kept a swift pace.

Finally, she reached the car. Amazingly, no one appeared to be watching.

Jenna leapt behind the steering wheel and ground the key in the ignition. She took off toward the estate, not knowing if she would find Danny helping Rafe to the car or if she was driving directly into an ambush.

She parked near the stucco wall and stepped out of the car. For a long, desperate moment she stood staring. Where were they? Had Danny failed? Was Rafe captured?

Then she saw them behind a juniper. Danny waved to her, and she ran toward them.

With Danny on one side and Jenna on the other, they managed to get Rafe to the car. When they leaned him against the passenger side, he stood erect. "I'm all right," he said. "It'll take a minute, but I'm going to be all right."

"Tell me about it." Danny glanced toward her and said, "When I tried to lift him, he woke up. Practically took my head off. That guy is plenty strong."

"Are you coming with us?"

"No, but I'll be in touch." He glanced back toward the stucco wall. "You'd better get moving."

"Danny." She touched his shoulder. "I'm sorry about your brother."

"Never should have happened." He swallowed hard. "Frank was a good man. Gentle. He didn't deserve to die."

"Was it the virus?"

"Hugh's freaking experiment," he said. "From death comes life. That's what he keeps saying, but all I see is death."

"The virus," Rafe said. "How is it transmitted?"

"I don't know anything about that scientific stuff."

"What happened..." Rafe paused to draw breath. "When Eddy came here, what happened?"

"We were out in the barn and he got bit by a pig.

Geez, only an idiot could have let that happen. Hugh gave him a shot of antibiotics before he left.''

"A shot," Rafe said. "What kind of shot?"

"It was antibiotics," Danny said impatiently. "I got the stuff from the first-aid kit myself. With all the wildlife on the property, we're prepared for anything. We've even got a rabies vaccine."

"But you're sure—" Rafe said "—that the shot didn't contain the virus."

"Damn sure. Eddy was a complete jerk when it came to handling animals, but his heart was in the right place. I didn't want him to get sick." Nervously, he looked over his shoulder. "I better get back."

On impulse, Jenna said, "Come with us, Danny. I know a place where we can be safe."

"Nobody is safe. Not until that bastard is stopped." He stepped away from the car. "I can't leave Nick here alone."

"Be careful," she said.

Rafe lifted his hand in a gesture of blessing. "Godspeed."

INSIDE THE SAFE HOUSE, Rafe was able to walk on his own, carefully placing one foot in front of the other. His vision had gone from hazy to acute—painfully so. Bright light hurt his eyes. In fact, the aching in his head seemed to have sharpened all his senses, causing the sound of his own feet walking on carpet to sound like an army on the march.

This must be what healing felt like. Gradually, his strength was returning. He paced through the kitchen to the front room and sank down on the leather sofa.

Jenna hovered nearby. "I still think you need a doctor."

"It's not going to happen. As far as I know, I'm mortal. However, I'm unwilling to submit to medical examination. Give me a chance to rest, I'll become an angel again, and my wounds will be gone."

"We'll see." She went to the kitchen and returned with a pint of bottled water. "Drink this."

"Why?"

"If you're not going to allow me to take you to the emergency room, at least let me play nurse. You drink water so you won't get dehydrated. I've noticed that when you're human, you don't drink enough water."

He took a sip. The cold liquid felt good inside his mouth. Dutifully, he swallowed again.

She returned to the kitchen, issuing another order as she left the room. "And you're also going to eat something."

"Yes, that would be good."

In his current debilitated state, he wasn't sure if he had enough energy to make the switch from imperfect human to angel. He needed to gather his power—every bit of strength and all the wisdom he had garnered through the centuries.

His adversary was strong. During his fight with the cowboy—a fight he should have won easily—Rafe had sensed the presence of the demon, a shadow creature. The cold fetid breath of evil had paralyzed his reflexes, distracted him, made him slow.

If he'd been in angel form, they would have battled head-to-head, and their clash would have shaken the heavens. The confrontation would have ended with either victory or eternal damnation. How Rafe longed for that fight!

For now, he was stuck as a human. Pathetic, really.

"Jenna? What should I do for the pain in my head?"

She emerged from the kitchen and stared at him. "Ever hear of aspirin?"

"Yes. But I've never taken any."

She strode past him toward the hallway that led to the bedrooms and bathroom, returning with a small, clear bottle. She tossed it toward him. "Take three or four. I'm going to call the movie lot and let my mother know I'm okay."

Rafe glared at the plastic container in his hand. Aspirin was a form of drug. Though he wasn't sure that it was wise to take this medicine, he wished to end the hammering pain that radiated from his right temple through his skull. He needed to be clear, to think.

He twisted the cap, but it wouldn't come off. This bottle must be defective. Heavily, he rose to his feet. "Jenna, something's wrong with this thing."

Chatting brightly on the cordless telephone, she came into the front room and took the bottle from him. With a twist of her wrist, she popped the cap off the bottle. "Childproof," she whispered as she left the room.

Rafe took four powdery white pills in his hand, placed them in his mouth and chewed. The taste puckered his gums, his tongue, even his teeth. He gulped down the entire pint of water and went to the kitchen for more.

Jenna hung up the phone. "What's wrong?"

"A headache is better than the taste of medicine."

"You're supposed to swallow them," she said.

He took another bottle of water from the refrigerator and opened the top. "Swallow them whole? Why didn't you tell me?"

"I thought everybody knew how to take aspirin. I guess that information didn't come in the Angel Handbook."

"I find nothing amusing in our situation," he said. "I have failed twice to destroy the virus."

"You don't have to tell me how serious this is. First, Eddy's death. Now Frank. If that virus is transmitted through the air, I've probably caught a dose myself. But it never does any good to dwell on the negative."

"So I've been told by countless cherubim." Over the centuries, he'd developed a reputation for brooding cynicism, an occupational hazard for Avenging Angels. He had seen too much evil to be naively optimistic. "And what, pray tell, are the positives?"

"We've got a man on the inside," she reminded him. "Danny Vincenzo."

"Which makes destruction of the virus all the more complex. If I could be sure that Hugh and all the people who worked for him were in the grip of evil, I would have no hesitation about blasting his laboratory to bits."

Her eyebrows raised. "And taking a chance on making the virus airborne? Turning it into a deadly gas?"

As soon as she spoke, he realized she was correct. To succeed on this mission, he needed more than brute strength. Penetrating the perimeter of the Montclair estate required the strategic brilliance of a general. To gain access to the virus, he should employ the guile of a Cold War spy. To obliterate the killing virus, he must operate with the skill of a genetic scientist.

"If you please," he said, "give me another positive."

"Well, we're pretty sure that Hugh is the murderer."

"Are we?" he queried. "We know that Hugh created the virus. We know that forces of evil protect it. But we can't be sure that Hugh murdered Eddy Benson."

"Are you suggesting that someone else used the virus?"

"It's possible," he said.

"Why don't you explain while I rustle up dinner?"

Rafe seated himself on a stool at the countertop and watched as she selected a dazzling array of fresh vegetables and fruit from the refrigerator. He hadn't realized how much he needed nourishment until he saw the food. Then his mouth began to salivate. His stomach twisted in a knot. This was hunger, a sensation so intense that he nearly forgot the pain in his forehead.

"Well, Rafe, how could someone else have murdered Eddy?"

"Consider the forensic evidence," he said. "The animal bite probably came from your pig. Therefore, the virus was not transmitted in that way."

"Right." She nodded. "I hope not."

"According to Danny, the needle mark came from an injection of antibiotics."

"Right again. So, Eddy wasn't poisoned by the shot."

"Therefore, Eddy was given the fatal dose of virus in another manner, possibly at another time."

"How?" Jenna asked.

"If it's a serum," Rafe said, "it might have been administered in liquid form. In a glass of water."

"Which anyone could have given him."

And there wasn't much of anything he could do—except speculation—until he regained his strength and became an angel. Frustration simmered within him. He wanted to fly, to discover the answers to this deadly puzzle. He needed action.

Instead, he sat on a kitchen stool, watching Jenna perform homey chores. She removed a container from the freezer and transferred it to the microwave. Deftly, she cleaned the lettuce and sliced tomatoes for a salad.

"Hungry?" she asked.

"Yes."

"That's another positive sign. If you have an appetite, you must be getting better."

"Is that your medical opinion?"

"It's something we poor humans call common sense. And here's a bit more of it. If you get yourself cleaned up, you'll feel like a new man."

Rising from the kitchen stool, he said, "I'd rather feel like a new angel."

"Maybe you will." She grinned mischievously. "Didn't someone once say that cleanliness was next to godliness?"

He knew she was trying to cheer him up, and he'd be rude not to respond to her efforts. "What else would you suggest, Jenna?"

"Enjoy yourself. Being human isn't all bad, you know."

He forced a slight smile as he strode from the kitchen. "I know."

In the bathroom, he peeled off his clothing. Though he was still aware of the headache, the sharp edge of pain had subsided. Apparently, his recuperative powers were functional, and Jenna would tell him that it was another reason to make a joyful noise. But that wasn't his job. Rafe was an avenger, strong and fierce. Seldom had he indulged in happiness, the most fleeting of emotions.

When he stepped into the shower and the hot water sluiced down his naked body, he gasped. Never before had he been in human form long enough to bathe. The sensation was remarkable, as if every fiber in his being had come alive. The combination of heat and wetness delighted him. His skin felt slick and supple.

After his shower, he dried himself, experiencing the friction of the towel against his flesh. In the bedroom, he looked for something to wear. In the top drawer of the dresser, his fingers touched a fabric that was soft and smooth. Why not pamper himself? He slid into these clothes and returned to the kitchen where Jenna was setting dinner on the table.

Without looking up, she said, "Sorry about the re-heated lasagna casserole, but I didn't want to take the time to thaw a steak."

"It looks delicious."

When she gazed at him, her mouth curved into a wide, adorable smile. "Black silk pajamas?"

"The fabric feels good against my body." He sat in the chair. "You told me to enjoy being human, and I think I'm beginning to get the hang of it. There's almost constant sensation and stimulation."

She heaped salad into a wooden bowl in front of him. "I guess you're right. An awful lot of the way we function is sensual."

"Through the senses," he clarified. The idea of sensual was too close to sexual, and he needed to avoid going down that road. "There's much to experience. I think I might enjoy cooking. The redolence of food. The textures and colors."

He plunged a fork into the salad and took a bite. A moan of contentment rose in the back of his throat. "And the taste!"

"When you're an angel, don't you taste the food you eat?"

"It's different."

He sampled the square of lasagna on the plate in front of him. The flavor aroused him and he wanted to take his time, savoring every bite, but his hunger demanded fulfillment. He ate quickly.

When he looked up, Jenna was gazing indulgently. "It seems that you've recovered."

"Somewhat."

And he was aware of another appetite, a hunger that was kindled by the warmth in her eyes. She was lovely. From the first moment he'd really noticed her, he had thought she was pretty. But now he realized she was more than that—so much more. Her actions enhanced her physical appearance, making her beautiful. Her intelligence and the trait she called "common sense" appealed to him greatly, teasing his all-too-human senses.

She pushed away from the table. "Now it's my turn to use the shower. When I'm done, we'll figure out what comes next."

But he didn't want her to leave the room. Stalling, he asked, "How are things at the movie lot?"

"According to my mother, it's all moving nicely. Alex has started the alien scenes."

Rafe barely heard her words. He was captivated by the shape of her lips as she spoke. He wanted to touch her, to inhale the clean fragrance of her hair. He wanted to taste her lips.

Clearing her throat, Jenna took a backward step. "I'll be in the shower."

An image of Jenna naked, with water gliding down her body, consumed his brain. With an effort, he forced himself not to groan aloud as he thought of her pale shoulders glistening. As he watched the sway of her hips walking away from him, he was driven to follow her, to take her into his arms and make love to her.

The temptation was greater than any force he'd ever felt. His human body responded. Beneath the silk pajamas, he was hard. Needing her, wanting her, he could barely contain himself.

If he'd been an angel, Rafe would have soared into the distant, rarefied atmosphere. He would have put a million miles between himself and Jenna.

But escape was impossible. From the bathroom, he heard the shower start. He remembered her graceful arms and shapely legs from the movie scene. Her torso tapered like an hourglass.

He had to see her in the shower. Too soon, he would be an angel again. The moment would have passed. Jenna would no longer be available to him.

He went down the hallway to the bathroom. His hand rested on the doorknob. Rafe was well aware that he was playing with fire. How could he see her naked and not make love to her?

"Jenna," he said.

"Rafe? What's wrong?"

"May I come in?" He suited the action to the words, pushing open the door and stepping into the steamy, tiled room.

She had pushed aside the rippled glass door to peer out at him. Her face and her long wet hair were clearly in focus. The rest of her body was a tantalizing outline. "What is it, Rafe?"

His throat constricted. He couldn't speak. Instead, he unbuttoned the pajama top and discarded it. The silk bottoms slid from him, puddling at his feet.

Her lips were trembling. Droplets of water shimmered on her long lashes. "Can we do this? What will happen?"

"I don't care."

He stepped over the porcelain edge of the tub into the shower. She stood before him, unashamed and beautiful. His eyes feasted upon her. Never in his existence had he wanted anything more than he longed for her. It was love that burned within him. Love for Jenna.

She whispered, "Are you sure that we should make love?"

"The truth?"

"Yes."

He closed his eyes, listening to the patter of water from the shower, allowing the damp warm moisture to permeate his skin. "I wish to become part of you. I believe we should be together for all time in all ways."

"Is it possible?" Her voice quavered.

He opened his eyes. "I don't know."

Her delicate hand reached toward him. She stroked the hair on his chest. With the soap, she lathered his body.

Pure sensation crashed through him. When he pulled her close and her slick wet body glided against his, the pleasure exceeded anything he had ever dreamt of. He wanted to prolong the sensations, to record them forever in his experience.

Gently, he helped her from the shower and towelled her dry. When he turned away from her to open the door, she gasped.

He was immediately alert to her mood. "What is it, Jenna?"

"Your back," she said. Her fingers touched his shoulder blades. "There are deep scars here. Like tattoos. Does it hurt?"

"My wings," he said.

Soon they would grow again. Soon he would be an angel, incapable of lovemaking.

Firmly, he gripped her hand and led her into the bedroom, where they lay beside each other on the sheets. His first kisses were tentative, curious.

She was so remarkable. Her long, damp hair spread in beautiful tendrils. Her eyes reflected the stars that flew overhead. Jenna was his entire universe. Her body was the most perfect vision. Her skin felt softer than rose petals.

When he tasted the sweetness of her breasts and felt her respond, he enjoyed her pleasure. Her excitement urged him to further exploration. Every touch, each caress, brought renewed wonder.

As he entered her, she cried out.

"Jenna, have I hurt you?"

"Make love to me, Rafe."

His thrusts brought him to the verge of ecstasy.

She arched. A fierce cry exploded from her.

Shuddering, he achieved climax. His satisfaction matched hers, and he fell away from her on the bed, breathing heavily.

Jenna snuggled against him and he held her.

Their lovemaking was over. Yet he sensed that it was just a beginning. Rafael Santini was changed forever.

Chapter Eleven

Jenna couldn't quite believe it. She'd just made love to an angel. A deep happiness warmed her from the inside. In her heart, she knew that she had found the perfect love she'd been seeking all her life.

From the example of her mother and father, she knew what true love, pure love, should look like. But Jenna had never imagined how wonderful this moment would be. Finally, she had discovered the masculine being who could complete her femininity. Rafe was everything she'd ever wanted or needed in a man.

Propped up on her elbow, she gazed down upon his handsome face, admiring the jut of his firm chin and the symmetry of his cheekbones. The contented glow from his blue eyes fulfilled her, because she saw her happiness reflected in him.

"Thank you," she whispered as she lightly kissed his forehead and combed through the silky texture of his thick black hair.

"Jenna, I don't know if—"

"Hush." She placed a finger across his lips, silencing him. "Let me have this moment."

"I'd give you anything. Jenna, I'd give you the world."

"All I want is...you."

Ironically, he might be the one thing she could not have. When Rafe became an angel again, she knew he would leave her and return to an existence weighted by duty and history. For now, at least, she could dream. He belonged to her, if only for a brief interval.

When the bedside telephone jangled, the noise called her back to another time and place. Reality intruded upon her blissful reverie.

She glanced at the digital clock on the nightstand. Though it seemed much later, it was only a few minutes after eight o'clock in the evening.

The telephone rang again and Rafe's eyebrows raised in a question. "Who knows this telephone number?"

"I gave it to my mother when I talked to her earlier." And that meant she had to pick up. Her mother might need her. Jenna reached across him to lift the receiver. "Hello?"

"May I assume that you're with Rafe?"

"You may." Jenna rolled her eyes. This was an interruption she didn't need. "Hello, Alex."

"Perhaps you'd be so good as to remind Mr. Santini that he has contracted to work on this movie. We're filming the alien sequences, and I need all my stuntmen."

Wasn't that too bad! "Sorry, Alex. Rafe can't come to the set right now."

"Could you possibly inform him that his employer, Hugh Montclair, is on the way to the soundstage?" His sarcasm dripped like molasses. "Your presence is also required, my dear."

"You don't need me. My mother can take care of the animals, probably better than I can."

"I want you here. Immediately," he snapped. "Both of you. You and your lover boy."

She was about to protest that Rafe wasn't her lover. But he was. Her incredible lover. "You'll have to work around us."

"Jenna, darling, don't be mutinous. I won't hesitate to fire you and your mother."

She should have cared, but she didn't. His threat was nothing more than an annoyance.

"I mean it," he said. "There are already two people who are lobbying to get rid of you."

"Does this mean I'll never do lunch in this town again?" Still, she was curious. "One of them is Taylor, I'm sure. Who's the other?"

"Nick Vincenzo."

Jenna could ignore Taylor and the silly movie, but she couldn't dismiss this information. Nick was too involved with the virus and the intrigues at the Montclair estate. "When did you speak with Nick?"

"Moments ago. Actually, I was planning to call it a day and wrap up, but Nick called to inform me that Hugh was coming. He asked after you specifically."

"And what did you tell him?"

"The truth, my dear." The tone in Alex's voice was haughty. "I said that I hadn't seen you for most of the day."

"And what did he say?"

"He remarked on your unprofessional attitude. Something about how you were too busy butting into everyone else's business to take care of your own."

Nick must still be angry about what he perceived to be her interference with Frank. It seemed odd that Nick would be concerned about her. His younger brother's death should certainly take precedence.

"However," Alex continued, "Nick also said I should make an effort to find you. Apparently, Hugh has some sort of test results he wishes to share with you."

The virus tests from her animals! That was something Jenna needed to know. "We'll be there, Alex, as soon as possible."

After hanging up the telephone, she gazed longingly at Rafe. "We need to go."

Briefly, she recounted her conversation, watching as his features took on a pensive cast.

"Interesting," Rafe said. "Nick doesn't seem too upset about his brother's death."

"We don't know that. This is hearsay from Alex." However, Alex seemed to have an inside track when it came to information about Hugh Montclair and his employees. Earlier, he'd been the one to inform her that Paolo Vincenzo had died of AIDS and that Hugh was seeking a cure. "Somehow, it seems like Alex is tangled up in all this."

"Maybe through his brother, Sean."

"Who was friends with Frank Vincenzo." The web of interrelationships started spinning again. "Hollywood seems like a big place, but it's so inbred. Everybody knows somebody who knows somebody else who goes to the same hairdresser."

"And one of them killed Eddy Benson."

"Hugh Montclair and Nick Vincenzo. Alex Hill and his brother. Dinah. Taylor." She sighed. "After all our investigating, we still don't know which one."

He reached up toward her, gliding his hand around her neck beneath her hair. "I never thought I'd say this, Jenna, but I don't want to think about murder and vengeance anymore."

"Nor do I."

"You're turning me into a dove of peace. Right now, I wish only to lie with you and count the evening stars as they light the skies above us."

"You haven't been in L.A. for long," she said. "With the smog and the lights of the city, there aren't many stars visible."

"We could soar above the clouds." He pulled her down to him, guiding her into a kiss. "I want to stay with you."

His words penetrated her consciousness and branded her soul. If only he could be with her forever, she'd be the happiest of women. But that was an impossible dream.

Tightening his grasp, he pulled her on top of him. She felt his hardness, his strength, his passion when he kissed her again. Gently, he said, "We should go."

"We should." She wanted to know the results of Hugh's tests on the blood samples. "But I don't want to share you with anyone else. I want you to be mine alone."

"Hold that thought. Wherever you are, whatever you're doing, you must think of me and the next time we'll make love."

Would there be a next time?

He rose from the bed, naked. His body was magnificent. He was a mature man, heavily muscled with a virile pelt of chest hair that arrowed down his torso. When he turned away from her, she noticed that the scars where there had been angel wings had disappeared.

THE FIRST PERSON Jenna saw when they entered Soundstage 7 was her mother. Kate's worried expression softened as she beheld her daughter with Rafe.

"You look like you've been having fun," she said.

Was it that obvious? "It's amazing what a good dinner will do for you," Jenna said.

Her mother nodded wisely. "Appetites need to be appeased. I hope you didn't eat anything that disagrees with you."

"It was all delicious. Right, Rafe?"

"The best I've ever tasted," he said.

Their coded conversation veered too close to the truth for Jenna, and she definitely did not wish to discuss Rafe's incredible lovemaking with her mother. Quickly, she changed the subject. "What's going on here?"

"Nothing much." Kate shrugged. "An alien invasion."

The set was populated with stuntmen in shiny latex that made them look as if their skin had been turned inside out. Veins and arteries scribbled up and down their limbs. Their torsos featured dramatically outlined musculature. The design was fairly simple, very human-like, except for the webbed feet, fins and gills.

Jenna looked at Rafe. "Is that what you're going to be wearing?"

"That's the costume."

Kate informed him, "Alex is looking for you. Something about jumping from a platform and doing a somersault in the air."

"I remember," he said.

Rafe wasn't sure that he could successfully perform the stunt he'd practiced earlier when he still had his angelic powers. Even if there had been time to attempt the switch back to that form, he'd already decided that he needed to be human for filming so his aura wouldn't be detected.

"I'd better check in with the new stunt coordinator," he said.

As if it were the most natural thing on earth, Jenna offered her upturned face and he casually kissed her before taking his leave. It was only a peck on the lips, but such a simple display of affection was foreign to Rafe, the loner, the avenging angel, the fierce being whose existence was devoted to vengeance.

Striding across the soundstage, he realized that he was part of her. Likewise, she was part of him. They had joined, not only physically, but also on a spiritual level.

He feared that precious bond would shatter when he became an angel again. But the alternative was unthinkable.

Alex accosted him. "You! I need you in makeup. Right away."

"First I want to try a run-through on the stunt," Rafe said. "We haven't had a chance to practice on the set."

"Fine, fine," Alex said. "I shan't rush safety precautions. Take all the time you need."

Rafe studied the black-clad director, who fidgeted while he nervously tweaked the patchy goatee on his chin. "I understand that Hugh is coming to the set."

"Yes." Alex scowled. "I was told, before accepting this project, that Hugh Montclair was a recluse who would not pester me. But he's been here constantly."

"What do you think changed his mood?" Rafe asked, leading toward discussion of the virus. "Maybe he's made progress on his AIDS cure. Are you familiar with his experiments?"

"I've heard far too much about Hugh and his chemistry set. Taylor Wannamaker has been haunting me, making inane threats about sick pigs."

"Pigs," Rafe said. Taylor might have finally figured out that Hugh was using his pigs for scientific testing. Though such a procedure clearly went against SPCA regulations, Taylor wouldn't be happy about confronting the powerful, influential Hugh Montclair. Innocently, Rafe asked, "What do pigs have to do with Hugh's research?"

"I'm an artist," Alex declared. "I pay no attention to commentary about livestock."

He charged back toward the lit set, leaving Rafe to wonder if the director was cleverly hiding his knowledge of the virus, or if he was truly ignorant of the lethal results of Hugh Montclair's AIDS research.

Before he could join the stuntmen, Jenna came up beside him. "You've got to come with me."

"With pleasure. I'm not looking forward to plummeting off a twenty-foot-high platform, doing a double flip and landing on my feet."

She gaped. "Why would you do that?"

"It's a stunt," he said. "When I did it before, I was pretty spectacular. Of course, I was also an angel with a different sense of balance and a certain buoyancy."

"Right," she said. "You could fly."

"Which is a useful attribute for a stuntman."

"Be careful, Rafe. I don't want you to hurt yourself."

"Don't worry," he said. "After I was beaten by that security guard, I decided that pain is nothing to laugh at."

"So to speak." She grinned.

"What did you need?"

"According to my mother, no one has heard about Frank's death. Since Frank gave us a message for Sean Hill, it seems like we ought to tell Dinah personally so she can pass the word. And then, maybe, we could go with her to tell Sean."

"I like the way you think," he said. "It would be

useful to meet this guy. If anybody had a real motive for wanting Eddy Benson dead, it's Sean Hill.''

''But everybody says he's not bitter.''

Rafe nodded. ''Makes you wonder why not.''

Together they strolled through casual groups of costumed aliens toward Dinah's dressing room. Again, Rafe was struck with the unusual, yet wholly comfortable, sense of being half of a couple. It felt right to have Jenna beside him, matching her shorter stride to his.

When he tapped on Dinah's door, she flung it open in a moment. Clutching a cell phone in one hand and a makeup brush in the other, the beauty queen was showing signs of irritation, slight cracks in her veneer.

''What?'' she demanded. ''What is it?''

''May we talk with you?'' Rafe formally requested.

''As if I have time for a chat?''

''It's about Frank Vincenzo,'' he said.

Grumbling, she bid farewell to the person on the phone, flipped it closed and came out of her dressing room. Beneath her terry cloth robe, she was still wearing her nearly naked costume. Her long chestnut wig tangled around her shoulders. ''All right, then. Talk.''

Jenna stepped forward. ''It might be best if you hear this in private.''

''Listen, Jenna, I don't have time for a deep and meaningful chat, okay? Just spit it out.''

''This afternoon,'' Jenna started, ''we had to go out to the Montclair estate. Frank met us at the gate, and it was pretty obvious that he was quite ill. It might have been the same disease that killed Eddy.''

''Wait a minute,'' she said. ''I thought Eddy was murdered. Isn't that right? He drank some kind of poison or something.''

''Not exactly,'' Jenna said.

"What does this have to do with me?"

Rafe suspected that every topic introduced to Dinah Aaron eventually got around to this focal point: herself. "Frank gave us a message for you," he said. "To pass on to your boyfriend."

"Which one?" Her laughter trilled. "At any given moment, I try to keep at least three on the line."

"A good strategy for you." With three boyfriends, none of them would become bored too quickly. "I'm talking about Sean Hill."

"He's a sweetie. Much better-looking than his brother, and he's amazingly well connected. So? What's the message?"

"Frank won't be able to meet with Sean," Rafe said. "Why not?"

Obviously, she had no idea of Frank's fate. And her utter lack of concern about Frank being infected with the same virus that killed Eddy led him to believe that Dinah was innocent of the murder. Her only crime was unadulterated selfishness.

"Frank Vincenzo is dead," Rafe said.

An expression of shocked surprise flitted across her lovely face. Her composure, though not lost, was shaken. "Dead?"

Another person had joined them. Silent as nightfall, he had crept to the edge of their group. In his deep, authoritative voice, Hugh Montclair said, "What are you talking about?"

Jenna whirled around to face him directly. "Frank's death. I was sorry to hear that the antidote didn't work."

"You're mistaken. Frank is tired, but he's recovering. Who told you he was dead?"

"One of the stuntmen," Rafe interjected quickly. If

they mentioned Danny, they'd be admitting that they were the trespassers on the estate. "It's not true?"

"Absolutely not." He stepped past them to place a protective arm around Dinah's shoulder. "Why would you upset her with these lies?"

Dinah did more than merely accept his comforting gesture. She reveled in the attention. Sniffling girlishly, she snuggled against his chest. "I'm so distraught."

"Well, of course you are." He frowned at Jenna. "You should be more careful of what you say."

His words sounded dangerously like a threat to Rafe, and he noticed a sharp edge to Hugh's naturally forceful manner. There was a twitch at the corner of his eye. He looked much older today than he had yesterday.

Rafe couldn't decide if Hugh's tension came from guilt or something else. A cover-up? Frank was dead. His brother had no reason to lie.

Jenna planted her feet firmly. "Did you finish with the blood samples, Hugh?"

"Your animals have a clean bill of health." Again, he warned, "Stop being so alarmist, Jenna. You're seeing danger where there is none."

"The blood samples weren't my idea," she said in her own defense. Gesturing toward the long-beaked blond man who loped toward them, she said, "It was his plan."

Taylor Wannamaker joined them with his hand outstretched. His officious manner was in full force when he introduced himself as the legal representative of the Society for Prevention of Cruelty to Animals. Vigorously, he shook Hugh's hand. "I've spoken to you on the phone. Delighted to meet you in person."

"Why?" Hugh barked.

"Because of your fine reputation." Shamelessly, Taylor flattered him. "In my legal work, I find it most useful to be involved with the influential, the renowned and the..."

"The wealthy?" Jenna suggested.

"Strangely enough," Taylor said, "I find that wealth seems to go hand in hand with influence and power."

"Nice to meet you." Hugh turned away from Taylor.

But the SPCA attorney would not be ignored. He continued, "It's because of your reputation, Dr. Montclair, that I can't believe these allegations."

Hugh Montclair's back bowed under the weight of more problems. "What allegations?"

"I'm sorry to be the bearer of unpleasant news, but we've had a complaint at the Society."

"Explain," Hugh said coldly.

"Apparently, you've given away several pigs or piglets. Is that correct?"

"Yes."

"How many?"

"Five or six," Hugh said.

"One of those pigs got sick, and the new owner tried to return it to your estate. While she was there, she spoke with a farmhand who suggested that you'd been using the animals for experimental purposes. Of course, that's illegal."

"Take this matter up with my attorney."

"Oh, that's not really necessary. Legal battles are so time-consuming, requiring investigation and a lot of inconvenience. A person of your stature shouldn't have to be bothered," Taylor said. "I'm sure that if you and I sat down together, perhaps over lunch, and discussed this situation, we could come up with a solution."

Rafe's natural dislike for the SPCA attorney blossomed into full disgust. Taylor was a complete moron, who didn't have the good sense to realize that he was over his head in trying to make a deal with Hugh Montclair.

"Call my assistant, Nick Vincenzo, for an appointment," Hugh said. "Please excuse me."

He went with Dinah into her dressing room and closed the door behind them.

Taylor rocked back on his heels, beaming like the fool he was. "I think that went well."

"Oh, sure," Jenna said. "He didn't reach down your throat and rip out your tonsils. That's a plus."

"What's that supposed to mean?"

She pointed out the obvious. "If Hugh Montclair is maltreating his animals, you can't just let him off the hook because you want to cozy up to his wealth and power."

"It's just a misunderstanding, I'm sure. The woman who brought the complaint was overreacting because her four-year-old daughter got attached to a sick pig."

"Were tests run on the pig?" Rafe asked.

"Well, no. She'd already returned the animal to the Montclair estate."

If the pigs were infected, the result could be catastrophic. A shock went through Rafe. Why hadn't he foreseen this danger? Nick had told him, the first time they visited, that several piglets had been given away, dispersed. If the virus was passed through the pigs, an outbreak could already be in genesis.

Rafe imagined the cute Vietnamese potbellied pigs, playing with children, infecting entire families. How quickly would the disease spread?

Rafe needed to transform back to angelic form. Gathering up the pigs would be a quick process if he could fly from place to place. In a few hours, he'd have the animals. The virus would be contained.

He took Jenna's arm. "We should be going."

Nodding good-bye to Taylor, she went along with him. "Do you think the Montclair pigs were infected?"

"We need to find those animals, round them up before someone else gets sick."

"How?"

"Danny gave me a phone number to contact him privately, without going through the main system for the estate. I'll talk with him, find out who received those pigs."

"Also, ask him about Frank," she added. "Why would Hugh lie about his death?"

"Hugh doesn't want an autopsy or an investigation into the cause of death. That would cause his virus to become known."

"But he can't just pretend it didn't happen."

Covering up Frank's demise would be easy. Frank had been unmarried and without children. Since he lived at the estate, there would be no problem with a nosy landlady. Nor was there an employer to miss his presence at work. Frank's disappearance could easily be explained to friends and acquaintances who contacted the estate. He would simply vanish.

Only his brothers, Nick and Danny, would be obstacles to such a plan. And Rafe had begun to wonder about Nick's involvement.

"I hate this," Jenna said under her breath. "Because he's rich, Hugh is a law unto himself."

"There is a higher authority," he reminded her. "That's why I'm here."

They had reached a distant corner of the soundstage, near where the detectives had set up their impromptu offices. Rafe twisted the door handle, discovered the office open, and escorted Jenna inside. He closed the door and turned on a gooseneck desk lamp.

In the dim light, he couldn't see Jenna clearly, but every detail of her face was familiar to him. The shadows caused a melancholy cast to her features. He held both her hands in his own. "It's time, Jenna. I need to pick up the pigs before anyone else is infected with the virus. I have to change back into an angel."

"Not yet." Sadness tinged her voice. "Stay with me for one more day."

"I'm not going anywhere. This is only a transformation." But he understood her fear. When he became an angel again, they could not make love. Their human passion would be only a memory. "I can shift back at anytime."

"Do you want to become an angel again?"

"It's who I am. My earthly experience as a human was centuries ago. Since then, I've been an avenger. That's my identity."

"But if you could change and become human forever, would you?"

To be mortal meant suffering, a lifelong struggle ending with death. But it also meant experiencing transcendent passion in her arms. "If I could choose," Rafe said, "I'd have it both ways."

"Whatever you are, whoever you are, my feelings for you won't change." She stepped away from him. "I'll wait outside, Rafe, to make sure you're not disturbed."

Sitting yoga-style on the thinly carpeted floor, Rafe was aware of his mortal aches and pains. The headache wasn't completely gone. A bruise on his arm twinged.

Sinking into meditation, he blanked these physical sensations from his conscious thought. His deep

breathing assumed a regulated pattern. His mind became
still. All of his energy focused on the core of his being,
the angelic spark.

But there was no connection.

His impatience caused him to lose concentration, and
he started again. Concentrating, he drew on the spiral
vortex of primal force. He was nothing and everything
at once.

He waited, praying.

The sudden explosion of transformation would not
come. He searched for the tunnel of light and found only
darkness, a thick void.

He could not change. His powers had forsaken him.

Rafe was trapped in a mortal body.

Gasping and sweating from his exertion, he lay flat
on the floor. He was gripped by equal parts of terror and
remorse. He would never fly again, never become one
with the wind and light. His vision would be limited to
objects in front of his eyes.

"Damn." The curse, forbidden to an angel, slipped
easily through his lips. He was only a man.

Chapter Twelve

"Rafe? Are you all right?" He heard Jenna tapping at the door. "Rafe?"

"In a minute."

He wasn't meant to be mortal. His only hope was that his human condition was only temporary. Maybe he was still too weak for the transformation.

That must be the answer. He couldn't believe he'd been stripped of his powers. Rafe was good at his job. He was the best. Saint Michael needed him.

An unbidden thought flashed before him: *Arrogance.*

"Mike, is that you?"

Pride will be your downfall, Rafael. Did you think you could partake of the pleasures of the flesh and still return to an angelic state?

"It wasn't lust, Mike. I swear."

Rafe heard a rumble, like distant thunder. He knew better than to argue with Saint Michael.

But he needed to explain. He hadn't been indulging himself when he made love to Jenna. His feelings for her were complicated. When they had lain in each other's arms, it had been pure and good, an ultimate fulfillment of divine destiny. Somewhere in his being, he'd always been a part of her, and she of him. Somehow, at a soul-deep level, they were meant to be together.

And yet he was also meant to be a warrior angel.

"Don't leave me, Mike."

Finish the job you were sent to do.

Was this a test? If Rafe succeeded, would he again become an angel? He could only hope that was Mike's plan. Rafe could only pray for deliverance from his human form.

Rising from the floor, he opened the door and confronted Jenna. Her eyes widened as she beheld him.

"You're still a man," she said.

"We have a lot to do, Jenna." He dug into his pocket and found the card on which Danny had written his phone number. "Call Danny and find out who has those pigs. We need to pick them up before anyone else is infected."

Confusion raced across her face. "I don't understand. I thought you were going to change into an angel."

"It's okay. Everything will work out for the best. Right now, I'm going to find Alex and talk my way out of this stunt."

Exuding a confidence he didn't feel, Rafe strode toward the set. When he was an angel, he had very little trouble in bending others to his will. As a man, he'd need more cunning, an ability to second-guess. He could do it. He had no choice.

As soon as Alex spied him, the director called out, "Get over here. Quickly, please. Where do you keep disappearing to? Never mind, I don't really care. Now, shall we go over your preparations and get you into costume?"

"It's late," Rafe said. "And you're paying all these

men overtime. Wouldn't it be better to wait until tomorrow?''

"Perhaps you're right." He frowned. "Dorothy? Where is that woman?"

She sauntered up beside him, clipboard in hand. "What's up, Alex?"

"Send the cameramen and technicians home. The only ones who need to stay are the stuntmen, so we can practice Rafe's dive."

"What time do you want to start tomorrow?"

"Regular schedule," he said. "A five a.m. makeup call."

"You got it, boss."

Alex motioned for Rafe to join him on the set. "A brief background. The aliens are attacking. The idyll in the Garden is ended. Adam must fight back. For this stunt, you'll be doubling for our star. The aliens are shooting at him. He's up in a tree. Up there."

Rafe's gaze went to where Alex was pointing at a high platform disguised as a tree branch. "All the way up there?"

"You're to leap into the fray. Rather like a swan dive. Flip twice and give the impression that you're landing on your feet."

"But what will I really be landing on?"

"That cushioned mattress. Quite comfortable, really. It's similar to the thing used by pole-vaulters." He clapped his hands together. "Let's give it a try, shall we?"

Rafe looked around for the stunt coordinator, hoping for another excuse to avoid performing a twenty-foot swan dive onto a pole-vaulter's mattress. Instead, he saw Hugh, accompanied by Jenna's mother. They were a couple that needed to be broken up, but Rafe would leave that unpleasant task to Jenna.

Hugh gestured to the flock of personnel who were vacating the soundstage. "Why are they leaving, Alex? Quitting time already?"

"We need to practice a few stunts so we'll be prepared to start shooting again in the morning."

Kate asked, "Will you be needing any of my animals in the morning?"

"Perhaps a bird or a monkey here and there, but we'll be concentrating on the alien battle."

"Well, Rafe," Hugh said. "Finally, we'll have a chance to see you work. I was beginning to doubt that you really were a stuntman."

"What else would I be?"

"I can think of a number of professions you might be qualified for." Suspiciously, he eyed the bruise on Rafe's forehead. "How did you injure yourself?"

"In the line of duty."

"You should be more careful. It's easy to be hurt when you don't know what you're doing."

With that cheerful thought ringing in his head, Rafe headed toward the rear of the set, where he briefly consulted with the stunt coordinator. Since Rafe's prior attempt at this stunt had been nothing short of an angelic miracle, no one was much concerned about giving him direction.

"What about rigging?" Rafe asked. "Isn't there some kind of harness I could wear?"

"Sure, we can hook you up. But why? When you practiced the other day, you were perfect."

Rafe wondered if Eddy Benson would have allowed this stunt without safety precautions. True, the dive and flip were simple gymnastics, but if Rafe misjudged the

distance or missed the landing mattress, he could be seriously injured.

"What's it going to be? Rigging or not?" The stunt
coordinator checked his wristwatch. "It's after ten
o'clock, and I've got to be back here by five in the
morning."

"We could put this off until tomorrow," Rafe suggested.

"Not a chance. Not while Alex is trying to impress
the producer with how efficient he is."

"Okay." Rafe resigned himself. "I'll do it without."

He climbed a rope ladder to the platform, and then
stood staring down, attempting to gauge the distance, to
visualize himself somersaulting through the air. Practice
would have been useful, gradually working up to this
height, but it was too late for that now.

"Ready when you are," Alex shouted.

Glancing heavenward, Rafe muttered, "If it's not too
much trouble, Mike, I could use some help on this."

He inhaled a deep breath. Like a platform diver, he
went up on his toes and launched himself into thin air.
He tucked and flipped. The world was upside down, dis-
oriented. He straightened himself and landed—dead center on the mattress—flat on his back.

Slowly, he sat up. His arms and legs were still attached. Nothing seemed to be broken.

Jenna was beside the mattress. "Are you okay?"

"Couldn't be better."

Alex shouted to him. "Not bad. Next time, I'd like to
see a complete triple flip."

"Sure thing," Rafe responded with a heroic wave. To
Jenna, he added, "There's not going to be a next time.
I can promise you that."

Kate and Hugh joined them. Kate offered congratulations, though she hinted that it might be smart to wear a safety harness.

Grudgingly, Hugh said, "Nice job."

Kate teased him by saying, "And you didn't believe Rafe was a real stuntman. I guess this proves it."

"Why?" Hugh asked.

"Because nobody else would be crazy enough to try something like that. It takes a certain kind of man. Like Rafe. He's a regular daredevil."

"He certainly is," Jenna said. "And everybody knows that daredevils need their sleep. We'd better hit the road."

After a quick round of good-byes, Rafe clasped Jenna's hand, and they left the soundstage, much sadder and wiser than when they'd arrived.

On the drive back to the safe house, Jenna told him about her conversation with Danny. "He can find out the names of people who got the pigs, and we can pick the list up at the estate in the morning. He said to come to the gate at exactly seven o'clock."

"Why couldn't he give you the names over the phone?"

"I don't know. He sounded furtive and anxious to get off the phone."

Were they walking into an ambush? "It's just as well," Rafe said. "We can use that time to look around the estate," Rafe said. "We still need to destroy the virus."

"We can't go inside," she said. "Danny said the guards are patrolling constantly."

"What about his brother's death? Did Danny have anything to say about that?"

"He was gruff—the way men get when they're hiding

their emotions. I didn't tell Danny that his employer is trying to cover up his brother's death.''

''And Nick? Did he say anything about Nick?''

''Not a word. And I didn't ask.''

Nick puzzled Rafe. No matter what was happening, Nick was always there, behind the scenes, handling the Montclair affairs and taking care of his younger brothers. The notoriously reclusive Hugh Montclair might have come to rely on Nick, especially in the difficult times when his best friend was dying. And reliance oftentimes developed into dependence.

The situation was not unlike that of Jenna and her mother, but Jenna truly cared for her mother and wanted the best for her. She'd encouraged Kate and hadn't gotten in the way, even when she thought her mother was making a mistake by dating Hugh Montclair. If Jenna had wished to, she could have shut down her mother's first venture into normal society. But her motive was love for her mother.

What was Nick's motivation? He seemed always to be nearby, pulling strings and controlling. He had a certain power when it came to his brothers and Hugh. Had he abused the relationship? Had he been influenced by the dark forces who held the Montclair estate within their fierce grasp?

Nick had been responsible for sending the infected pigs into the community. Why?

''Rafe? What happens next?''

''We wait until morning to gather up the pigs. If I were an angel, I could have picked up the list from Danny and flown,'' he said. ''Now, we'll have to use more conventional means.''

As he pulled into the driveway and parked, Rafe forgot about the murder and the pigs. He and Jenna would be here at the safe haven, alone all night.

She reached across the console and touched his arm. ''Are you all right?''

''Just thinking.''

''About the virus?''

''Right at this moment, Jenna, I'm thinking about you.''

His observation of mating rituals had left many questions of protocol unanswered. Men, indulging in locker-room talk, liked to brag about their stamina and how many times they were capable of making love in one night. But he had never heard women speak of such things, and he had the impression that they performed sex as a wifely duty.

Would it be proper to make love to her again? Would she be offended? The need grew strong within him, but he wanted to please her. ''Before we go inside,'' he said, ''we need to talk.''

When she nodded, the streetlight reflected shimmering highlights in her hair.

''Before today, it had been a long time since I made love to a woman. I'm unfamiliar with the procedure.''

''You were wonderful, Rafe.''

He took her hand in his, marvelling at how small and delicate her fingers looked against his darker skin. When he brushed his lips across her knuckles, he caught the scent of peach from her flesh.

''Jenna, may I make love to you, again?''

She reversed the position of their hands and kissed his fingertips. ''I'd like that very much.''

He exhaled in a whoosh, relieved that they were of one mind. ''What are we doing here in the car?''

She purred, "We'll be much more comfortable in the bed."

Joyfully, he followed her inside. Tonight, he would sleep beside Jenna. Tonight, they would make love again. Being mortal definitely had its rewards.

THE NEXT MORNING, Jenna felt as if the dawn skies had been painted just for her, as a reflection of her own rose-colored contentment. Though it was selfish to hope that Rafe would always stay mortal, she couldn't help her desires. He was the best lover she'd ever known—the perfect combination of gentleness and strength.

As they drove toward the Montclair estate, she couldn't take her eyes off him. He was wearing black again. His black cotton shirt tucked into black Levi's. His thick black hair was pulled back in a tight ponytail at his nape. He looked dark and determined. Only the lively blue of his eyes contrasted and reminded her of his tenderness.

A light sigh escaped her lips.

"You're quiet," he said. "Is something wrong?"

"Everything is wonderful. Look at this sunrise! And the birds are chirping. Even the air seems fragrant."

She inhaled so deeply that she began coughing. "Gosh, I hope too much happiness isn't bad for me."

"You look a bit tired."

"Well, we didn't get much sleep." She grinned broadly. "I'm fine."

"I've been thinking," he said. "When we get to the estate, we should go inside. No sneaking around, just march up to the door with Danny."

"And then what?" She swallowed another cough. Her throat felt scratchy.

"We'll go directly to the lab, break into the refrigerator and find the virus. If we can get a sample to the police, they can run tests. Then, Hugh Montclair and his killer virus will be a police problem.''

"I'm all for that," she said.

Though his plan was far less dramatic than swooping through the heavens and striking down electrical generators, she liked it. Even though it seemed highly unlikely that they could simply walk in and take the virus sample, Rafe was thinking in rational steps—more like a sensible man than a raging angel.

She took his reasoning one step further. "We could call in the authorities right now. Dial 911 and tell them about Frank's death. If the police had a call saying there was a dead body, wouldn't they need to search?"

"Not at the Montclair estate," Rafe said. "Right or wrong, the wealthy have privileges. Hugh has enough influence to keep the cops at bay until he can dispose of the body and hide the virus."

They parked beside the front gate, in the shadow of the gray stone gargoyles. When they reached the iron bars, Danny was waiting. His posture seemed furtive. His eyes were haunted. He wore a gold Saint Christopher medal around his neck, and he touched the edges with shaking fingers.

Jenna felt terribly sorry for this young man whose brother and father had so recently been taken from him. She wondered how old he was. Early twenties? "How are you holding up, Danny?"

"I don't know." He looked away from her.

"It's hard," she said.

When he met her gaze, his eyes were watery. "I don't know what to do."

"I understand," she said. "I lost my father. Not too long ago. In a car accident. He died in my arms."

"When Papa died..." His thick black eyebrows scowled fiercely, fighting back tears. "That's when everything started going bad. We should've left—me and Frank and Nick—we should have moved back to the winery upstate."

"How is Nick taking Frank's death?"

"He won't talk to me. He's the oldest, and he feels like he's got to protect the rest of us. He told me not to say anything about Frank being dead, and when I went up to the bedroom last night to sit with Frank's body...he was gone."

She wasn't sure what he was saying. "He was dead?"

"Gone. Frank's body is missing." He gestured helplessly. "I asked Nick what happened, and he told me not to worry about it. He said he'd take care of everything."

"And you believe him?"

"He's my brother," Danny said. "Anyway, I can't give you this list of people who have the pigs. I shouldn't even be talking to you."

"Why not?" Jenna asked.

"Nick wouldn't like it. He told me I couldn't trust you."

"Me?"

"That's right. Do you remember that night when I slept at the studio? I was helping you with the animals."

"I remember," she said.

"Do you remember when Nick stopped by?"

It was Nick! He was the dark stranger who appeared in the night and drugged her.

Danny continued, "I told him it was late and that you were asleep, but he said it was important that he talk to you. And he said you told him lies."

The conversation had never happened. Nick had

joined her, all right. But they shared no words. He'd
drugged her into a stupor. Nick! Of course, she thought.
Who else would Danny have allowed to come into her
room?

"You lied to him about Eddy's death," Danny said.
"Nick knew that Eddy had come to you for a reason.
He left something with you or told you something. But
you wouldn't tell Nick what it was."

"Eddy said one word before he died. Francis."

Rafe stepped forward. "Eddy called upon Saint Francis of Assisi to avenge his murder."

"Or else," Jenna said, "he might have been trying to
warn me that something was wrong with your brother
Francis."

Danny shook his head. "Nobody called him Francis."

"You can trust me," Jenna urged. She wouldn't even
try to explain that Nick had drugged her, had lied about
the conversation. "Please, Danny. I don't want anyone
else to die."

"I won't give you the list."

Rafe grasped the iron bars. He looked ferocious
enough to rip them apart with his bare hands. "Listen
to me, Danny. This is serious."

"Don't you think I know that?" His voice was low
and intense. "I've got to do what my brother says."

"Heed my words," Rafe said.

Jenna's head turned sharply. There was a sonorous
tone to Rafe's voice. He was still a man, but he was
speaking with the authority of a higher power. His presence magnified.

"Daniel Vincenzo." Rafe addressed him with a
strange formality. "You know the right thing to do.
Your brother Francis was a gentle soul, a botanist. If he
were here, he would tell you that no one else should die.

Work with me, Danny. Take your stand beside me. Avenge your brother's death.''

"But what about Nick?"

"You know the right thing to do." Rafe's blue eyes shone with compelling light. "I'm on the side of the angels."

Danny's hand clenched the St. Christopher medal he wore on a golden chain.

"Give me the list," Rafe said.

Moving slowly, as if in a trance, Danny reached into the hip pocket of his jeans and took out a piece of paper. His hand passed between the iron bars as he held out the list.

Rafe took it from him and caught hold of Danny's hand. "I feel the courage in you, Danny. Open these gates."

Danny tried to pull back his hand, but Rafe held tight. "I can't let you in here."

"You know I'm right," Rafe said. "You know that Frank's death should have been reported to the police."

"Why? He wasn't murdered. He was just real sick."

"Like Eddy Benson," Rafe reminded him.

Danny's complexion paled. "I'm scared. I just want to bury my brother."

"It's all right, Danny." Rafe let go of his hand. "I'll help. Let me in."

Quickly, Danny unlocked the gates and ushered them inside. "Now what?"

"We need to get up to the house and take samples from the refrigerated unit inside Hugh's lab."

"The lab is locked up tight. I can't get in there," Danny said. "Nick can, though. He has keys to everything. Maybe we should find him."

"No," Rafe said. "We'll find a way."

As dawn became daylight, they followed the winding road through the gardens in a small golf cart that Danny was driving. the put-put of the motor sounded too loud to Jenna. She was afraid they would attract attention and be stopped before they even got to the house.

She had never before sensed the evil that Rafe said was inside this place. But she felt it now. Her skin crawled, and she shuddered at the thought of what they might find. What had Hugh done with Frank's body? Surely he wouldn't hide the corpse on this property where the police could find it.

"Duck down," Danny said. "We're going past a place where there are a couple of security men. They won't pay any attention to me, but if they see you, we're in trouble."

How could they miss seeing them? Jenna curled up on the floorboards of the golf cart, trying to make herself very small. She still had her gun in her purse, but she didn't want to attempt a shoot-out.

"Hey, guys," she heard Nick call out.

Would he betray them? Had he brought them in here so he could turn them over to Hugh?

But the golf cart kept rolling.

Miraculously, they reached the house without being discovered, and Danny led them to a side door below the lab. When they were inside, he whispered, "Go down this hallway and take a right. There's a staircase that leads to the lab. But it's locked. I'll go find Nick and get the key."

"Stay with us," Rafe said.

"What about my brother? I got to watch out for him, even if he thinks he's the one who's protecting everybody."

"Be silent."

Rafe was already down the hall, approaching the stairs. He moved so stealthily that he didn't even seem to disturb the flow of air. Focused on his mission, Rafe was more formidable than Jenna had ever seen him, more impressive than when she came into the room and saw him in his full angelic splendor.

Though he wasn't an angel, he had centuries of experience in espionage. He was in total control, and his confidence shielded her as surely as when he had raised one of his wings above her head to protect her from the rainfall.

When he climbed the stairway and reached the door to the lab, he knelt down and studied it. "The lock isn't difficult, and this room isn't wired to the central alarm system. Is that right, Danny?"

"We unhooked it because Hugh kept accidentally setting it off. But the refrigerated units are connected. There's no way to bypass."

"What kind of lock?"

"It's a computerized system. Sometimes Hugh changes the code, like when we have an electrical blackout."

Rafe produced a set of lock picks, and he fiddled with the lock for only a few seconds. He twisted the doorknob and it opened.

Inside, with the door closed behind them, Jenna felt safe from detection, yet terrified at the same time. This break-in was like hiding inside a cage with a tiger that might lash out at any second and tear them limb from limb.

Rafe went immediately to the separate room with the walk-in refrigerator. The lock on that unit looked like it was as unbreakable as the security system on a bank vault.

"Computerized," Rafe said. He turned to the monitor and keyboard on the shelf opposite the refrigerator. "I hate these things."

"Can you get it open?"

"I can try. I'll try to override the security, but there's a good chance I'll set off alarms." He glanced at Danny. "If I can get inside, I'll need something to transport these vials."

Danny pointed to a black doctor's bag in the corner. "How about that?"

"Perfect."

His fingers flew across the keyboard, and the screen flashed with a dizzying series of numerical codes. Jenna had no idea what he was doing, until he went to the keypad beside the door and punched in five numbers.

She held her breath, waiting for the shrill of alarms. But there was no sound.

Rafe opened the stainless steel door, releasing a blast of arctic air and a dim glow. The light had switched on automatically when the door opened.

Peeking around the edge of the door, she saw that the unit was larger than an average walk-in closet. Wire mesh shelving lined the wall. Though Rafe had already entered, she and Danny held back. A premonition warned her that she didn't want to see what was inside the unit. But she had to know. Jenna knew that danger wouldn't go away just because she hid from it.

Resolutely, she pushed the door wider so she could see within. Stretched out on the cold floor was the motionless body of a man. The skin on his hands was tinged blue.

"What the hell?" Danny said. "Who the hell is that?"

She moved closer. There was a bloody wound in the center of his chest. His eyes stared, unseeing, in death.

"Taylor," she whispered. "It's Taylor Wanna-maker."

Her hand rose to cover her mouth. Her throat constricted, choking back a scream. She was aware of Rafe, moving efficiently among the marked vials on the shelves.

"The antidote," he said. "We'd better take this, even though it didn't work on Frank."

How could he still concentrate on his mission? In the face of murder, Rafe was unperturbed.

Shaken to the marrow, Jenna trembled. Cold, clammy fingers tore at her heart. She felt faint. Her vision blurred. Lurching into Danny, she tried to escape the cold steel walls that felt like they were shrinking to entomb her with the dead man.

"Careful now," Danny said. "You're going to knock stuff over."

"Get me out of here."

He wrapped his arm around her shoulders. "It's okay, Jenna. You're okay."

Danny helped her into the outer room, and she was grateful for his support. Her legs seemed paralyzed, stiff. He helped her to a tall stool, and she balanced precariously.

"You just sit there," Danny said. "I'll get you some water."

She blinked slowly. *Water. Every time she'd come here, she'd had water.* Behind her eyelids, she saw swirling colors, a whirlpool that threatened to pull her down, drowning her in unspoken panic.

Rafe appeared in the doorway of the refrigerator. In his hand, he carried the black doctor's bag. "Got it!"

He closed the door. With a few strokes on the computer keyboard, he relocked the system. "Let's get out of here."

He paused in the lab, looking through the windows toward the barn. Then he clasped Jenna's hand, dragging her forward. "Come on, Jenna. We have to escape before we're found out. Danny, you need to drive us to the gate. Hurry."

Drawing on a strength she didn't know she had, Jenna staggered after him. She felt numb. Her legs trembled with each jolting step.

Somehow, they made it back to the golf cart.

With Danny driving, they again passed the guards without notice or incident.

At the gate, Rafe spoke to Danny. "Will you come with us? You'll be safer."

The young man drew himself tall. "I can't leave my brothers. I have to find Frank, and Nick needs me."

Gently, Rafe said, "Nick may be working with Hugh."

"Then I'll get him to change his mind," Danny said. "The only way I'll leave here is if Nick comes with me. You understand? I can't lose him, too."

"He may already be lost."

"No," Danny said.

"I pray that you're right." Rafe stepped through the iron bars of the gate. "This is very important, Danny. You must tell no one, not even Nick, that we were here. Things may start happening very quickly. The police might be here today. Tell no one."

The two men clasped hands in an iron grip.

Rafe said, "You've done the right thing."

Back in the car, Jenna collapsed in the passenger seat beside him.

"Are you okay?" he asked as he started the powerful engine.

"No, I'm not." She was chilled to the bone and sweating at the same time. Their break-in had a surreal quality, as if it were a nightmare, and she wondered if she was suffering from shock. "I'm not accustomed to finding dead bodies before breakfast. What happens next?"

"First, I'm giving a sample of the virus to the police and the coroner's office. Then, I'm going to round up those pigs."

He drove efficiently down the hillside, not at all bothered or upset.

"How can you be so calm?"

"I can't afford to be nervous. We were blessed today with incredible good luck, and I've got to take advantage of that. It won't be long before Hugh realizes what's happening."

"And then what?"

"No one else is going to die, Jenna. I promise you that."

Chapter Thirteen

When Rafe went into action, he made a fairly impressive showing. In record time, he'd dealt with the coroner and the police, arranging with Detective Metz to obtain a search warrant for the Montclair estates and to shut down production on *Alien Age* until further notice.

Most amazing, Jenna thought, was that no one questioned his authority. Officials—who would normally require dozens of forms to be filed and references to be checked—responded to Rafe as if he were a commanding general and they were his foot soldiers.

When they were back in the car, driving toward the studio, she asked, "Are you hypnotizing these people?"

"Of course not."

"How come everybody jumps to do what you tell them? I'm glad they do, but I don't get it. I mean, they could just as easily dismiss you as a troublemaking lunatic."

"A lunatic? You know me better than that."

"Do I really?" There was an awful lot about him that she would never know or understand. "Come on, Rafe. How do you get everyone to cooperate?"

"Before I started on this case, Mike hinted that it might be more complex than I expected."

"Who's Mike?"

"Saint Michael, the archangel."

"Well, sure."

"I figured I might need authorization at a high level. So, I kept the cover I had set up for a previous case in the Pacific Rim."

"Your cover?" Now Rafe was sounding like James Bond, secret agent. "What kind of cover story are we talking about?"

He flipped open a wallet she'd never seen before and displayed a badge and credentials.

"Special Agent, C.I.A.? With direct authorization from the Joint Chiefs? Oh, really." She wrinkled her nose. "I can't believe nobody has called you on this."

"It's backed up. I wouldn't use a half-baked cover story. This holds true, all the way to Quantico."

"How did you—"

"Don't question an angel, Jenna."

"You're amazing," she said. "Arrogant as hell, but amazing."

"I know."

"Why didn't you use this stuff before? You could have had Detective Metz do a search of Hugh's labs."

"I had no evidence," Rafe said.

"But you could have pulled the special agent story to get the investigation moving in the right direction."

"Is it absolutely necessary for me to explain every detail of my psyche to you?"

"I'd say...yes."

"All right, it was my arrogance," he admitted. "When I still had my angelic powers, I preferred to work alone. I could get more done—at least, I thought I could. Also, Jenna, the avenging business is different from police work. As an angel, when I'm certain of guilt, I don't need a trial and jury to exact justice.''

''And are you sure now?'' she wondered. ''Hugh murdered Eddy, and Nick Vincenzo is in charge of the cover-up. Right?''

''Hugh is guilty of many sins, Jenna. But I don't know if murder is among his transgressions.''

''Who else could it be? Whoever killed Taylor had to be inside the estate. And they had to have access to the computerized refrigerator locking system.''

''Not necessarily,'' he said. ''Whoever *hid* the body was on the estate. But Taylor wasn't killed in the refrigerator. There was no blood except for his wound.''

''So, he was murdered somewhere else. Then, some person hid the body.''

''Correct.''

At the gates of the R.I.P. movie lot, Rafe drove through with only a wave to the guards. Like everyone else, they were delighted to extend special privileges to him. Driving slowly, he navigated through the busy pedestrian traffic.

''Thanks for coming back here,'' she said. ''I wanted to be sure Mom understood what was going on.''

''And we also need your truck,'' he said, ''to pick up the pigs.''

A policeman was posted at the door to the soundstage. He checked Rafe's credentials and spoke into a cell phone before allowing them to enter.

Jenna hurried across the empty building to the room where the animals were kept. ''Mom? Are you in here?''

Kate peeked around the edge of the door. In her arms, she held one of the spider monkeys. ''Hello, dear.''

''I don't want you to be alarmed, Mom, but there's something dangerous going on, and I think Hugh might be involved. Whatever you do, don't go anywhere with him. Do you understand?''

Kate's eyebrows arched. "Don't patronize me, Jenna. I'm not a doddering old hen. I've figured out a few things for myself."

Taken aback by her mother's rediscovered assertiveness, Jenna asked, "Such as?"

"For one thing, I'm not surprised that Hugh is mixed up in something illegal. The years haven't been good to him. He used to have integrity and a hunger for knowledge." She scratched the monkey between his tiny shoulder blades. "Somewhere along the way, Hugh began to believe that he knew it all, more than anyone. Nobody could teach him anything."

"I thought you liked Hugh?"

"We have a bond from knowing each other for such a very long time. I'm concerned about him."

"So am I," Jenna said.

"For another thing," Kate said, "I know that your boyfriend, Rafe, is some kind of policeman."

"How did you figure that out?"

"Through Hugh. Yesterday he told me Rafe was faking it as a stuntman and he was really a cop. When he said that, I got to thinking. Unless Hugh was up to no good, why would he be worried about the police?"

For the second time that morning, Jenna found herself pleasantly amazed by the behavior of another. First, Rafe turned out to be as clever as a secret agent. Now, her mother—who had been so depressed that she could barely stand to leave the ranch—was confronting life with her former sharpness and wit.

"You're doing so much better, Mom."

"I needed to get back to work." She chucked the monkey under the chin and returned him to his cage.

"After your father died, I thought I'd never be happy again. And I suppose I never will, in the same way."

Her words echoed hollowly in Jenna's heart. *Never again be happy.* Though it seemed preposterous for Jenna to compare her one night with Rafe to her mother's twenty-six years with her father, Jenna knew she'd feel a similar desolation when Rafe left her and became an angel once more.

"I couldn't hide from life anymore," Kate said. "Do you remember when you were little and I'd take you to Pacific Ocean Park?"

Jenna nodded.

"You loved the merry-go-round. I never got on with you because it made me dizzy. So, I'd stand outside the railing and watch as you and your father and brothers went round and round. I always felt left out."

"I remember."

"I was afraid to take a chance on getting sick. Afraid. Do you understand what I'm saying, Jenna? My fear kept me from participating. Well, this job has shown me that it's time for me to buy a ticket and get on the ride, even if I'm alone on my painted pony."

"You'll never be alone, Mom. I'm here."

Kate opened her arms, and Jenna stepped into her warm hug. "You don't have to take care of me, sweetie. I think Rafe might be the man you've been waiting for. Buy the ticket, Jenna. Go with him on the ride—wherever it takes you."

But she couldn't ride on that carousel. Regret tightened her throat, and she coughed. Though Jenna was ready to follow Rafe anywhere, she couldn't go with him. He lived in a place she could only imagine. Someday, she would explain to her mother why she couldn't be a part of Rafe's life. But not right now.

Now there was too much to do. Though Rafe was nowhere in sight, she could intuitively feel his eagerness for action. She pulled away from her mother. "Are you going to be all right?"

"Heavens, yes! I have two policemen protecting me." She shrugged. "It's too bad that production had to be closed down, but we weren't doing anything, anyway. Alex didn't show up this morning."

"What?"

"You heard me. After all that racing around yesterday, our esteemed director called in sick. Dorothy was so mad that she almost smashed her clipboard."

"He said he was sick?"

"The flu." Kate frowned at her daughter. "You feel a bit hot to me. Are you sure you don't have a touch of flu yourself?"

"I'm fine. Be careful, Mom."

Jenna hurried through the soundstage where she found Rafe talking with a policeman. "I'm ready," she said.

"We'll take your truck."

She tossed him the keys. "Guess what Mom told me. Alex didn't come in today. He called in sick. You don't suppose he's been infected, do you?"

"I hope not." He turned the key in the ignition, frowned at the chug-chug noise of her aging truck and spread a street map of Los Angeles across the steering wheel. "Is there any way we can reach him? I kept a couple of vials of the antidote."

"I don't know," she said.

He handed her a cell phone. "Try."

After a series of calls, she finally contacted Alex. His voice was low, filled with dismay.

"It's Jenna," she said. "Are you feeling ill?"

"I'm as well as any man who has consumed his body weight in alcohol," Alex said. "What do you want?"

"I'm concerned, Alex. You know about the virus that killed Eddy. Is there any chance that you might be infected?"

"No one has injected me," he said. "Nor have I petted any of your nasty pigs."

"My pigs aren't spreading the disease." But the Montclair pigs might be a whole different story. She thought of the symptoms she'd seen in Eddy and in Frank. "Are you running a temperature?"

"Afraid not. My brow is not fevered. My hands do not shake. I called in sick because I needed a mental health day. Leave me alone."

She still wasn't convinced. Frank hadn't thought he was dying until the last stages of the illness. "Where are you, Alex?"

"Not that it's any of your business, but I'm staying with my brother in Sepulveda. Sean is also a picture of health."

She glanced at Rafe. "He's with his brother in Sepulveda. Is that anywhere near where we're going?"

"It's one of our destinations," Rafe said. "Sean Hill is on the list. He has one of the Montclair pigs."

She informed Alex that they would be coming to see him and his brother, then rang off. To Rafe, she said, "He says he's not sick. How would we know until the last stages?"

"I'm not sure," Rafe said. "We'll give Alex the antidote, and we need to move fast. It's going to take a while to gather up all these pigs. There are six of them."

"I don't suppose they're all in the same area."

"They're all over southern California. From looking at the map, I think we can pick them up in a loop. We'll start in the north with Sean, then we'll need to swing far south to Compton, then Irvine, east to Riverside, circle back to Pomona and end up where we started, near Olvera street.''

"Shouldn't we stay close to the Montclair estate? In case the police need your help?''

"Detective Metz has the number of that cell phone. He's promised to call when they're ready to enter the estate with a search warrant. Right now, he has a couple of men posted outside, ready to follow Hugh if he takes off.''

It was one-thirty-seven in the afternoon when they found the address. Sean Hill lived in a small adobe house, surrounded by palm trees on a double lot. There was a ramp leading to the front door. Two cars were parked in the breezeway—a van with a handicapped license plate and a BMW.

When Rafe knocked, Alex answered the door. "I can't believe you've bothered to track me down.''

"Frankly, Alex, I'm more interested in the pig than in you.''

"The pig?''

On cue, a brown-and-white spotted Vietnamese pot-bellied pig waddled toward them, making contented grunting noises. Like many of his species, he was curious. His piggy little eyes seemed to squint, and his mouth turned up in what looked like a grin.

"Come here, Hambone. Don't be rude.''

The speaker was a dark, handsome, broad-shouldered man in a hand-pushed wheelchair. His British accent gave a dignity to his words, but a devilish grin curved his generous lips, and Jenna couldn't help responding with a smile of her own.

"You must be Jenna,'' he said. "I'm Sean.''

"Pleased to meet you." She liked him immediately. He had a boyish aura of mischief, a common trait among stuntmen who never got over playing "double dare" with each other. But there was also a maturity and solidity, a sense of true courage. Sean Hill would be a good friend—solid and fun at the same time.

Jenna understood why he was so popular with the flighty, shallow Hollywood crowd. True integrity was so rare that they tended to be drawn to those few individuals who had it.

"Dinah says you like snakes," he said.

"And pigs." She pointed to Hambone.

"Come in," he said. "May I offer you a drink? I'm afraid my brother has laid claim to the vodka, but I have wine and beer."

"Water," Jenna said. "I'd love a glass of water. Or bottled, if you have it."

"You're like Frank," he said. "I've never seen anybody drink as much water as he does. You know him, don't you? Frank Vincenzo?"

"Yes," Rafe said, following her into the room. "We'd like to talk to you about Frank."

"Don't say anything to them," said Alex as he flopped into a chair by the front window. "I have reason to believe that this gentleman—Rafe the stuntman—is actually a cop."

"Fine with me," Sean said. "I've got nothing to hide. Rafe? Can I get you something to drink?"

"Nothing, thanks." He turned to Alex. "Why do you think I'm a cop?"

"Hugh said so."

Rafe took a seat beside Alex. His blue-eyed gaze was cool and steady. His posture was casual, and his manner suggested easygoing conversation as he and Alex discussed the progress on *Alien Age*.

Jenna knew Rafe would shift his tone, that he intended to probe Alex for information. She admired the skill with which he passed smoothly from chatting to questions.

Rafe's arrogance, she thought, was justified. Not only was he a natural leader who had instigated action on the homicide investigation and with the Los Angeles coroner's office, but his manner was persuasive. People wanted to tell him everything.

He became direct. "When was the last time you talked to Hugh?"

"Late last night. He called and told me that he wanted changes in the script. Also, he had some concerns about the casting."

"Did you go to the estate?"

"Yes, I did. And Hugh, that interfering old bastard, wasn't even there. I ended up talking with his assistant."

"Nick?"

"An annoying twit. When I left, I was fuming. I came here for a brief discussion with my brother, and our thoughts flowed deep and melancholy as we jointly contemplated the demise of my brief Hollywood career."

Sean returned from the kitchen with Jenna's bottled water which he tossed to her. "He got blitzed."

"I had reason," Alex protested.

"Last night at the estate," Rafe continued, "did you talk with Taylor Wannamaker?"

"Who? Oh, Wannamaker. That SPCA idiot. Actually, he was there, poking his gargantuan nose where it didn't belong."

"Was he with Hugh?"

"He was waiting in the front room while I enlightened

Nick Vincenzo on why I didn't care to stay and listen to opinions from Hugh Montclair.''

Alex took a long sip from a crystal tumbler half filled with clear liquid. "I require complete artistic control. I told him that Hugh could take his noxious aliens and shove them.''

"You quit?" Jenna asked.

"I did," he said with a dramatic flourish.

Sean added, "Then he spent the rest of the night wishing he hadn't. Might have been a bit hasty.''

"It's all your fault," Alex said to Jenna. "As soon as your mother showed up on set, Hugh had to start showing off, flexing his muscles.''

"You're better off without this job," Sean said. "It's an unlucky show, what with Eddy being murdered. Poor old guy. He never forgave himself for what happened to me.''

"But you forgave him?" Jenna asked.

"Life's too short to be bitter.'' His expression turned contemplative, but just for an instant. Then the sparkle returned. "What did you want to know about Frankie Vincenzo?''

"How long have you been friends?" Rafe asked.

"Since before my accident. Frank was trying to be a stuntman, but he wasn't the type. Not crazy enough.''

"What do you know about his brothers?''

"Danny's a good kid. A little rough round the edges, but basically okay. Nick is the typical domineering older brother. He's even more of a control freak since their father died. He tries to take care of everybody. Even Hugh.''

"How so?"

Sean gestured. "My pig is a prime example.''

"Your pig?"

"Hugh was using the pigs for experimentation with some kind of virus that would cure AIDS."

"Do you know that for certain?" Rafe asked.

He shrugged. "That's what Frank told me. Anyway, that kind of experimentation is illegal. Somebody found out about it and threatened to report him."

"Do you know who that someone might be?"

Sean rolled his eyes toward his brother.

"Not me," Alex said. "I'm an artist. I don't need to blackmail my way into a job."

"You blackmailed me," Jenna said.

"And aren't you glad that I did? Those sequences of you two frolicking together, almost naked, are the best bits done for this stupid film."

"Naked," Sean said. "I'd like to see those rushes."

"They're very tasteful," Alex informed him. "You'd be disappointed. Go on with your story, Sean."

"Right. The story of Nick and the pigs. Anyway, Hugh said that he couldn't care less about being reported. He's a wealthy man and nobody is going to bother him. But Nick got all worked up and decided to disperse the pigs. So, Frank showed up on my doorstep with Hambone under his arm and asked if I wanted to give the little beast a good home. Luckily, we hit it off."

"Mind if we take him for a while?" Rafe said. "We're gathering up all the pigs for a health check."

"No problem," Sean said.

He called Hambone, and the pig dutifully waddled over to him. Reaching down from his wheelchair, he scratched under the pig's chin. "You be good, Bacon Boy."

Rafe turned back to Alex. "While we're here, I'd like to give you an antidote to the virus. Just in case."

Nervously, Alex pushed his glasses up on his nose

and stroked his goatee. "Do you think that's necessary? Eddy's death was murder. He was purposely poisoned."

"Do you have any idea why?"

Alex nodded toward his brother. "I believe Sean mentioned that someone planned to blow the whistle on Hugh's experiments. The someone might have been Eddy."

That made perfect sense, Jenna thought, especially since Taylor had been murdered after making the same threat.

Alex demanded, "How could I be infected?"

"Possibly by accident."

"That's rather bad news, isn't it? Are you suggesting that this virus might be running out of control?"

"Frank Vincenzo is dead." Rafe turned toward Sean. "I'm sorry."

"My God." Sean bowed his head. For a moment, he seemed to concentrate on his hands, laced together in his lap. A deep sigh lifted his shoulders. "I'll miss Frankie."

When he looked up, his jaw was tight. But Sean was in complete control. He wasn't the sort of person who would succumb to sorrow. "Did Frank die of the virus?"

"We believe so," Rafe said.

Sean spoke to his brother. "Take the antidote, Alex. I don't want to lose you."

Alex was already holding out his hand. "Nor do I wish to be lost. What should I do with this vial?"

Rafe handed him a card from the coroner's office. "If you start to feel ill, contact these people and tell them. They can inject you with the antidote."

Before they left with the pig, Sean spoke quietly. "I don't know if you're a cop or not, Rafe. But you've got to catch that bastard. Stop him."

Chapter Fourteen

Three men were dead. Eddy Benson. Frank Vincenzo. Taylor Wannamaker. Though Jenna hadn't known any of them well, she regretted their passing. A veil of sadness covered her thoughts, and she was determined to do anything she could to prevent other deaths.

Back in the truck with Rafe, she read the map and directed him from the Hollywood Freeway to the Harbor Freeway. Their drive to Compton took over an hour, when it felt like every minute should count. Another twenty minutes was required to locate the house.

The new owner of the pig—a woman who worked at home and cared for her three small children—quickly turned over their piglet when Rafe explained that there might be a need for health tests. He questioned her briefly, and discovered no suspicious connection to Montclair. She had responded to a small ad in a local newspaper offering free piglets. The next thing she knew, a nicely dressed man had appeared at the door with their free pig.

The second piglet joined Hambone in the rear of the truck as Jenna directed Rafe toward the Artesia Freeway.

"This is taking too long," Rafe said. "It's almost four o'clock. We're hitting rush hour."

"There's an airport in Compton," she said. "We could charter a plane to fly from here to the John Wayne Airport near Irvine."

"Excellent," he said.

"It might be a novelty for you to fly in a plane," she commented.

"I've flown commercial," he said. "Don't much like it. I'm always nervous when somebody else is at the controls."

After a few minutes on the cell phone, Rafe had made arrangements. Jenna noticed that he didn't inform the charter pilot that their cargo would be piglets. As they boarded the twin-engine Beechcraft in Compton, both Rafe and Jenna carried a pig under their arm.

"Whoa," the pilot said. "What's this?"

Jenna held up Hambone. "A pig."

"I can see that. Why are you bringing pigs on my plane?"

"We don't have time for a chat," Rafe said. He flashed his C.I.A. credentials. "This is a matter of national security."

The pilot rubbed his forehead. "Make sure your national security doesn't destroy my cabin, okay?"

After Jenna had found an appropriate crate for holding the piglets, she slipped into her seat across a narrow aisle from Rafe.

"Flying was a great idea," he said as he fastened his safety belt for takeoff. "We'll get these animals picked up before Hugh has any idea of what we're doing."

"Why would we be worried about Hugh?"

"If they're infected, they're evidence that can be used against him," he said. "More importantly, I'll be able to breathe easier only after I feel like we've got the virus under control."

She had the idea he was holding back. "Is there another reason?"

Sheepishly, he said, "I think Saint Francis would want it this way. If there's a cure for this virus, I don't want the pigs to suffer."

"I like the way you think."

Jenna leaned back in her seat. She hadn't flown on small planes too often, and this felt like a real adventure. The static from the pilot's radio in the cockpit mingled with alarmed squeaks from the pigs and the whir of propellers. When they swept into the skies, above the clouds, Rafe took her hand.

She remembered watching him in flight with his powerful wings spread, soaring majestically. Was he yearning for that angelic freedom?

"I'm feeling strong, Jenna. I might try the transformation, again."

"You are strong," she said. "The most determined, courageous man I've ever known."

"I'm an angel."

Tension prickled through her, alerting her to the inevitable moment when he would metamorphose and fly away. It was always so dramatic in the movies when the hero had to leave his darling. In *Casablanca*, she remembered Humphrey Bogart saying to Ingrid Bergman, "We'll always have Paris." In real life, such sentiments seemed less romantic, especially when she was the one being left behind.

"Do you have a choice?" she asked. "Could you decide not to change back into an angel?"

"I don't know." He turned his head to peer through the porthole window. "I miss it, Jenna."

"Suppose you could choose. Would you stay with me?"

"If I were an angel, I could have flown from place to place and picked up these pigs in an hour."

"Well, that sure puts me in my place," she teased. "Are you saying that it's more important to have a speedy pig pickup than to be with me?"

"No." He turned to face her. "No one is more important to me than you."

"Then don't go. Stay with me forever."

Over the whir of the airplane engines, he said, "I love you, Jenna."

He'd never expected to fall in love with her. In his angelic existence, he never contemplated what it meant to be blessed by the love of a good woman, to see the warm light shining from her and to know her happiness was a part of him. "If I were mortal, I'd marry you. I'd want for you to be the mother of my children."

His children? Rafe swallowed hard. Could it be possible that he would sire children? The idea expanded within him until he was consumed by a vision of the two of them, together, raising a family, growing old together.

When he looked at her, he wanted that future, that chance for a gentle, peaceful life. He'd been a warrior for so many lifetimes. Was it possible that now, finally, he could hang up his sword?

"I love you, Rafe." With a contented smile, she leaned back in the seat and closed her eyes. "Everything's going to work out perfectly. I know it is."

"Are you tired, darling?"

"Exhausted."

"Get some sleep. I'll take care of the pigs."

In a quick hop, the plane sped to Irvine where Rafe and Jenna caught a cab and tracked down the next pig. Now there were three. Only three more to go.

By the time they picked up the next piglet in Riverside, the pilot had developed a fondness for the animals. He'd made makeshift leashes and took the herd for a walk while Rafe and Jenna made their run.

Four piglets. Two were left.

At the next to the last stop in Pomona, Rafe left Jenna resting in the cab as he approached an attractive home where a young woman with magenta-streaked hair sat on the front stoop.

"Is this the Ferdinand residence?" Rafe asked.

"Yeah."

"Do you have a Vietnamese potbellied pig?"

"Yeah. Her name's Punky. That's what my Dad calls me sometimes. He thinks it's funny."

So did Rafe, but he didn't say as much. He pressed the doorbell.

A harried-looking woman answered. She looked from her daughter to Rafe. "Now what?"

"Mrs. Ferdinand, I'm here about the pig you received from the Montclair estate. There's a possibility that the pig might be infected with a virus, and we need to take it for a health checkup."

"A virus, huh? Well, the pig seems fine, but my husband has been throwing up since early this morning."

Though vomiting had not been among the symptoms shown by Eddy or Frank, Rafe was alert. "May I see your husband?"

"Is he really sick?" the daughter asked. "I mean, I thought he was just, like, in a bad mood."

Rafe didn't want to tell her that her father might be dying. "May I see him?"

The man of the house was in bed. Unlike Eddy and Frank, he wasn't feverish, but his complexion was pale and he was wheezing.

"To be on the safe side," Rafe said, "I want you to report to the coroner's office."

"The coroner?"

Rafe flipped open the black doctor's bag and took out a card. At each stop, he'd been advising people to contact the coroner's office if they noticed any unusual symptoms. He scribbled down a name and phone number. "Tell this man that you might be infected with the Montclair virus and do exactly as he says."

Additionally, Rafe took his last vial of antidote and gave it to Mrs. Ferdinand. "This might be a cure, but don't use it unless you're instructed to do so."

The teenaged girl regarded him with wide, frightened eyes. "Is this stuff dangerous?"

"Yes," Rafe said. He didn't tell them that the virus could be lethal within forty-eight hours. To Mrs. Ferdinand, he said, "You need to act on this right away."

"I knew the free pigs were too good to be true. There had to be a catch."

"Was your pig delivered by a well-dressed man?"

"Yes. Mr. Vincenzo," she said.

Rafe returned to the cab. As he deposited the squealing piglet in the back seat beside Jenna, the cabbie groaned.

"Don't worry," Rafe said, "I'll pay extra."

"Yeah, but what about the pig?"

Rafe went nose to snout with the piglet. "He looks like a real big tipper."

Jenna laughed. "That's five. Only one to go."

IT WAS AFTER NINE O'CLOCK at night when their plane touched down in Compton, and they loaded the pigs into the truck. For the last pickup, near Olvera Street in downtown L.A., Rafe decided they could drive.

By now, the pilot had developed an attachment and was gushing with baby talk for the herd.

"So, Jenna," he said, "you get in touch with me. Okay? I want to get one of these guys for myself."

"Sure thing," she said.

"Bye, fellas." He waved. "You be good, little snookum-wookum piggies."

When Jenna climbed into the passenger seat, she seemed to be dragging. Though she'd slept through most of the day, she still didn't seem rested.

Rafe reached across the seat and touched her forehead. She seemed warm. "How are you feeling?"

"A little chilly." She fished around behind the truck seat until she found a gym bag. Inside, she found a sweatshirt and slipped into it. "All better."

"Are you sure?" He'd given the last vial of antidote to the Ferdinand family. There was no way of treating her if she'd caught the virus. Even if he had the antidote, it hadn't succeeded in curing Frank. "Maybe we should go to the coroner's office and see if they can help you."

"Why? Do you think I might have been infected when we were with Frank?"

He counted the time backward in his head. Roughly, it had been a day and a half since she'd helped Frank into the rear of the car. "The timing seems right."

"But if the virus is airborne, why aren't you showing symptoms? For that matter, why not Hugh? And all the other people on the estate? It doesn't make sense that I'd be the only one to catch it."

He thought back to their prior encounter with Hugh at the estate. They'd taken Frank inside, gotten him into bed. They'd gone to the kitchen. "The water," he said.

"What?"

"While you were at the estate, you drank bottled water."

Her eyes widened. "And Sean said that I was like Frank. He drank a lot of water, too."

"The water must be how the virus is transferred."

This final deduction paled in importance when he realized that Jenna was infected.

She shook her head. "I don't really feel bad. Let's get the pig."

"Absolutely not. If you were infected when you drank the water, it means you only have half a day left. We can't waste any time."

"First, get the pig," she said. "If I don't feel better by then, I'll check in with whomever you want me to see."

Though it went against his better judgment, Rafe headed toward Olvera Street. He was right about the water. He knew it. And he didn't want to take chances where Jenna was concerned.

Even if he couldn't be with her, he wished for her to have a long, productive mortal life, to draw every pleasure from that existence. He wished she could have every experience, that she could see every sunrise, taste every succulent fruit.

"Stop fussing," she said. "Get the pig."

"Damn the pigs. Jenna, if you've caught this virus—"

"I want to finish what we've started."

His heart pumped at double the normal rate. A sensation that Rafe deduced was panic spread through him. He couldn't stand to have anything happen to her.

He drove through the streets of downtown Los Angeles, keeping a careful watch for signs of her illness worsening. But she appeared to be better. Either she was putting on a great show or he had overreacted.

Rafe parked outside a small apartment building. Could there be a pig here? Why would Hugh give a pig to someone who lived in the middle of the city? "Come with me, Jenna."

"I should stay here and keep an eye on the pigs. In this part of town, they're bacon. Somebody might take them for lunch."

When she climbed out of the truck to stand in the back, near the pigs, he noticed that her usual energy was gone. She moved slowly, weakly.

"I'll be right back," he said, racing into the apartment building.

When he climbed the stairs to the second floor and found the appropriate apartment number and asked about a pig, the woman looked at him as if he was crazy. She had no pigs. Nor did she want one.

This address was a setup.

In a flash, Rafe knew exactly what had happened. Danny had given them the list, but Danny wouldn't betray them. This list came from Nick Vincenzo. Nick had been in charge of dispersing the pigs. Nick had always been at the center of operations, the only person besides Hugh who had access to the refrigerated unit in the lab.

Rafe charged down the stairs and into the streets in time to see Jenna arguing with a man. Evil was thick around them. Rafe could smell the fetid stench. The demons had gathered for their final assault.

As if alerted to his presence by an unheard shout, Nick Vincenzo whirled to confront Rafe. In his fist, he had a gun. "I've come for the pigs," he said. "Give them to me, and you won't be hurt."

Rafe knew better. Nick couldn't let them walk away. He and Jenna knew too much. "Why did you kill Eddy?"

"Eddy was a fool."

Rafe eased closer to him, hoping Nick would drop his guard. "You were protecting Hugh," he said. "Eddy threatened to inform the SPCA about the experiments on pigs."

"Dr. Montclair is a good man. He's been good to my family." Nick shuffled nervously, but held the gun steady. "He tried to save my father. He discovered the second virus. Nothing else was his doing."

"Then it was you," Rafe said. "You killed Eddy to protect the good doctor. You gave Eddy the virus in bottled water. The same kind that Jenna likes to drink."

Nick glanced toward her. His lip curled in a predatory sneer. He was trembling, unaware that dark forces beyond his comprehension directed him toward evil.

Rafe continued, "You tried to kill her. You had already prepared the water for the next time she visited. Or maybe you were planning to leave the bottle in her refrigerator on Soundstage 7."

"Shut up," Nick said.

"But Frank drank the water, instead."

"My brother shouldn't have died. It was an accident. He took the wrong water bottle." Nick's chin lifted. "But his death was not in vain. When he succumbed to the virus, we learned that the antidote that worked on pigs was useless on humans."

Rafe was horrified. Nick had used his own brother for experimentation. "And Eddy? Did you try the antidote on him?"

"I watched him. I waited for my chance. He didn't seem to be infected. Then the symptoms arose. He was violently ill. When I approached him, he fled to Jenna."

So, Eddy was another experiment. Like the pigs. Rafe

glanced toward the truck. "Why didn't you just kill the pigs?"

"They all had the virus and had been cured by the antidote. They might have been useful for further experimentation. I didn't think anyone would track them down through anonymous ads in a local newspaper."

"Why?" Rafe asked. "Why have you done these things?"

"No one should have to suffer the way my father did. The experiments were necessary. Don't you understand? They were necessary to find the cure."

Nick's voice quavered. Confusion distorted his face as he looked down at the gun in his hand, wondering where it had come from.

Though Rafe was no longer an angel, he saw the struggle that raged within Nick Vincenzo. His soul was the battlefield for good and evil.

Rafe stepped toward him.

Nick raised his gun. His eyes burned. "Get away from here. Am I going to have to shoot you?"

"Don't shoot." Rafe held out the car keys. "Take the truck. The pigs are in the back. That's all you want. The pigs. The evidence."

A small crowd had gathered around them, and Rafe was concerned for their safety. He began gesturing for people to get back, to give Nick room.

As soon as Nick left the rear of the truck and climbed into the front seat, Rafe pulled Jenna out of the way. "Stay here," he ordered.

He returned to the truck and grabbed one of the pigs from the rear. He started running. There was a church on the corner, the same adobe church where he'd come to find Eddy Benson's guardian angel. Nick's evil angels couldn't follow into the sanctuary. In the church, Rafe might have a chance.

He was shocked when he turned and saw Jenna running right behind him. She hadn't looked strong enough to stand. Now, she was sprinting with all her might.

He clasped her hand as they charged up the steps and pushed open the heavy wooden doors. Inside were rough wood floors and simple pews. There was a confessional, and a stand with holy water. A wooden statue of the Madonna stood outside the altar rail to the left. Dozens of votive candles were lit at her feet.

Rafe led Jenna toward the front.

"In here," he said. "Lie down on this pew. Don't move."

The exertion had taken its toll on Jenna. She was gasping for breath. Her face was waxen. Her hands, ice cold, shook uncontrollably.

He freed the piglet and herded it toward the front of the church where a Franciscan priest in woolen robes had appeared.

"Get back, Father," Rafe shouted.

"What is the meaning of this?"

"Take the pig and get out of the way."

Rafe barreled down the center aisle of the church. He was running full tilt when the door opened and Nick stepped inside. Before he had time to react, Rafe had crashed into him, knocking him off his feet. The gun fell from his hand.

Rafe picked it up. He stood over Nick Vincenzo.

It was time for vengeance.

"Nick Vincenzo," Rafe said. "You murdered Eddy Benson. Your actions caused the death of your brother, Frank. With a gun, you killed Taylor Wannamaker."

Nick covered his face with his hands. "I only wanted

to protect the people I love. My father left us. It was up to me."

"In the name of Saint Francis of Assisi." Rafe lowered the gun and aimed it at the man who cringed on his knees before him. "You will meet your justice."

But Rafe couldn't pull the trigger.

So many times before he had delivered punishment to the wrongdoers. But now he could not kill with impunity. He was no longer an Avenging Angel. Rafe was mortal. Justice was not his right.

At that moment, he knew that he could never return to that existence. Forever until death, Rafe Santini was only a man. It wasn't his place to decide the fate of other men.

"Hey, Nick."

When he looked up, Rafe delivered a heavy blow to the chin, sending him into unconsciousness.

He returned to the front of the church where the votive candles seemed to burn more brightly. And he knelt beside Jenna. Her breathing was labored. She shivered convulsively.

Gently, he pulled her into his arms, trying to impart his bodily warmth to her.

But Rafe could see death in her eyes. She was going to leave him. "I love you, Jenna. I love you with all my heart. Don't forget me. Please, my darling Jenna, don't forget me."

Tears fell unchecked from his eyes. Never before had he wept. Never before had his body wrenched with such agonizing sorrow.

"I swear, Jenna, I'll find you. Even death won't keep us apart."

Arrogance.

The word rumbled, shaking the walls of the church.

"Saint Michael," Rafe whispered. He bowed his head. "Help her, Michael. I pray. Please don't let her die."

When Rafe looked up, he saw a swirling of light, a glow so brilliant that it hurt his eyes. It passed down the center aisle of the church and descended in a funnel cloud to Nick. Silhouetted against the light were multicolored shapes, writhing in heinous torture. The evil was dying. Rafe could hear the piercing screams of demons as they were vanquished, one by one, burned in the fire of Saint Michael's fierce illumination.

There was a flash, almost an explosion.

He leaned across Jenna, shielding her. In his arms, her body went limp.

"Michael," Rafe cried, "take me instead. Let her live."

Her breathing ceased. He could feel her soul departing, drawn to the celestial light.

"No," he cried. "Jenna, don't leave me."

He clutched her body against his. It couldn't be her time to die. It couldn't be. She had so much more to give.

He poured all his love into her, all his hopes, all his prayers.

And Jenna gasped. Her delicate eyelids fluttered and opened. As her chest rose and fell in steady breathing, he saw the color return to her cheeks. Her arms tightened around him.

"Rafe? What happened?"

"You've been given back to me," he said.

His tears streaked, shamelessly, upon his cheeks. He was humbled in the presence of their miracle.

She snuggled against him. "You're not going to become an angel and go flying off, are you?"

"From the first moment I truly recognized you, my choice was made," he said. "I choose you."

He kissed her forehead. The fevered skin had begun to cool.

"I'm all right," she said. "I can sit up by myself."

He gazed at her in wonder, and stroked her long blond hair. Her fragile beauty overwhelmed him. "Are you sure you're all right?"

"I think so."

He placed his head on her breast, hearing her heartbeat. As he listened, Rafe imagined that he heard the tiny echo of another heart beating within her. A child?

The priest, accompanied by a potbellied pig came to stand beside them. "My son, what happened here?"

"A miracle, Father."

"Is there anything I can do?"

Rafe gazed into Jenna's soft brown eyes. "We'll be needing your services, Father."

"We will?" Jenna said.

"For a wedding ceremony."

In his mortal heart, Rafe had already made the vow. They would be together forever.

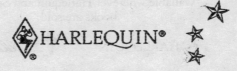

Look what Santa brought!

CHRISTMAS DELIVERY

Capture the holiday spirit with these three
heartwarming stories of moms, dads,
babies and mistletoe. *Christmas Delivery*
is the perfect stocking stuffer featuring three
of your favorite authors:

A CHRISTMAS MARRIAGE by Dallas Schulze
DEAR SANTA by Margaret St. George
THREE WAIFS AND A DADDY by Margot Dalton

**There's always room for one more—
especially at Christmas!**

Available wherever Harlequin and Silhouette
books are sold.

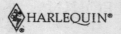 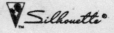

DEBBIE MACOMBER

invites you to the

HEART OF TEXAS

Join Debbie Macomber as she brings you the lives
and loves of the folks in the ranching community
of Promise, Texas.

If you loved Midnight Sons—don't miss
Heart of Texas! A brand-new six-book series
from Debbie Macomber.

Available in February 1998
at your favorite retail store.

Heart of Texas by Debbie Macomber

Lonesome Cowboy	February '98
Texas Two-Step	March '98
Caroline's Child	April '98
Dr. Texas	May '98
Nell's Cowboy	June '98
Lone Star Baby	July '98

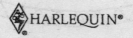
HARLEQUIN®

HPHRT1

WELCOME TO *Love Inspired* ™

A brand-new series of contemporary inspirational love stories.

Join men and women as they learn valuable lessons about facing the challenges of today's world and about life, love and faith.

Look for:

Promises
by Roger Elwood

A Will and a Wedding
by Lois Richer

An Old-Fashioned Love
by Arlene James

Available in retail outlets
in October 1997.

LIFT YOUR SPIRITS AND GLADDEN YOUR HEART with *Love Inspired* ™!

Steeple
Hill™

LI1197

Every month there's another title from one
of your favorite authors!

October 1997
Romeo in the Rain by Kasey Michaels
When Courtney Blackmun's daughter brought home Mr. Tall,
Dark and Handsome, Courtney wanted to send the young
matchmaker to her room! Of course, that meant the single
New Jersey mom would be left alone with the irresistibly
attractive Adam Richardson....

November 1997
Intrusive Man by Lass Small
Indiana's Hannah Calhoun had enough on her hands taking
care of her young son, and the last thing she needed was a
man complicating things—especially Max Simmons, the
gorgeous cop who had eased himself right into her little boy's
heart...and was making his way into hers.

December 1997
Crazy Like a Fox by Anne Stuart
Moving in with her deceased husband's—*eccentric*—family
in Louisiana meant a whole new life for Margaret Jaffrey and
her nine-year-old daughter. But the beautiful young widow
soon finds herself seduced by the slower pace and the much-
too-attractive cousin-in-law, Peter Andrew Jaffrey....

**BORN IN THE USA: Love, marriage—
and the pursuit of family!**

Available at your favorite retail outlet!

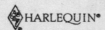 

Look us up on-line at: http://www.romance.net

BUSA3

Harlequin Historicals presents an exciting medieval collection

THE KNIGHTS OF CHRISTMAS

With bestselling authors

Suzanne
BARCLAY

Margaret
MOORE

Debborah
SIMMONS

Available in October
wherever Harlequin Historicals are sold.

Harlequin® Historical

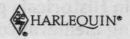

Not The Same Old Story!

 Exciting, glamorous romance stories that take readers around the world.

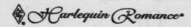 Sparkling, fresh and tender love stories that bring you pure romance.

 Bold and adventurous—Temptation is strong women, bad boys, great sex!

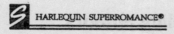 Provocative and realistic stories that celebrate life and love.

 Contemporary fairy tales—where anything is possible and where dreams come true.

 Heart-stopping, suspenseful adventures that combine the best of romance and mystery.

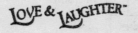 Humorous and romantic stories that capture the lighter side of love.

Look us up on-line at: http://www.romance.net   HGENERIC